2100

ROBERT PHILLIPS

Map of Australia Flag design by Robert Phillips
Copyright © 2025 by Robert Phillips

Paperback: 978-1-967820-44-3
eBook: 978-1-967820-45-0
Library of Congress Control Number: 2025909354

This is a work of fiction.

Ordering Information:

Prime Seven Media
518 Landmann St.
Tomah City, WI 54660

Printed in the United States of America

TABLE OF CONTENTS

CHAPTER ONE

WHO AM I?

There were vague sensations. Pain? Pulling and pushing … stray thoughts … all random … just odd moments. No feelings.

Then feelings. Cold? Warm? Warm and pleasant … languid. Sounds? Was I hearing voices? I dreamt of a Japanese garden. Was I hearing an Asian accent? Speaking in English? Something about lifting him slowly?

More sounds. Were they from my lips? As in a dream, I tried to move, tried to talk, but was paralysed.

There was a blinding flash, first in one eye, then in the other. The Asian voice again. I blinked. There was something pressing rhythmically on my chest, and I was breathing steadily.

I hadn't been aware of the darkness until it started to disappear. There was a warm, relaxing red blur in which forms began to take shape. Someone was leaning over me. Red face and dark hair. I gasped.

'How are you?' The voice was precise and clipped, yet with a trace of Aussie drawl.

'Uh, OK.' My vocal cords were clumsy and sluggish.

'I did not hear that clearly. Please try again.'

My vocal cords were better at the second attempt. 'I'm OK.'

'What is OK?' My questioner seemed more puzzled by the word than by how I felt.

'All right.' I could focus my eyes now to look at my questioner. He was a short man with Asian features. His greying hair was glowing an odd colour in the redness.

'Why … everything red?'

'You are in the heat treatment room until you warm up properly.'

I looked around. The other people in the chamber were too preoccupied with massaging me or taking readings from instruments to be aware that I was watching them.

There was tingling in my arms and legs, like pins and needles. Slowly, feeling was coming back into my body. I felt my muscles tense and relax.

'Wha … happened?' My voice was still clumsy. 'Where am I?'

'Please relax. I will explain when you have rested.' I heard a faint buzzing sound. 'When you wake up, you will nexus.'

●

When I woke up again, I was in a well-lit room with sunlight streaming through the windows. It was about midday. It wasn't my bedroom. Where was I? Some sort of hospital. Then I remembered the strange dream about an Asian doctor in a red room.

I tried to think back. One word came to mind: Cryosleep. What did it mean? Ah, yes, hibernation. Had that really happened to me, or was it just a dream?

I took a good look around the room. On the wall were two sets of numbers, 11:95 and 01002100. Below them, a caption read:

HAPI NU YEAR.

When I tried to move, I was very stiff. Was I paralysed? I tried to call out, but all that came from my throat was a garbled form of 'help'. Someone must have heard me, because a moment later, the door opened and a nurse walked in. She was young and pretty, short and tanned, with a round face.

'Are you feeling better?' Her voice was clipped, husky, but distinctly Australian.

'Can't move,' I groaned.

'Repeat.'

'C-can't move.' I was starting to find my voice. 'Can't move.'

'That's better,' she said. 'You're learning to talk again.'

'What happened?' I asked, relieved that my vocal cords were returning to normal. I lifted my head a little. 'Where am I?'

'Doctor Ohira will explain everything to you at the proper time.' She walked to a spot on the wall and called his name.

'Yes?' The doctor's voice was so loud and clear that it filled the room. I stared at the numbers on the wall. 'What's all that mean?' I asked.

'It means,' explained Dr Ohira as he walked into the room, 'that it is just before noon on New Year's Day of the year two thousand one hundred.'

'Twenty-one hundred?' I sank back on my pillow. I tried to think. 'I … I … Can I ask a question?'

'Certainly.'

'Who am I?'

CHAPTER TWO

MEMORIES

'Your name is James Lawson.' The doctor consulted his clipboard. 'You are a Canberra businessman who has been in hibernation for sixty-five years.'

'Sixty-five years,' I repeated slowly.

Looking back at the wall, I saw that one of the numbers now read 11:99. It changed to 12:00. 'I think I was only supposed to be in Cryosleep for ten, maybe twenty years until they found a cure for … what was it I needed a cure for?'

'A glioblastoma. An inoperable brain tumour.'

I felt a surge of alarm. 'Is it still there?'

He nodded. 'We have injected some clusters of nanites that will find their way into your brain. They will destroy the tumour, but it will take some time.'

I sighed. 'Oh, that's a relief.' Truth to tell, I didn't feel that relieved. I probably wouldn't believe it until I saw the x-rays.

Dr Ohira and his assistant massaged my limbs and fed me some soup. 'Ugh,' I complained. 'That's lukewarm.'

'We don't want to take any chances with your intestines at this stage,' he explained. 'You haven't used them for so long.'

The soup had an odd taste. I could detect a hint of some vegetables, and it was a bit salty. 'When am I going to get some real food?'

'Solids? Not just yet. In two more days.'

By now, I was recovering the use of some of my limbs. Yet my arms felt stiff and sore, and it wasn't easy holding the cup of soup. 'Whereabouts am I?'

'The Belconnen Community Hospital. West Canberra.'

'But you're Japanese, aren't you?'

'Actually, I was born in Wagga.'

I could now move the upper part of my body easily. I had some more soup and tried to think about what had happened. When was I going to recover the use of my lower limbs?

After the doctor and his nurse left, I nodded off to sleep again. I had strange, disconnected dreams that didn't seem to make any sense. Yet the same characters kept turning up. I eventually recognised them as my parents and my sister Kylie. There was also a young woman with a long face. Who was she? Jane … Janice … Janet! I think she was my girlfriend.

When I awoke, the hospital room now felt familiar. By then it was around sunset, and the time was 19:77. I suddenly realised why I had woken up. The soup had run its course, so to speak. I called out for the nurse, who arrived immediately.

'It's all right,' she said, 'I was just coming.'

I was able to sit up in bed, and move my legs a bit. 'Where's the bedpan?

'Just coming.'

Dr Ohira arrived with a large receptacle.

'You want me to pee in that?'

'All specimens must be collected,' Dr Ohira insisted as he pulled back the sheets. I was shocked to discover how white I was. He helped me to swing my legs over the side of the bed so I could give the necessary specimen. Then, he and the nurse carried me over to a chair. My legs felt as though they were made of lead. They gave me some more soup while they ran a scanner over the bed sheets.

'What's so important about the bed sheets?' I asked.

'We are taking readings from them,' he explained. 'Skin temperature, perspiration, heartbeat, muscle pressure. They have all been recorded.'

'How?'

'The sheets are impregnated with micros.'

'Micros?'

'Clusters of nanites that form microprocessors. Hence, we call them "micros". There are more in the walls around you.'

I examined the wall. It had a funny, papery feel. 'Is it some sort of wallpaper?'

He was too absorbed in his readings to bother to explain anymore. I asked, 'Was I really in Cryosleep for sixty-five years?' He told me that he would explain later.

He and the nurse put me back into bed and massaged my limbs. Feeling was coming back into my legs, and I could wiggle my toes. I asked him again about the 'micros'.

'Do you know about parallel processing?'

I nodded. 'It means lots of computers working together.'

'Or, in this case, many clusters of micros, each with a discrete function. The wallpaper of this room contains micros that can detect sound, movement, temperature.'

'Sound? Is that why, if you want to call someone, you just shout at the wallpaper?'

'Correct.' Dr Ohira nodded, which seemed to be his way of showing he was pleased. 'You nexus well.'

'Nexus?'

'Nexus … link … understand.'

'Oh. I nexus.'

Dr Ohira smiled and nodded. 'Good. Rest for now. I will explain more to you tomorrow.'

After he and the nurse left, I settled back between the microprocessing sheets, which felt like any other set of sheets. At first, I wasn't sleepy. Then I heard a faint buzzing sound and was aware of a slight vibration behind my ear.

●

That night, my dreams, or memories, started to become more coherent. But Dad's hair kept changing: one minute he had black, wavy, swept-back hair, the next it was grey and receding. Then, there was Darren – a gangly fair- haired lad of ten, and my kid sister Kylie. Hang on, Darren was Kylie's child. Kylie then promptly transformed into a woman in her twenties.

Next morning, I woke up feeling fine. I was no longer surprised at being in the hospital room with its 'micro' wallpaper. The wall said it was 6:00 and Mu01012100. Then another date flashed into my mind: 29/2/00. It was the rarest day in the calendar. It only happened once every four hundred years. I was born on that day in 2000. That was why I was special.

Outside, the sun was already shining. I yawned and stretched. Without thinking, I got out of bed, and sank to my knees. Easing myself up by holding on to the bed, I was able to stand up.

A few moments later, my nurse and Dr Ohira walked into the room. They helped me into a chair. While they ran their scanner over the bed sheets again, I asked, 'How did I get to be here? Shouldn't I be in the Cryosleep Centre?'

'Who? Oh, them.' Dr Ohira shook his head. 'They went out of business many years ago. The Centre was taken over by the government, at least until you could all be revived. You were the last, because yours was the most difficult case.'

'How could they have gone out of business? I think we were paying Cryosleep a fortune to be kept in hibernation.'

The doctor hesitated. 'There were difficulties.' I could see he was bracing himself to tell me some bad news. 'How did you pay Cryosleep?'

'Erm … I must have been rich. That's right. I made a fortune out of climate change.' I noticed the sour look on the nurse's face. 'My executors paid Cryosleep through a trust fund. The interest alone should have paid for its fees. I should have a nice nest egg of a couple of million.'

Dr Ohira shook his head. 'Probably not. Economics and history are not my strong points, but it's likely your trust fund would have exhausted decades ago.'

'What? Nothing left?'

'Probably not.'

I was dismayed. 'How is that possible?' It was coming back to me, now. 'I had gilt-edged investments, blue-chip stocks, preferential shares, hedging against currency fluctuations and inflation.'

'I'm not an economist,' he retorted. 'I know the financial system collapsed, some years after you went into cryosleep. I don't know the reasons. I grew up in difficult times, and we've had to work hard to restore equilibrium.'

'Equilibrium with what?'

'It means a steady-state economy. I'll see if I can get an economic historian to explain it to you.'

I sighed in exasperation, while I let it all sink in. Then a thought occurred to me. 'Why wasn't I revived when my money ran out?'

'They did revive three of the sleepers. But they had suffered some mind damage.'

'Mind damage?' That was a new one on me.

'The mind is a dynamic thing – the result of many neurons firing,' he explained. 'In hibernation, the brain structures remain intact, but many neural pathways are lost.'

'So what happened to these people?'

'Amnesia, mood swings, even delusional paranoia. They did eventually recover their faculties, but they spent a long time in institutions.

'Therefore, the revival program was suspended. Cryosleep went into receivership, and the government took over the facility. The remaining nine of you remained in hibernation until such times as a means could be found to successfully revive you.'

I could see that he was eager to continue his explanation, but I decided to savour the moment. I stretched before asking, 'So how was that done?'

'By means of a device designed for a quite different purpose. It occurred to us that it could be used to stimulate the neural pathways of the sleepers when they were revived. So it was then used successfully to revive eight of the nine remaining patients.

'We weren't sure if it would work on you, because of your tumour, but we knew that there was only one way to find out. Eventually, we got consent from your current guardian to revive you in time for your one hundredth birthday, at the end of next month.'

'You mean, you revived me without knowing whether it would work?'

Dr Ohira nodded. 'Apart from some-short term amnesia, it has worked so far.'

'So far? And what is this new device?'

He beamed. 'Put your hand behind your right ear.'

I discovered there was something pressing against it. 'Feels like a hearing aid.'

'It's an emotional regulator,' he explained. 'Within limits, it can alter your brainwave patterns. So when we had thawed you, I programmed it to revive you.'

'What's an emotional regulator?'

'I will explain its workings later.' He helped me back to the bed. 'Your leg muscles are not yet able to support your weight. They must work in easy stages.' He nodded to the nurse, and left the room.

'I don't suppose there's any point in asking you,' I said to her.

'Doctor Ohira can explain it better than I can. Don't worry. It's good for you.'

I didn't find that reassuring, but she started massaging my legs, gradually working up towards my thighs. She smiled as she did so, and my expectations rose. Just when she reached the interesting parts, however, she told me to turn over. She worked on my shoulders and neck. Then she stretched my fingers, tested my joints and gave me a thorough workover.

'What's your name?' I asked.

'Mara.'

'That's an unusual name.'

'Is it? Before Gaia's curse, perhaps.'

'Before what? Ouch.'

'Before climate change got really bad.'

'Why is it called Gaia's curse?'

'Because the Earth goddess is punishing us for what your generation did to the planet. Many people believe that, anyway.'

'It started long before my generation came along. Ouch.'

'If you say so.'

'What do you believe? Ooh, that's nice.'

'I believe it's my job to look after patients. It's not for me to judge how bad you were.'

'Charmed, I'm sure.'

I lost interest in the conversation when she rolled my head around on my neck. By the time the massage ended, all of my joints and muscles ached. Mara assured me that I would be in good physical shape for tomorrow.

'What happens tomorrow?'

'You will walk properly. No more cramps.'

With that, she departed, leaving me to my thoughts. Despite her offhand manner, she was sexy. I might have to educate her as to what early 21st century people were really like.

Then I remembered the device. With difficulty, for my arm was now stiff, I reached behind my ear to touch the regulator. Trying to control my mind, were they? If I could remove it …

Quickly and painfully, I moved my hand away as another nurse walked in. I managed to turn my grimace into a smile.

The new nurse wasn't as pretty as Mara. She was red-haired and freckled. Prim and proper, she carried a tray with some soup and a glass of orange juice.

'How are we today?' she asked, very correctly.

'Fair to middling.' I grinned at her puzzled reaction. 'What's your name?'

'Helen.'

She helped me to sit up and placed the tray on a small bedside table. The orange juice was real orange juice. While she straightened the bedclothes, I ate the soup reluctantly. It was slightly warmer than before, and had a hint of meat as well as vegetables.

'We'll gradually increase the temperature of your food,' Helen explained. 'And introduce solid food.'

'Because I haven't eaten for so long?'

'It's just a precaution. I don't think anyone has been in hibernation for as long as you have.'

'Really? Have I set a world record?'

'Is that important to you?'

'Well, if I've set a world record, where's the press?'

'The … I don't nexus.'

'The press. You know, the newspaper reporters, the journos. TV cameras. Am I going to be interviewed?'

'Great Gaia! I don't know. Perhaps when you have rested.'

'Gaia? That name rings a bell. Was it a type of perfume?'

She looked at me as if she were a devout nun whom I had just told that the pope was actually a radical Muslim. 'You don't know about Gaia?'

'Enlighten me.'

'The earth goddess. Many of us worship her. I thought that even in your day—'

'I remember the Gaia theory now. The Earth is like some sort of organism that—'

'It's much more than a theory,' she insisted. 'It's our creed. The air we breathe, the soil and water that give us nourishment, the heart that beats within the human breast. All are part of Gaia's grand design.'

'And the whole world is one you-beaut ecosystem.'

Helen pondered over my antique language. Then her eyes lit up. 'Yes. I can see that you nexus.' She touched my arm, as if to say 'Poor dear, there's hope for you yet.'

'I'm sure you'd love to explain it to me. Some other time perhaps.'

'Of course. I nexus. When you have rested.' With that, she picked up the tray, and departed with a smile. As she was leaving, I saw the small rectangular object behind her right ear.

CHAPTER THREE

PARANOIA

hen Helen had gone, I again reached for the device behind my ear. It came away easily in my hand. Now, I was free because they couldn't control my mind anymore.

I didn't feel anything much at first. I thought about the people I had met in this strange new world. How different they were: Dr Ohira, cold and precise; Mara, sensual, if unfriendly; and Helen, prim, proper and religious.

The way she had spoken about Gaia as the Earth Goddess made it sound like a pagan cult. I knew that the Gaia theory was based on the concept that the world behaved as if it were a single organism.

From what Helen said, it sounded like a theory had been turned into a religion. She spoke as if she had been brainwashed. Yet she obviously knew about the regulator behind her ear. Maybe she believed it was making her happy when actually it was controlling her thoughts. Perhaps the Gaia cult was a fraud, used to enable a small group of people to control everyone else. In their holy writ, there was probably something about the sacred regulators.

I could feel the terror lurking. I had woken up in a sinister world where you couldn't be sure that your thoughts and feelings really were yours. A world of mind slaves.

What had they woken me up for, apart from clearing up my tumour? What were they going to make me do? Perhaps they wanted me for experiments. Wouldn't an early 21st-century man be a good guinea pig?

I had to escape. I had to run away into this strange new world and find a place where they couldn't get at me. Somewhere outside there may be other people who had also escaped. We could get together and fight back. Maybe I could get access to my accounts and find out what had really happened to my money.

It occurred to me that the world outside might not be totally strange. If this was still Canberra, the city in which I had lived most of my life, then there were places I could get away to – the Stromlo Forest or the Brindabella Ranges perhaps.

First of all, I had to get my bearings. Sitting up, I winced. Mara had done a thorough job. Had she been trying to immobilise me?

Pulling back the sheets, I swung my legs onto the floor. There was plenty of feeling in them now. Painfully, I tried to haul myself upright, only to fall back onto the bed.

I tried and failed a second time. It was like being a prisoner in your own body. This made me more determined. I almost hurled myself onto my feet, toppled, and fell to the floor. It hurt, but nothing was damaged.

I dragged myself over to the window, reached up, and grabbed the ledge. Slowly, I hauled myself upright, to stare out into the world beyond.

The sky was deep blue and cloudless. The ground was parched and brown. There were some stands of stunted trees and bushes, with white shapes that looked like domes protruding above them. Perhaps they were rooftops.

Before I could get my bearings, my legs gave way in spasms. Dr Ohira caught me as I fell. The wallpaper had obviously warned him of my movements. 'Tomorrow,' he said. 'Tomorrow.'

Despite my protests, he pressed the regulator behind my ear. I soon realised the meaning of the buzzing noise I had sometimes heard: the same device that had woken me from my hibernation could also be used to send me to sleep.

●

For the rest of the day, I slept fitfully, weak and sore from the exertions and the massage. Helen fed me twice more, each time making the soup a bit warmer and thicker. I thought of asking her about her regulator, but I felt I was in enough trouble as it was.

In the evening, Mara gave me a light massage with a machine with a very weak laser. I noticed that she wasn't wearing a regulator. 'Are you one of the bosses?' I asked her.

'Bosses? I don't nexus.'

'You're not wearing a regulator. So they can't be controlling your mind. You might be one of them.' When she again said that she didn't nexus, I demanded, 'What is it you people want from me?'

'To make you healthy again. Have a good night's sleep, and you'll feel better in the morning.'

'When you've finished brainwashing me? Like you did to poor Helen.'

'You—' Mara's eyes glistened as if she was about to cry. 'That's a very cruel thing to say, James.' With that, she left.

Were they brainwashing me or weren't they? Yet if they were, then why was I having these suspicious thoughts when I wore the regulator? If they did brainwash me, would I know it? And if brainwashing me made me happy, did it really matter?

●

My dreams that night were more coherent. I started to piece together the story of my life.

I was born in Sydney but I don't remember much about it. We left there just before I was due to start school. I know we lived in an apartment near the beach. I can remember the Harbour Bridge, the Opera House and the CentrePoint Tower, mainly from later trips to Sydney.

Dad worked as a mechanic there, but we moved to Canberra when he got a job as a bus driver. Mum was pregnant again and my sister Kylie was born just after I started school.

Things went OK for the first few years. Dad was earning enough money to take out a mortgage on a three-bedroom 'ex govie'. At school, I was a bright student, especially at arithmetic. I could do sums faster than any other kid in class. The only problem was that I was short. Some of the bigger kids used to pick on me. I took up cricket so I could be 'one of the boys'.

●

When next I woke up, the sun was already shining through the window. I felt a warm, contented weariness as I looked at the numbers on the wall: 06:00 Tu02012100 – the same time as yesterday.

Helen, who came in with my breakfast and a dressing gown, was more cheerful. 'How are we today?'

'Fine.'

The soup was warmer and more tasty. I could almost smell the beef. 'Have my taste buds returned, or has the soup really got some flavour?'

'A bit of both, I should think.'

I looked at the time again. 'Is there an alarm?'

'Alarm? I don't nexus.'

'Both days when I've woken up, the time has been six o'clock.' I motioned towards the numbers on the wall. 'At least, I assume they're telling us the time.'

'That's when your regulator is programmed to wake you. It fits in well with the hospital schedule.'

'Is your regulator programmed to wake you up, too?'

'When I am on shift.'

'What about at other times?'

'Sometimes. When I remember …' She seemed sad for a moment. Then she was back to being the efficient nurse again. 'Finished?'

'Mm.' I handed back the breakfast tray. 'What's on the agenda for today?'

'More walking exercises. And some visitors.'

At precisely 09:00, Dr Ohira walked in with two visitors, whom he introduced.

'This is Doctor Ron Bushell, historian.' He was a big bloke with a bushy black beard. He shook my hand as he greeted me heartily, in an almost convincing accent, 'Gidday, 'owyer goin', mate?'

'Orright.' I liked him immediately.

'And this is his assistant, Ms Imogen Smith.'

She was a tall, young woman, slender, with short, dark hair and keen blue eyes: beautiful in a classical way, but as cold as marble. She had about as much sex appeal as a piece of soggy lettuce. She looked down at me as if I was an interesting specimen.

'Historians?' I queried. 'Is this a historical occasion?'

'In a manner of speaking,' Ron replied.

'All right, James,' said Dr Ohira. 'You can get up now.'

'Up?'

'You can walk.'

'Oh. Can I?' Getting out of bed, I stood up, and was surprised at how easy it was. The unsteadiness of yesterday had gone.

I walked tentatively at first, as if trying out a new pair of shoes, or even a new pair of feet. Feeling no soreness or clumsiness, I wandered over to the window, and squinted outside.

'Is the light troubling you?' asked Imogen.

'No. It's OK.'

'O … K?' She furrowed her brows.

'All right. I feel fine.'

'Ah, yes. OK.' She smiled, briefly. I turned to look through the window which I had struggled so desperately to reach the day before.

The sun was now some distance above the horizon. Shading my eyes, I tried to get my bearings. There was a low range of hills to the southeast, but… I gasped. I saw the familiar needle shape of the Black Mountain Tower, one of Canberra's most famous landmarks. It was a shock to see something so familiar in this alien world.

I looked to the left, trying to make out some of the suburbs of Belconnen. All I could see were trees, with a few curved white shapes in the midst of them. 'Where are all the houses?'

Dr Bushell joined me at the window. 'Most of the houses are partly underground. You'll get a chance to see some later.'

'Mm.' I stepped back from the window and stared at the three of them. They had to be part of the group of people that was controlling this world. I put my hand up to the device behind my ear.

'You can take it off if you want to,' said Dr Ohira.

'Why? Have you finished brainwashing me?'

He was puzzled. 'Brain … washing?'

'An archaic term,' Dr Bushell explained. 'He thinks we've been controlling his mind. Reprogramming his thoughts.'

'I did warn that paranoia is often one of the side effects of the hibernation process,' Dr Ohira reminded me. 'Reprogramming someone's thoughts is impossible because everyone has their own mental context. Even with a normal human being, the contextual fields would be too complicated to calculate.'

'And with an abnormal one?' I demanded, as I took off my regulator. 'How does this thing work, anyway?'

Dr Ohira explained that it had three components – a set of receivers, a processor and a transmitter.

The receivers had sensors in contact with the skin. They could measure changes in temperature, blood pressure, perspiration, lactic acid, and adrenaline.

The processor interpreted the receiver signals and matched them with the wearer's known brainwave patterns to determine if the person was depressed or agitated. If so, then it programmed the transmitter to send signals to the brain to modify the brainwave patterns and therefore change the emotional state.

'Thus, while you are wearing an emotional regulator,' he assured me, 'you will not become too depressed or angry.'

'It still sounds sinister to me,' I insisted.

He put a hand to his ear. 'Not at all. Apart from using it to wake you, and to stabilise your neural pathways, we thought it wise for you to wear one because we were not sure how you would interact with your new environment. It is for your own protection.'

'Against culture shock?'

The three of them were puzzled. They muttered among themselves for a moment. Then Dr Bushell nodded. 'Your fears are nothing new. Most people felt that way when regulators were first marketed. Like you, they feared that the government might use them to control their minds.'

I looked at Dr Ohira. 'And you say that is impossible.'

'It can only control the mind to the extent that emotions influence thoughts. If you are happy, you are likely to have positive thoughts. But the human mind is far too complex to be controlled by such a simple device.'

Bushell took his regulator out of his pocket and pointed to the adhesive- receiver surface of the tiny device. 'Look, it's too small for a single, external device to do anything drastic.'

'At first,' Ohira continued, 'they were used in psychiatric clinics and prisons for the treatment of violent or chronically depressed patients. Later, their use spread through councillors giving them to out-patients. People suffering from bereavement traumas, for example.

'After that, they became accessible to the general public. You consult a psychologist, who does some brain scan tests, and prescribes a regulator designed to your psyche.'

Dr Bushell added, 'A bit like going to an optometrist in your time.'

'Did they catch on?'

'Oh, yes. Most people have got one. They were very effective in solving the problem of what you would call hard drugs.'

'Like heroin and ice?'

'Yes. Though I thought the main problems were with alcohol and nicotine.'

'An emotional regulator can be programmed to cure smoking and other bad habits like over-eating,' Dr Ohira said proudly. 'Whenever you feel the impulse, it transmits a counter signal. Alcohol addiction is not so easy, because of its social uses.'

'Besides,' added Dr Bushell, 'it's not a bad idea to get a little drunk now and again.'

Imogen frowned, and Dr Ohira's face reddened. I decided that Dr Bushell and I were going to be good mates.

I looked closely at the device in my hand. It was flesh coloured, rounded to fit the curve of the ear, and made of plastic, except for a soft felt pad on one side. 'What about you people? I notice Ms Smith is wearing one. Do you wear them much?'

'We don't usually need to,' Dr Ohira replied. 'Our lifestyle is not as stressful as in your day. I wear one when I need to stay calm and precise during an operation, such as bringing you out of hibernation.'

I looked at the bearded historian. 'And you, er …?'

'Ron. Not very much. I resisted them for years until I was sure there were no long-term side effects. But it's a comfort to have one. It's a bit like having a glass of water by your bedside at night. If it's there, you probably won't need it; if it isn't, you get thirsty. So, if I'm upset about something, just the thought that I've got a regulator is usually enough to calm me.

'Sometimes I put it on if I'm listening to music. I become aware of subtle overtones that I wouldn't notice otherwise.'

'Besides,' added Imogen, 'it's appropriate that you should experience all of the emotions, even the unpleasant ones. That's all part of being human. It's when depression and anger persist to the extent of being debilitating that someone needs a regulator on a long-term basis.'

I was annoyed with Imogen. There was something smug about her. Was she being patronising (sorry, matronising)? I objected, 'It doesn't really solve anything, does it?'

I was pleased to see that she went a bit red in the face. 'I don't nexus.'

'Well, if you're upset because your world is suddenly turned upside down, like, you discover you've got a terminal illness or you've lost all your money, then it's not going to change anything, is it?' I realised that there was a bitter edge to my voice.

'James,' warned Dr Ohira, 'you are getting heated. Please put on your regulator.'

'Heated?' I snapped. 'Like her?'

Imogen's face had resumed its icy coolness. Ron leant casually against the wall. 'I don't know,' he said. 'In his day they had their own emotional regulator. It was called "letting off steam", wasn't it, James?'

I put the regulator back on.

'It helps in two ways,' Dr Ohira explained. 'It reduces the effect of the initial shock. Then it brings you gently but steadily back to a calm state. With your mind clear, you are able to accept your problems and examine them in a state of equanimity.'

I was going to snap back that I didn't want to accept them in a state of equanimity, but the impulse left me as soon as it came. I changed the subject. 'What about Helen?'

He paused for a moment. 'Helen's love partner was killed in an accident last year. Also, she is by nature sensitive and, as they used to say, "highly strung". The regulator keeps her emotions in equilibrium, and the Gaia cult is a great comfort to her.'

'So Gaia has been turned into a religion?' I laughed. 'Janet would have loved that.'

Dr Ohira looked briefly at his guests, then folded his arms. 'Dr Bushell will tell you more about the Gaia cult later. I think you should rest for now.'

With a faint smile on her lips, Imogen asked, 'Do you still believe that we're trying to take over your mind?' Her blue eyes were staring straight into mine – piercing, yet strangely inviting. I didn't answer.

'Feel free to experiment with the regulator,' said Dr Ohira. 'Wear it as often or as little as you like. You might be surprised what you learn about yourself.'

To my surprise, I was almost overflowing with joy. Was the regulator compensating for my earlier aggression? I felt tempted to bait the almost ever-so-cool Imogen. 'Just one thing,' I asked her. 'Are these regulators any good while you're making love?'

Her brows arched over those inquisitive eyes. There was a warm smile on her lips as she replied, 'You'll have to find that out for yourself, James.'

With that, the three of them departed, leaving me wondering why I had been visited by two historians. But they said that they would be back someday.

After they had gone, I experimented with the regulator. I took it off to concentrate on my feelings. At first, there didn't seem to be any. Then I felt uneasy. I put the regulator on, and the uneasy feeling almost went away. It was still there, but it didn't seem to matter.

Next, I played with my emotions. I tried to feel angry and resentful about losing all my money. I could kick myself for not asking Ron what had happened to the economy during my Cryosleep. Yet I was viewing it as a detached, abstract thing. Strangely, I probably always felt that way about money. It was always a means to an end, never an end in itself.

Taking the regulator off, I felt slightly angry and resentful, but the feelings were forced and unnatural. It still seemed unreal. I did have that feeling of unease again, though. I realised that it was probably anxiety about whether the nanites implanted in my brain really were killing the tumour. I hadn't had any headaches or blackouts since I was revived.

Putting the regulator back on, I again asked myself how it felt to lose all my money. I was philosophical, remembering that we had used mid-range estimates of rates of return when forecasting the long-term value of my portfolio. But if rates of return were just one percent lower, then the value of my portfolio would have dropped sharply in real terms. Hmm. I still shouldn't have run out of money though. I would have to find out who my guardian was, and examine the trust accounts for myself.

What about Janet, my girlfriend? How did I feel about her? I searched for my feelings but couldn't find many. I was fond of her, and would have been happy spending the rest of my days with her. But was that genuine love, or just an amicable convenience?

The only feeling I had was one of slight nervousness when I decided to take the regulator off. How did I feel about Janet now? I felt … I felt … that I was fond of her.

This discovery came as such a shock to me that I put it back on. I ought to have felt something more about Janet than just fondness. My feelings for my friends, my parents and my sister weren't much stronger. Maybe I had always felt that way about them. Perhaps I just wasn't the loving kind. It had always been about me.

I felt exhilaration: I was free – free from all obligations to friends and relations, free to be what I wanted to be, to do what I wanted, and to have what I wanted. As long as I had my little friend perched behind my ear, and could find new ways of making money.

And there was something I wanted, something for which I suddenly had a great craving. I wondered if I could get it in the late-21st century.

CHAPTER FOUR

DOMES

For the rest of that day, as on the previous one, I slept fitfully during the afternoon, and soundly at night. When Helen had brought me some soup for lunch, she explained that my tiredness was an after-effect of the shock to my body when I was revived. She said the effects would pass in a day or two.

That night, I dreamt about the accident. *As far as I can recall, Dad was a careful bus driver. Yet, even the best of them make mistakes. Maybe he was distracted by a passenger: he didn't look properly in his rear vision mirror when pulling out from the kerb. He hit a cyclist who was going past the bus at the time.*

The cyclist got concussion and broken legs. Dad got charged with negligent driving, and was suspended from duty.

We noticed the change in Dad almost immediately. He used to be a very confident driver, taking us in the family car to all parts of Canberra, as well as to the snow fields, and the occasional trip to Sydney to catch up with 'the relos'.

When he was allowed to drive again after the accident, he was a changed man. He had lost all his confidence. He became paranoid about looking out for bikes and motorbikes and just about anything else on the road, even if he was just taking us to the local shopping centre.

He went back to bus driving for a while, until his paranoia got the better of him, because he quit after a few weeks. A friend of his, a former bus mechanic who had started up his own garage, gave him a part-time job. It didn't pay very well, but at least it gave Dad something to do. Kylie had started school by then, so Mum got a part-time job as well.

Between them, they made enough for us to get by. They had to renegotiate the mortgage a couple of times, and we couldn't afford a flat-screen TV, smart phones or school excursions. My first car was an old bomb that Dad had restored in his spare time. At least it got me to cricket practice and matches. I had my own cricket gear, paid for by the paper route that I ran.

By world standards, I guess we weren't poor, but we weren't comparing ourselves with the rest of the world. Compared to our schoolmates, Kylie and I were poor, and we felt it too.

●

When I woke up the next morning for my fourth day in this new world, We03012100, I felt fine, even when I removed the regulator.

Remembering my craving of yesterday, I allowed my emotions free play while I worked out if I had any other desires. My thoughts turned to lust. It wasn't Janet whom I desired, nor the enigmatic Imogen. I was startled when the subject of my desires walked in.

'Good morning,' said Mara. 'It's time for your massage.' She whipped off the bedclothes to reveal my nakedness. 'Great Gaia. Who have you been thinking about?'

'You,' I confessed.

'Really? Then I'd better use the microlaser.' This meant that she ran the massage machine, rather than her sensual hands, over my body.

I sensed a certain coldness about her. Then I remembered the sour look on her face when I said that that I made money out of climate change. 'There's something I need to explain to you. I got my words muddled the other day. I meant to say that I made money out of dealing with climate change.'

'Oh.'

'I ran an energy efficiency company called Climate Changers. We helped people to become less wasteful of energy, thereby reducing their amount of greenhouse gas emissions.'

'I see.' She still didn't seem too impressed. 'Everything seems to be in perfect working order.' She handed me my dressing gown. 'Time to get up.'

I put on the gown and followed Mara to the door. She led me down a corridor to a shower block. The shower cubicles looked much the same as they did in my day, except that there weren't any taps or soap, only a sponge. Mara called out, 'Press the blue tile.'

I found a blue tile and put my palm on it. A steady shower of water fell – not too hot, not too cold, nor too much, nor too little.

'It lasts for five metric minutes,' Mara added.

'What about soap?'

'You can have some soup later if you like.'

'Not soup. Soap. You know, to clean yourself within the shower.'

'The water and sponge contain all the cleaning and sterilising agents you will need.'

The shower lasted for about three minutes. By that time, I had found a red tile, and guessed what would happen when I pressed my hand on it. I was soon able to dry myself in the gentle streams of warm air that filled the cubicle.

Feeling like a new man, I stepped out of the cubicle and into a pair of slippers and my dressing gown. 'Is this thing full of – what do you call them – micros?'

Mara looked at the tag at the back of my gown. 'No. Cotton and polyester. Belconnen Laundry Coperative.'

When I walked back to my room, Dr Ohira was there to meet me. 'It's nearly seven,' he remarked. 'Are you hungry?'

'Ravenous.'

'Come. It's time for breakfast.'

He led me down another corridor and into a bright, sunlit room that looked like, but did not feel as warm as, a glasshouse. It contained a sunken Japanese garden. At least, it was Japanese in the orderly way the shrubs and Eucalypti were arranged among the rocks by a small pond.

There were half a dozen tables with, bless them, red and white checkered table cloths. There were also about a dozen diners, who on seeing me enter, stood up and bowed to me. I bowed back. They bowed again. I bowed again and sat down. So did they.

I felt important because I was the tallest person in the room. About half the diners were Asian, and the Japanese custom of bowing had evidently caught on in Australia.

I found out that they were a mixture of staff, patients and visitors.

Some were there for community health programs – it was a community hospital, after all. Relationships between doctors, nurses and patients seemed to be a lot more casual than in the regimented hospitals of my time.

Dr Ohira sat down beside me and pointed to the servery. I could see a few salads on display, tastefully arranged in patterns of red and green. I could also see that cooking was done in a wok – steamed or stir-fried vegetables were the order of the day. The powerful aromas from the wok were blending with the fragrance of the adjoining garden, creating a distinctive scent that I would always remember.

For the most part, the canteen was self-service. But the manager, obviously chuffed at having an honoured guest such as me, came over personally to ask what I would like.

I remembered my craving from the day before. 'Any chance of a Big Mac and french fries?'

Dr Ohira told the puzzled manager that I would have a salad sandwich and an apple.

I told Dr Ohira that in my day, I was slightly below average height for a man. Why were people shorter now?

'Because of the diet,' he explained. 'I believe we eat about half as much meat as you did in your day. Not only is it better for your health, but it is more energy effective.

'Animals use much energy and eat a lot of vegetation. For meat, we mainly eat fish and poultry. Red meat is for special occasions.'

When breakfast arrived, it was palatable. The bread was wholesomely wholemeal, and the salad and the apple were crisp and tasty, if a bit dry. But I wanted to sink my teeth into a nice, juicy steak.

After we had eaten, Dr Ohira said it was time to go outside to see the big, wide world. First, however, we had to put on some sandals, long- sleeved, loose-fitting robes, broad-brimmed hats and sunglasses.

'For protection against ultraviolet radiation,' Dr Ohira explained. 'We will not stay outside very long.'

Outside, I breathed the fresh air. My senses were keen to the deep blue sky, the scent of flowers, the buzzing of bees, the singing of birds. Once or twice I thought I heard the hum of a car. Otherwise, there was no traffic.

Dr Ohira took me around to the side of the building, which was a large, white dome, similar to the ones that I had seen in the distance on previous days. He led me to a complex of greenhouses. Viewed from without, and from within, they were grey-green translucent. As we walked along rows of luxuriant plants and ponds, I felt as though I was strolling at dusk.

'It's dark for a green house,' I said. 'How do the plants get enough light to grow?'

He took me over to the side of the greenhouse and asked me to touch it. I was surprised that it had a warm, plastic feel.

'It is made of a complex organo-plastic,' Dr Ohira explained, 'with numerous micros to regulate the temperature and its transparency. That way, the energy of the sun is trapped and evenly distributed. The walls glow for a time after sunset.'

'Neat. I wish I had come up with that idea. I used to run an energy efficiency company, you know.'

'Yes, I did,' replied the doctor. 'That is why I thought you would find this place, and the next place we visit, interesting.'

'Which reminds me, do you think you could have a word with Mara. She seems to think I was an evil polluter who caused climate change. Actually, I was the opposite.'

Dr Ohira nodded. 'I'll see what I can do.'

We wandered for a while among hordes of cress, carrots and silver beet. My companion bent down to prod some cress, which bobbed up and down. 'Have you heard of hydroponics?'

I nodded. 'Growing things in water. It was a hobby people had in my day.'

'Today,' he explained as he flicked the water droplets off his fingers, 'with ten billion people to feed, and good soil stripped away by erosion, it is essential.'

When I muttered something about the population explosion, he went on. 'The world's population has stabilised, but fluctuates slightly. Nearly everyone has enough to eat, and even in the poorer countries, life expectancy is about seventy to eighty years. In Australia, it is nearer eighty- five.'

'So all the gloom and doom pessimists were wrong?'

'Why? What did they say?'

'There would be droughts and floods because of climate change, affecting food production. With the population still growing, there would be too many of us, and we would starve.'

Dr Ohira nodded. 'All of these things happened, to a degree. Doctor Bushell will tell you about that someday, if you are interested.'

'That's something I meant to ask you. It wouldn't have surprised me if you had brought along another couple of doctors to examine me. But why historians?'

For a moment, he looked uneasy. 'Their role will become clear later. Because they know about your world, they will help you to adjust to living in this one.'

By now, we were amongst a small grove of fruit trees, surrounded by dense foliage. The glass was much clearer; clouds passing overhead were casting their shadows on the ground.

I bent down to feel the soil, which was soft and moist. 'This part isn't hydroponics?'

'No. An experiment in undercover permaculture. We are proud of it.' Plucking a mandarin, he peeled it, and threw the rind on a compost heap. He gave me part of the fruit: it was dry, but edible. I told him that the food I had tasted was a bit dry.

He seemed surprised. 'Food has always tasted the same to me. But we do have to be careful with water. Australia is even more of a desert country than in your time. I am told that our ancestors wasted water, and did not recycle it.'

The truth about Australia being a desert country struck me when we walked outside again. Apart from the odd pockets of trees and other greenery, which looked as though they were carefully tended, the ground was bare and brown. I didn't feel out of place wearing a long, loose-fitting robe. But for the broad-brimmed hats, we could have been Arabs.

'With all this ultraviolet,' I surmised, 'I don't suppose people do as much swimming or sunbathing as they used to.'

'Not outside. But swimming will be a good exercise for you.'

We went back inside the dome, and took an elevator to the top section. 'I presume the buildings are dome-shaped to minimise the ratio of surface area to volume.'

He nodded. 'Domes do not gain or lose heat as quickly as rectangular buildings. Does the shape surprise you?'

'Not at all. Funnily enough, this is how I always imagined the future. Gleaming white domes and automated walkways, and little flying cars. That's how it looked in pictures.'

The elevator door opened and we stepped out on to the top floor. Through tinted windows, we had a commanding view of the countryside. The white shapes I had seen in the trees were domes. But there weren't any automated walkways or little flying cars. The whole area was made up of small green and white islands in a brown sea of parched earth.

Tinted or not, the windows let in a lot of warmth. 'I guess this place is solar-powered, but where are the panels?'

'Panels?'

'The solar panels.'

'How quaint. We haven't used them for decades. With insulation micros in the walls, we can regulate the temperature and air flow evenly. This, by the way, is the solarium.'

I heard a splash: it was only then that I became aware of giggling and laughter. Part of the solarium was partitioned by a set of panels painted with seaside themes. The pictures on the panels were of Australian beaches, yet the style was Japanese.

'Come', said Dr Ohira enthusiastically. We walked behind the screens and came upon a large swimming pool. There were several people splashing about in the pool, having a good time. They were all naked, including Helen, whom I noticed was well-endowed, but freckled all over.

Standing by the edge of the pool, wearing only a bathrobe, was Mara. Dr Ohira had a brief word with her, hopefully on my behalf. It seemed to work because she smiled at me.

'Hello, James.' She let the bathrobe slip from her shoulders. She lingered for a moment while I admired her firm, rounded breasts and thighs and her even, coppery tan. Then she dived into the pool.

To my surprise, Dr Ohira also stripped off and dived in. He was soon splashing about and laughing along with the rest of them. Looking up at me, Mara winked. 'Come in, James. The water's fine.'

I hesitated, partly because I felt embarrassed, but mainly because I don't like chlorinated swimming pools. After some encouragement, I stripped off and took the plunge. The water was cool and clear, with only a hint of chlorine. Air bubbles were forming on the bottom and tickling me as they rose. It was effervescent: like swimming in sparkling wine.

The effervescence affected the other swimmers as well. They were playing a high-spirited game of tag. Dr Ohira was playing with all the abandon and vitality of a child. Nor was anyone surprised by this. There didn't seem to be any social barrier between the doctor and other staff, or with patients, for that matter. I later discovered that social bathing was part of the culture of 2100.

One young man came over to shake my hand. 'Hello, I'm Simon. I'm the libarian,' he explained. 'You must come and visit the library while you're here. I'm sure there are many things you'll want to find out about.'

'Simon the Librarian?' I said, a trifle mockingly. He was a weed of a man with lank, dark hair.

'Libarian,' he corrected me. 'The spelling has changed since—'

'Tag!' I felt a hand in an intimate place. Mara had snuck up and caught me unawares. I lunged, but her nubile form eluded me. I was soon caught up in the game of tag with everyone else.

I chased the girls, and didn't try too hard to elude them when they were chasing me.

One by one, the others left the pool until only Mara and I remained, playing our own private game of tag. When I tried to get my arm around her, she slid tantalisingly just out of reach.

When we were alone, Mara got out of the pool and crooked her finger at me. I followed her to the sunniest part of the solarium, where we lay for a few minutes, soaking up the sunshine.

'Massage?' she asked.

'Yes please.'

'It seems that I have misjudged you,' she admitted as she began her work.

'You mean, I'm not the evil polluter you thought I might be.'

'Apparently.'

'Global warming was already a problem when my generation was growing up – heatwaves, bushfires, floods, and other extreme weather events. We knew that we would have to deal with those problems for all of our lives.'

It was a teasing massage: she worked her way up my thighs, then headed off in a different direction before returning there again. Barely able to contain myself, I reached out and grabbed her, a little more firmly than I had intended.

Just for a moment, she quivered and her eyes went blank. Then she regained her composure. 'Come with me,' she said.

Mara took me by the hand and lead me to a shower cubicle. Surely she didn't want us to do it standing up? She took up a container from the sponge rack in the other.

'What's this for?' I asked suspiciously.

'A sample,' she explained. 'We want to know whether all those years in hibernation have affected your fertility. I'll leave you to it.' I must have looked disappointed because she added, 'Don't worry. I may make it up to you one day. Perhaps.'

CHAPTER FIVE

TEST

was 15 when I worked out the secret of life. The whole point and purpose of human society was very simple: to maximise wealth. Money really did make the world go around, and I was determined that my destiny was to make as much money as I possibly could. Becoming a test cricketer faded into boyhood dreams, although in my twenties I did become a competent second-grade player.

I went to uni to study accountancy and IT. Despite the COVID pandemic, I got through my degree, although, as it turned out, my first job when I entered the big, wide world had nothing to do with accounting or IT. During the summer holidays at uni, I helped out in the garage where Dad worked for a time, which was a useful summer job even if I didn't get paid much. But the mechanical skills I learnt helped me to get a job installing solar panels on people's rooftops.

Then I joined an accounting firm. Yet I soon found double-entry bookkeeping to be dull. It was the IT side of my job, designing algorithms for financial planners, that got me into systems planning.

Later, I joined a firm that specialised in energy systems management. We would go into offices, factories, even private homes, to set up sensors that would detect when areas were in use, and when they were not. That way, lighting, heating and air conditioning could be regulated *from a central control. It reduced power usage and bills. As a bonus, it also reduced the carbon footprint, which is why the firm was able to get funding under a government scheme to deal with climate change.*

I was sceptical about climate change at first. It didn't fit in with my world view. I wanted the economy to go on getting bigger and better so I could make lots of money. While installing solar panels, and later when working for that firm, I realised that I could make money out of dealing with climate change, so I became a believer.

In time, I did make money out of climate change, or at least out of our attempts to combat it. I designed some apps for energy management systems. Then, I set up my own company, cheekily called Climate Changers, which became a household name in energy management schemes. 'Are you paying too much in power bills? Call Climate Changers.'

For professional reasons, I bought an electric car. It had the Climate Changers logo on it, which consisted of a map of the world, without ice caps. I was able to claim it against tax, of course.

●

Next morning, Th04012100, Dr Ohira called me into the laboratory to run a brain scan.

'Well?' I asked expectantly.

The doctor showed me some 'before' and 'after' images. It didn't look to me as though the tumour had shrunk at all. 'It has shrunk by about ten percent.'

'Well, that is encouraging.'

'Ten percent in diameter. That means its volume has shrunk by around thirty percent. All being well, it should be completely gone in another week or so.'

'Oh, good. That will soon be one less problem to worry about.'

He may have been surprised by my off-hand response to the good news. Truth to tell, I'd always found the tumour to be an annoying distraction. It hadn't fitted in with my business plans. Speaking of which, what I had to do next was to sort out what had happened to my money.

But yesterday's incident with Mara had piqued my curiosity. 'So what were the sperm samples for? AIDS or something?'

'We needed some of your sperm for research. To see if there have been changes in fertility levels since your time. Did you have any children?'

'No. Janet and I discussed it, but we never got around to it.'

Dr Ohira nodded, as if mentally checking off an item on a list. 'As for AIDS, you need have no fear of that.'

'You've found a cure for it, have you?'

'Not entirely. We have prolonged the lives of its victims by many years. With the neutralising effects of superblood, the chances of new infections are rare. The disease, with its victims, is dying out.'

'Superblood?'

'We realised many years ago that we could not cure all of the diseases that infect the human system. Instead, we found it more effective to modify human blood. Before birth, and two or three times during their life, each person is given an injection of micros that are programmed to identify many diseases. The micros not only attack the diseases themselves, they activate the natural immune system to do likewise.'

'How many diseases can you cure like that?'

'Almost all of them. New diseases can be quickly diagnosed and the appropriate treatment programmed. So you need not fear contracting AIDS or COVID or Ganges Fever or even Chicken Pox. Nor are you likely to get a recurrence of your tumour.'

'I've got superblood?'

'You now have superblood and a comprehensive set of micros.'

With that reassuring news, Dr Ohira bade me good morning, and told me that I was free to move about the hospital.

I took off my regulator because I wanted to give my feelings free run. I sensed two things: I was hungry, and I wanted to know about my money.

I wandered into the cafeteria for breakfast – orange juice, muesli and toast. I tried to strike up a conversation with one or two of the staff. They were guardedly polite, but kept their distance. Were they embarrassed about talking with the man from the early 21st century?

In a quiet part of the Australian-Japanese garden, I sat down in a small alcove by some fragrant frangipani, to enjoy the sight and sound of a small chain of ponds, each one pouring clear water into the pond below. Some big carp were gliding in and out among the water lilies.

I became aware that I was feeling anxious. What was I anxious about? The tumour was still there, even if it was smaller. Was I worried about that or my investments? Also, I had an unfulfilled craving for a Big Mac and french fries (and Mara), and I had a sore throat and a slight headache.

But there was something deeper. Perhaps I was too busy being worried to work out what it was I was worried about. I put my regulator back on in the hope that if it took away my feelings of anxiety, I might be able to work out its cause. All it told me was that I was sleepy. So I went up to the solarium, and snoozed in a deck chair.

When I awoke, I noticed for the first time the sign LIBARI. I walked into a pleasant area with a skylight. I thought it was a waiting room because there were an elderly Chinese man and woman sitting in easy chairs and reading tablets.

It occurred to me that these were the only other patients I had seen in the hospital. They nodded politely, then waited expectantly for me to say something. I felt foolish. 'Hi. I've been asleep for over sixty years. Erm, where's the library?'

They stared at me. 'Here,' explained the elderly Chinaman. I scanned the walls. I couldn't see many bookshelves, and their contents contained more videos than books.

I did, however, see Simon the Libarian, who got up from a desk in the corner and came over to greet me. I was glad to see him, because he was at least a familiar figure.

'Welcome, James.' He then turned to the elderly Chinese couple. 'Mr and Mrs Chan, this is Mr James Lawson, from early this century.'

Mr Chan rose from his chair with surprising agility, bowed, and shook my hand. Mrs Chan also bowed. I bowed in return: it was contagious.

'The Chans are here as part of a gerontology research project.'

I looked around the room. 'I know this might seem like a silly question to you, but if this is the library, then where are the books?'

Mr Chan smiled. 'There are not many hardcopy books as you would know them. But I have finished reading today's Canberra Times.' He handed me a tablet, on the screen of which I could see that the newspaper was dated Thersday Januri 4, 2100.

I scratched my head. 'How come, if I was awakened on New Year's Day, and I've been here five days, that today is the fourth?'

'Decades ago,' Mr Chan explained, 'we changed the calendar. New Year's Day became a separate day – neither a day of the week nor a day of a month. So it is no longer Januri one.'

Simon gave me a calendar. After Nu Year's Day, set in a box on its own, the weeks ran neatly from Munday to Sunday. The first of Januri, April, July and October all began on Munday. They were now the only months with 31 days. All the rest, including Feburi, had thirty. This meant that I no longer had to celebrate my birthday on the 28th of February in non-leap years. Also, there were ninety-one days, or thirteen weeks, in each quarter.

'There's no year on this calendar.'

'We haven't needed a year-specific calendar, because all the days on each year's calendar have been the same.'

'What about Leap Years?'

'We haven't had a Leap Year since 2080, and won't have another until 2124.'

'Why?'

'Because it has enabled us to align Nu Year's Day with the solstice.'

'Why is that important?'

It was Mrs Chan who spoke up. 'To please Gaia.'

I went back to the Canberra Times.

The thing that surprised me as I scrolled through the news section was that, for an Australian paper, it spent as much space talking about floods in Bangla Desh or the bumper crops in Sri Lanka as it did about pest control at the Kimberly Korporashn Komplex or the plan to save the Sydney Opera House from flooding.

I learnt that Australia was part of a large region of the world called the Eastern Zone, and that the rest of the world was also divided into zones.

There weren't as many ads in the paper as I expected, and most of them were in the Classified Sekshn. There were jobs for nano-computer organic chemists, hydroponics experts, motor car programmers, earthmoving contractors, rooftop gardeners and Globall coaches.

There were some ads for houses in community cooperatives, for long robes and large hats like the ones that Dr Ohira and I had worn on our trip outside, and for personally compatible mainframe systems. The motoring section extolled the virtues of cars' computer systems rather than their appearance, speed, horsepower, interior comfort or road-handling qualities.

The Public Notices Sekshn had announcements for various summer Gaia festivals, and many notices for community groups: the Woden Valley Korporashn, the Tuggeranong Society of Hydroponics, or the Downer Community Markets.

'Where's the Stock Exchange section?' I asked.

'The what?' Simon looked at me blankly.

'He means the share market,' Mr Chan explained. 'Not many people have shares now.'

'Why?'

'Nearly all gone. When the economy fell over.' He shook his head sadly. 'Very bad times.'

'You must have lived through them. What happened? Why did the economy fall over?'

Mr Chan thought for a moment. 'Boiling frogs.'

'Boiling what?'

'Boiling frogs. You put them in a pot, heat them slowly. They don't notice until it's too late.'

'Yes,' I replied doubtfully, and went back to the paper. I scrolled to the Sports Sekshn. It wasn't as big as I would have expected, and much of it was taken up with a sport called Globall. In the one picture the paper published about it, I could see a group of players with what looked like tennis rackets, running around a large, indoor court.

Then, under Traditional Sports, I came across something so familiar that I cried out in joy. When Simon asked me what the matter was, I was pleased to show him a conventional, old-fashioned, cricket scorecard: South Australia vs the MCC.

'Oh, cricket,' he said in a matter-of-fact way. 'I believe some of the traditional sports do have a few supporters. I think there's a – what do you call it? – test soon.'

There certainly was. According to the Canberra Times, the Third Test against England was due to start in Adelaide on Munday, which seemed an odd day on which to start a test match. Even odder were the playing times: 14.00 to 16.00 and 16.50 to 18.50. 'Only four hours' play,' I complained. 'And why such a late start?'

He looked at me as if the answer was obvious. 'It would be unwise to play outside before then. Because of the heat.'

'Why not continue under lights, then?'

Simon cleared his throat apologetically. 'I don't think the cricket association could afford it. To light an area as large as a cricket ground would be expensive. Cricket is a cultural heritage sport, which means it needs government support to survive.'

'That's very sad.' I looked down at the paper. 'It only goes for three days. How do they expect to get a result?'

'Is that important?'

'Not in test cricket. Even so, I'd like to watch it. Is there a TV set here somewhere?'

Simon was nonplussed. 'A what?'

'Ah.' Mr Chan piped in. 'He means television. My grandfather had a set long ago. Very quaint. Two dimensional. Today, we watch holovision.'

'Well,' I asked, 'is there a holovision set?'

'There's a holovision room,' Simon corrected me. 'But first we'll have to check if anyone is covering the test.'

I was indignant. Surely every test match in Australia was covered as a matter of course.

Simon went over to a blank screen and asked, 'Does any holovision channel cover cricket matches?' The screen lit up and displayed some data. 'Hmm. You may be lucky. There's an ABC cable channel that covers cultural events for special groups. It's expensive, though. If you are a registered player with a cricket club, we may get a discount.'

'I used to be. But I suppose my membership lapsed a long time ago.'

'Then I will ask Dr Ohira. We may be able to pay for it from a special purpose fund. You are a special case, after all.'

I wasn't sure whether to feel pleased or patronised.

I bade farewell to the other library patrons and went to the canteen for a wholesome, if unappetizing lunch. Then I retired to my room to rest.

I still felt uneasy, anxious even. And I felt off-colour. Putting my regulator on, I soon felt calm again. Whatever was nagging me had gone away.

●

Before tea, Dr Ohira and I went for another walk in the greenhouses attached to the hospital. We came across a large pool that I had not seen before.

'Do you enjoy fishing?' he asked.

'Sometimes. I used to go to Googong Dam with a couple of mates. We'd sink a few beers, catch a few carp, sometimes a trout.'

'Fishing is an indoor sport today.' He disappeared into a small shed, and returned with a couple of nets.

'Why indoors?' I asked. 'Are the rivers too polluted?'

'No. But we prefer to leave natural systems alone as much as possible. To give them time to recover.'

'Recover from what?'

Dr Ohira looked at me sadly, then turned his attention to a notice on the side of the shed. 'Four trouts are our quota for tonight.'

Netting fish was his great hobby. He could crouch, absolutely still, for a long time, then swoop on his prey with great speed. Every time he caught a fish, or just missed, he was very excited. I managed to catch one that blundered head-on into my net. But it wasn't the same thrill as having a bite on a fishing line.

Having caught our quota of trout, we took them to the hospital kitchen. For tea, we had fish and chips, which was evidently quite a treat. Because he was in a good mood, I asked Dr Ohira if I could watch the test match on Munday: no problems.

After tea, feeling off-colour again, I went to bed early. I turned on my regulator, and was surprised at how much better I felt.

●

By the time I was 30, I was a multi-millionaire. It was time, surely, to start paying more attention to other areas of my life, which I had largely neglected.

I hadn't yet settled down to raise a family. I still lived in a modest, if comfortable, two-bedroom apartment because I was putting most of my profits back into the business. As far as my love life was concerned, I had the disadvantage of not being tall, handsome or athletic. So I relied on charm and being a snappy dresser. I had some flings and a couple of longer term relationships, which ended when they raised the dreaded word: commitment. I wasn't ready to settle down yet.

Then I met Janet. She came to work for us as a receptionist. While she wasn't very pretty, she was a kind soul whose heart was in the right place (just beneath her ample bosoms). She thought the world of me, and caught me just at the right time, when I was ready to settle down. She was into saving the planet. She moved in with me, and we made plans to buy a piece of land, design and build a carbon-neutral house, raise two carbon-neutral children, and be an inspiration to others in a world of global warming.

Then, one day, our plans came crashing down, and so, literally, did I.

●

Next morning, Fr05012100, I had a sore throat, a headache, and a runny nose. When Helen came in with my breakfast, I told her the symptoms. All she could offer me was a nasal spray and sympathy. The doctors of the late- 21st century could cure just about everything from AIDS to Ganges Fever. The one thing they still couldn't cure was the common cold.

The emotional regulator gave me an effective treatment for the cold: it sent me to sleep. So I slept through much of the cold, and was right as rain by Munday.

During my recuperation, few people came to visit me. Nor did they talk to me much when I went to the canteen or other parts of the hospital. It was as if they were waiting for something to happen. I felt uneasy.

Munday lunchtime, I was sitting by myself in the canteen when Helen asked if she could join me. The sultry Mara hadn't been about lately. I was beginning to think I would have more success with the plain but sympathetic Helen.

'Are you nervous about the cricket match?' she asked.

'Just a bit,' I confided. 'England holds the Ashes and the first two tests were drawn. There's only three in this series, so if Australia doesn't win this one, they've missed their chance.'

'Ashes?'

'A sacred urn.' I thought the terminology might please her.

'I don't know much about these traditional sports. Would you like me to show you how to operate the holovision?'

'Yes, please. And I'll show you some of the finer points of the game.'

The holovision room was on the top floor behind the library. It was a fair-sized room, with blank white walls and a few benches. On the wall by the door, there was a small panel with several buttons.

'It's very simple to operate,' Helen explained. 'You press the green button and ask for the channel you want.'

'Er … Culture Four, I think.'

'Culture Four,' she echoed into a small mouthpiece. I thought I could hear a faint dial tone. When an amber light came on, she spoke an account number into the mouthpiece. I sat down and waited for something to happen. Helen sat beside me, and removed her regulator.

'I thought you always wore it.'

'For an exciting game, I might. But I'm told this is a quiet game. If I'm bored, the regulator would send me to sleep.'

'It can be slow. But you won't be bored if you know what the game is about.' Even so, I removed my regulator.

Helen smiled. She took a cloth from her pocket with which to wipe hers. 'They should be cleaned frequently. Would you like me to clean yours as well?'

As I handed it over, I felt strange.

The walls lit up. I gasped. Suddenly, there we were, by the players' race on a bright, sunny afternoon. One or two of the stands had changed, but the Mt Lofty Ranges in the background meant that this was definitely Adelaide Oval.

'It's just like being there,' I exclaimed.

The view changed to a slow pan around the ground. The few spectators that I could see were wearing a mixture of 19th- and 20th-century costumes. They were having jolly picnics in the stands.

Then we were back by the players' race, watching the toss between the captains, Ramesh Mahmud of Oxford and England, and Dr Rahman Singh of Queensland and Australia. England won the toss and decided to bat.

When the scene changed to show the pitch – a traditional, firm Adelaide batting wicket, I groaned. 'Blind Freddie could make a ton on that pitch. They'll be lucky to get a first-innings result in three days.'

I spent the next few minutes explaining the intricacies of cricket to Helen. I'm not sure if she understood very much. By the time I had finished, the Australians were already out in the field. The England openers were walking to the wicket.

Our vantage point shifted to behind the bowler's arm. We were now in front of the sight screen, about one-third of the way in from the fence. The ceiling of the holovision room had become the blue sky, the floor had become green turf, and the wicket was on the wall at the other end of the room.

Ambrose Pendexter, a tall, black right-hander, took guard. He was facing Andrew Anderson, reputed to be the fastest bowler in Australia. Yet there were only two slips: neither they nor the keeper were set very deep.

Nor did the England batsmen wear helmets. I soon found out why: Australia's demon bowler operated off a shortish run-up at a gentle medium pace. As he ran in to bowl, I felt the adrenaline surging. Tensing, I crouched forward, hands in front.

The first delivery strayed down the leg side. Only an athletic save by the keeper stopped it from going for four byes. The second delivery wasn't much better.

'I don't know about this Anderson bloke,' I complained to Helen. 'His footwork's all over the place and his arm's not high enough at the top. If he's Australia's best bowler, I reckon I could get a bowl with this mob. I always wanted to be in the test team.'

When I said that, I started to feel something … something lurking … coming to the top … like a dream turning into a nightmare. Helen sat quietly cleaning my regulator.

I was going to ask for it back, but Anderson was on his way in again. This time, he pitched it in line with the stumps. Pendexter, whose footwork was as bad as Anderson's, took a wild swipe at the ball. It struck him on the pad, plumb in front.

'Owzat!' I screamed. I leapt to my feet and raised the finger. Anderson made a polite inquiry of the umpire, who shook his head and said it was 'a tad high'. Feeling foolish, I sat down again. 'Sorry. Got a bit carried away.' Helen sat there quietly.

Anderson came in faster the next time and bowled a full toss. Pendexter whacked the ball high in the air, straight towards us. I could see it was going to drop short. I dived, rolled on the floor, and came up clutching thin air. This time, I felt very silly. Very silly indeed. Applause. I looked up as the umpire signalled four. Seeing something so familiar I … I … welling up inside of me … exploding … 'I want to go back.' I burst into tears. 'I want to go back.'

As I grovelled on the floor, Helen towered above me, cold, stern.

'Gimme back my regulator,' I demanded.

'No.' There was a grim smile on Helen's face. 'Not this time.'

CHAPTER SIX

CRYOSLEEP

had landed a big contract with a firm called Cryosleep. They put terminally ill people into hibernation at low temperatures, with the idea of reviving them years or decades later when cures had been found for their ailments.

When I was born, suspended animation was just an idea in science-fiction. Scientists set to work on larger animals, and finally, people. By the time I was a young man, doctors had been able to put people in stasis for up to two weeks. The director of Cryosleep was actually the first person to be put into hibernation and revived – a world-first for Australian technology.

Cryosleep developed a technique in which they put their clients into a catatonic state, where their metabolic rate slowed right down, to perhaps one heartbeat per minute; in effect, an extreme form of hibernation. After that, their bodies were kept on life support at low temperatures to be preserved, for years if necessary, before being revived. This meant that, legally, they were not dead, so the staff could not be charged with murder.

The Cryosleep Centre was in a remote valley near Canberra – geologically stable, well above the food plain, and with not many trees and grasses that could spread bushfires. The headquarters and *offices were comfortable enough: the spooky part was the cooling halls, where the clients were at rest in their 'coffins'. The halls were built underground, where the ambient temperatures would be more stable.*

Maintaining stability was where I came in. From time to time, technicians would go into control rooms to check that everything was OK, and make repairs if necessary.

Otherwise, the equipment had to monitor itself, optimising energy flows to minimise power usage while maintaining critical temperatures. The whole plant was solar-powered, with batteries and backup generators that could cut in automatically.

Cryosleep paid me well for my services. I had no idea at the time how much I would have need of theirs.

●

Tu09012100. The three of them were there again: Dr Ohira, Dr Bushell the historian, and his assistant, Imogen Smith.

'How are you feeling?' asked Imogen.

'Much better,' I said. This was true. When I had my breakdown, Helen and two orderlies had taken me back to my room. After I had calmed down, they gave me back my regulator. I had slept soundly. Now, the following morning, I was much calmer.

'I suppose,' I confessed, 'even though I knew I went into cryosleep, part of me still thought it was a dream. I'd wake up one day and find myself back in my own time.'

The historian nodded. 'What do you think now?'

'That this is 2100, and I can never go back.'

'Good.'

I turned my attention to Dr Ohira. 'Were you waiting for me to crack?' He looked puzzled.

'A mental breakdown,' interpreted Dr Bushell.

'No, not a breakdown,' Imogen insisted. 'The point of nexus between past perception and present realisation.'

'Yes,' said Dr Ohira doubtfully. 'I thought the crisis might come when I took James outside to see Black Mountain Tower and other familiar landmarks.'

'I did feel weird then,' I admitted. 'And I wasn't sure if this 2100 stuff was for real. I thought that maybe this was some sort of funny farm.'

Dr Bushell once again had to translate for his colleagues.

'For patients revived from hibernation,' Dr Ohira explained, 'there is usually a delayed reaction time of three to seven days before the shock hits them that they are living in a new age. That shock, when it happens, is often traumatic.'

'I had the feeling,' I explained, 'since the day we went outside, that something wasn't right. As long as people were wearing strange clothes and using funny words, I could accept it as a game. But the test match was so familiar … so real.'

Dr Bushell nodded. 'Your mind couldn't pretend anymore.'

We were quiet for a moment or two. Then I asked, 'So what happens now? What do you do with me?'

'The question is,' Dr Bushell replied, 'what do you do with yourself?'

'Now that you have recovered from post-cryonic shock,' explained Dr Ohira, 'you can see more places. We will still monitor your tumour. Once that has gone, you will be free to leave.'

'Where would I go?'

'I can help you there, James,' said Dr Bushell. 'You're welcome to stay with my family for a while.'

'With your family?'

'Yes. We live in a community a few kilometres from here.'

'A community? What sort of community?'

The other two looked at him. 'In James's day,' he told them, 'people often lived in houses on separate blocks of land, and I understand, lived independently of their neighbours.'

Then he told me, 'Today, we live in communities, and spend part of our lives working for them. I will explain it to you in more detail if you come to live with us.'

I thought for a moment. To me, community life sounded like people living together in one big building, which didn't appeal to me. On the other hand, I didn't fancy spending much longer in the hospital. 'Where is this community?'

'Not far from here. In North Canberra. We know you might have to come back for the occasional test.'

I generally don't take long to make decisions. Since I was probably penniless, where else could I go? 'OK.'

●

Janet probably saved my life. I'd been having headaches, which I had put down to working too hard. One afternoon, my headache was really bad, so I went home early. I don't actually remember getting there and going inside. Janet came home later and found me lying on the floor.

I can vaguely recall being put into an ambulance and driven to hospital. They conducted x-rays and other tests on me, and told me that I had an inoperable brain tumour called a glioblastoma.

'How long have I got?' I asked the specialist.

'It's difficult to predict. With treatment, we can slow down the rate of advance. You've got about a 50:50 chance of surviving for a year.'

The threat of impending death focuses the mind wonderfully. I contacted Cryosleep to find out how much it would cost to put me into hibernation: about one hundred thousand dollars a year.

I informed my employees that I was retiring, and putting Climate Changers on the market. I jokingly told them they could have it for three million dollars. Within a month I had sold it to a consortium that included my employees, for two and a half million.

I consolidated all my assets into a trust fund. We assumed an annual rate of return after tax of eight percent. We also factored in a rate of inflation of four percent, even though the long-term trend was only three. However, governments were predicting another financial crisis, and were planning to introduce pre- emptive quantitative easing to avert the crisis, with the proviso that it should not add more than one percent per annum to inflation. The upshot of it all was that my trust fund should earn enough to keep me in hibernation for decades, and still leave me with plenty to spare whenever I was revived and cured.

I also had to tell my parents, of course. And Kylie and her son Darren. Kylie had married and divorced. I told them that I had some bad news and a ray of hope. Treatment was keeping the beast under control, but it could 'erupt' again at any time. The ray of hope was Cryosleep.

'Once I go into hibernation,' I explained, 'I could be there for many years until they find a cure. So, in all probability, you won't see me again for quite some time.'

Darren was a precocious boy of ten. 'Uncle James, will you dream?'

'I don't know. Even in hibernation, there will still be some low-level electrical activity in my brain. Way below the threshold of consciousness.'

'What about your soul? Where will it go?'

'If I have one … I don't know that either. See, I won't quite be dead, so I suppose it would stay attached to the rest of me.'

●

I spent the next few days wandering about the hospital and its greenhouses, or swimming, or visiting the library. One morning, I did some research on economic history in the late-2030s and 2040s, and was appalled at what I discovered.

The world's financial authorities had indeed managed to forestall another Global Financial Crisis by using 'pre-emptive Quantitative Easing'; in effect, printing lots of extra money to make credit freely available before a crisis could hit. The problem was, once they started, they couldn't stop: the demand for credit by governments, business and private individuals was insatiable.

Bit by bit, during the late-2030s, Quantitative Easing crept beyond the one-percent contribution to the inflation limit that the authorities had promised to maintain. People got used to incremental increases in inflation, just as Mr Chan's frogs got used to boiling water.

But the expanding global economy put great demands on the world's dwindling sources of fuel and other scarce commodities, forcing prices even higher, thereby creating even greater demand for credit. In the 2040s, a series of severe droughts, probably caused by global warming, pushed food prices through the roof. There was runaway inflation, and the whole financial system came crashing down, taking my trust fund investments and those of the other 'Cryosleepers' down with it.

Even with my regulator on, I was in shock and disbelief. How could the politicians and financiers have been so idiotic? Come to think of it, I had probably thought that when I read about the Global Financial Crisis of 2008.

Whether due to the emotional regulator or my natural resilience, I soon calmed down. Other entrepreneurs had made fortunes, lost them, and made them again. I could do likewise, once I had 'learnt the ropes' of what the society of 2100 was about, and what sort of marketing opportunities would be available.

That afternoon, brain scans showed that my tumour had shrunk to less than half its original size.

●

Although there were several female staff at the hospital, Mara and Helen were the only ones I could strike up a friendship with. The other people were friendly enough, but they kept their distance. About the only time they wanted me was when they were having a game of water polo or aquatic volleyball.

Once every few days, Dr Ohira and his staff gave me a rigorous physical examination. They tested the strength of my muscles, weighed me, made me run on a treadmill, tested my reflexes, and took blood and other samples.

They also tested my eyesight and hearing, and my senses of smell, taste and balance. I was put on a fitness program. Instead of lying by the pool, or splashing about in it, I had to swim so many laps.

On a cool, summer evening, I went out with the hospital running team. It was the first time I had been outside the confines of the hospital and the greenhouses. I was excited because this gave me a sense of freedom.

We ran at a steady pace along a well-worn track that threaded its way through two rows of stunted eucalypts, and round a playing field that was more dust than grass.

We stayed within the perimeter of a cyclone fence, beyond which I could see a road, more trees, and the roofs of what looked to be houses. Unlike the white domes of the hospital and other buildings I had seen, these roofs were flat, dark and low.

After a few days, I started to enjoy my fitness routine. I became what I called 'disgustingly healthy', an expression which puzzled the medical staff. It would have been good pre-season training for cricket, a game that none of the staff knew much about. Because of my unpleasant experience of the test match in the holovision room, I was no longer so keen on it either. For the first time in my life, I really didn't care who won the series.

I had decided by then, wrongly as it turned out, that the people of 2100 didn't have a sense of humour. Most of the time, they were relaxed but serious, and so damn precise in what they said. It was only when they stripped off and mucked about in the water that they let their hair down.

I figured that Simon was probably the most serious of the lot of them. One day, I asked him, 'What do you blokes do in your spare time?'

When he had worked out what 'blokes' meant, he explained that he spent most of his spare time studying to improve his qualifications.

'Yes, but what about entertainment?' I insisted. 'What do people do at home at night? Watch HV? Play computer games? Go down to the club with their mates, get stuck into the booze, chat up the sheilas and play the pokies?'

I was deliberately being a provocative ocker, knowing full well that Simon wouldn't know what I was talking about. But people like Simon were so damned proper that I enjoyed taking the mickey out of them.

'All of the above, I suspect,' he replied, 'in moderation.'

'So you still have clubs and pubs, then?'

'If pubs is the old-fashioned word for tavern, yes. Although, more often we have community parties. People may drink at them if they wish.'

'In moderation.'

Simon nodded.

I said wistfully, 'I could do with a beer right now …'

I asked for a bottle of beer that evening at meal time. It went down rather well. I noticed, though, that not many other people drank. When I asked for another one, there was a discussion between Dr Ohira and the cafeteria staff. I thought I heard the word 'budget'.

'One is enough for now,' the good doctor told me. 'It is the first alcohol you have had for many years.'

I felt like telling him that was a perfectly good reason for having some more. As I was leaving, I scanned the cafeteria menu board. A bottle of beer (from the North Canberra Brewing Cooperative) cost twelve Australs.

'How much is an Austral?' I asked Dr Ohira.

'It replaced the dollar, if that is any guide to you.'

'Hmm. Twelve bucks is a bit steep for a bottle of beer. Especially given that incomes are a fraction of what they were.'

'You are aware of what beer is made from?'

'Hops and barley.'

'Both are in short supply. So are grapes for wine. All of our foods have to be rationed. Although alcohol may be pleasant, it is expensive.'

'Why are things in short supply?'

'Because of the damage to crops caused by drought and ultraviolet radiation.'

'When we were running round the hospital grounds, I thought the grass looked sick.'

'We can't afford to waste water just to make the grass look pretty.' He pointed to the waterfall in the Australian-Japanese garden, which was quietly flowing in the background. 'Even with that, we are very careful with water. Conditions are improving, but slowly.'

●

I handed over my flat and car to Janet. 'You've earned it,' I said as I gave her the keys on that tearful last day before we drove to the Cryosleep Centre. 'Find someone else, have a family, and save the planet for when I return.'

As we drove up into the hills, I looked back at the Canberra I knew and wondered if I would ever see it again. If so, what would it be like?

At the centre, I had hoped to have a hearty meal before they put me to sleep. Instead, I had to fast for two days and take laxatives to clean out my system. I wasn't sure whether the headaches I felt then were due to the tumour or the fasting.

Finally, the time came. My relatives and Janet were in attendance when I was given an injection to put me to sleep before the staff started 'processing' my body. The last things I saw were the faces of my loved ones, before I drifted off into oblivion.

●

My conditions, however, were improving rapidly. Next day, scans showed that my tumour disappeared altogether, hopefully never to return.

That evening, when we had a small party to celebrate, I learnt more about how the people of 2100 spent their leisure time. Once again, I was in the holovision room, this time with my regulator. In fact, everyone had their regulators on because they wanted to enjoy some music. The usual gang was there, including Dr Ohira, Helen, Mara and Simon.

The occasion was the live broadcast of a concert from the Sydney Town Hall by the Sydney Simfony Orkestra. It started with the orchestra materialising in the wall opposite us. Then the conductor walked onto the stage and into the middle of our room. Everyone around me stood up and applauded. They seemed to be as 'taken in' by the hologram as I was.

The conductor was Japanese, as was the first piece of music the orchestra played.

It was all done with short bursts of sounds, accompanied by patterns of light that played around the room. At first, it didn't appeal to me. It was like some of the weird modern music of my time. Yet, in its abstract way it had a rhythm to it which left me strangely contented.

The second work was called 'Lament'. Helen said that it was one of her favourites, and took off her regulator. Again, it was made up of weird bits and pieces of music, accompanied by spectacular photography of rainforests and swamps, which then turned to desert. When it was over, I felt sad. Weeping, Helen chanted a prayer to Gaia.

I turned to Mara, whom I managed to sit alongside. 'What's the matter with her?'

'She is crying for the lost rainforests.'

'Why? What happened to them?'

'Almost all gone,' Helen blurted out. 'All cut down. Then the fires and the desert winds came.'

I was going to say that if she got worked up about things like that, then why did she take off her regulator? Then I noticed that everyone was looking at me expectantly. 'Well, don't blame me. I wasn't a lumberjack.'

'We do have some rainforest left,' Simon chipped in, as if trying to be cheerful. 'But not much, I regret.'

Mercifully, it was the intermission. We had some cheese, biscuits and coffee. I asked Mara why Helen took off her regulator if she knew the music would upset her.

'It's her form of atonement,' Mara explained.

'Atonement? Why, what did she do?'

'Nothing. She does it on behalf of the human race. Or maybe she finds it therapeutic to have a good cry about something.'

'Women.' I shrugged my shoulders. 'They haven't changed much since my time.'

'Aren't you glad?' Mara patted me affectionately on the knee.

After the intermission, the music was more classical. I don't know much about classical music, but I was told the first work was a Brandenburg Concerto (without any fancy lighting or scenes from nature).

Even I knew the second work: Bolero. I recognised it when the repetitive drum beat started. I was soon seeing red – the whole room was bathed in it. Everyone around me was swaying or clapping with the music. Redness … Dr Ohira's white coat glowing red … Red faces … Silvery hair … Warm …

They carried me out into the cool night air to recover. When I came to, I saw the stars. They hadn't changed much, not that I expected them to. Dr Ohira was asking me what had happened.

'I don't know. A flashback. When everything turned red I thought I was back in the heat treatment room. You know, when you brought me out of hibernation.'

Dr Ohira nodded. 'That is why I think it wise for you to stay with us a little longer. Other cryonics patients have had flashbacks, but we cannot predict when and where they will happen. It can take a month to recover from hibernation.'

●

During the remainder of my stay in the hospital, I had no more flashbacks, traumas, or breakdowns. Nor did my tumour show any sign of returning. I ate, slept, exercised, read the Canberra Times, and harboured lustful thoughts about Mara. My only real problem was that I was bored and restless.

I had another session with Dr Ohira, Ron and Imogen. It was a friendly, informal meeting. Even Imogen was more relaxed. We all agreed that I should leave the hospital at the end of the month, to go and live with Dr Bushell and his community.

CHAPTER SEVEN

CELEBRATION

On Fr26012100, some of us went to the holovision room to watch a documentary.

A caption appeared on the wall: An ABC Creative History Unit Presentashn. Two familiar figures materialised, large as life, Dr Ron Bushell and Imogen Smith. They explained in a serious, formal way, that the program we were about to see was an accurate reconstruction of the landing of the First Fleet in 1788.

Next, we were on board ship with Captain Philip and his cronies, sailing into Botany Bay. They spoke in what we were assured was 18th-century English. I found it hard to listen to. My companions couldn't understand it at all.

The scene shifted to shore, to a group of aborigines who spoke in their local dialect.

'Why aren't there any subtitles?' I asked.

'Because two-dimensional letters aren't effective in three-dimensional space,' answered Simon.

The scene shifted back to the ships, then back to the shore, and so on, until the Union Jack was hoisted, and three cheers were given for King George. It was so low-key it was comical.

This was followed by a brief tour of Sydney Harbour since 1788. It had certainly changed since my time: gone were many of the luxury apartments that used to line the shores of the Harbour. When I saw the water lapping almost up to the edge of the Opera House, I realised the sea level had risen palpably.

Later, we saw another familiar landmark – Parliament House, Canberra. The 'house on the hill', as we used to call it, was still recognisable. Yet, fluttering from its massive flagpole was a green flag, with gold stars in the same arrangement as on the old flag, and a gold map of Australia in the top left-hand corner.

A small, dark, stooped figure stood on a podium in front of the House to give a speech to a crowd of a few hundred people. It was a speech about the trials and tribulations that people had experienced in this harsh land over umpteen thousand years. European settlement was but one chapter in the great saga of Australia.

I thought at first that the speaker was a doddery old woman until a close-up revealed her lively and determined face, with its deep-set character lines and flashing dark eyes.

'I have seen the President,' I remarked, 'and she is black.'

●

Late that day, I was told I had a visitor – my guardian.

'Good,' I said, as I was taken to a consulting room. 'I have a few questions to ask them about my finances.'

My guardian turned out to be a sprightly man in his seventies, with clear, blue eyes. There was something familiar about him. He smiled at me. 'Hello, Uncle James.'

I thought for a moment. 'Nephew Darren?'

He nodded, and we embraced. I looked at him closely. 'It's hard to believe. Last time we met, you were a boy of ten.'

'While you haven't changed a bit.'

'And the others? Mum and Dad and Kylie?'

We sat down while he told me that Dad had passed away soon after I went into Cryosleep, while Mum lived on for another decade. Kylie had passed away about twenty years ago. 'And Janet? If she's still around, she must be in her nineties.'

His expression was vague. He thought for a moment, then said, 'I couldn't say.'

He noticed that I kept eyeing a folder which he carried with him. 'This, as you may have guessed, is your portfolio, or what is left of it,' he said as he opened it. 'Have you heard of the Great Write Down?'

I nodded; I had read about it. When the economies went spiralling down while inflation went soaring up, all debts were written off, and governments transferred all depositors' savings to accounts in the Reserve Bank or equivalent. In Australia, they were subsequently devalued and converted to a new currency, the Austral. Other banks and financial institutions were left to 'crash, burn and die'. Insofar as it was possible to determine what constituted 'real terms', the economy shrunk to about one- fifth of its former value. Since then, modest real growth of about one percent per year had seen the economy increase to one-third of its former value.

'So, how much have I got?' I asked bluntly.

'Well,' he hedged, 'given that much of your share portfolio was rendered worthless due to many companies going out of business, and the soaring inflation before conversion to the Austral—'

'How much?' I demanded.

'About twenty thousand Australs. Which is now equivalent to average annual earnings for a full-time employee.'

'But that's less than one percent of its original value,' I protested.

'You were lucky to get that. Many trust funds were liquidated entirely. Fortunately, you had some investments in property, which were eventually realised for a fraction of their original value.'

I stared at him blankly. My regulator was working overtime. Then I looked at the bleak set of figures before me. Eventually, I sighed. 'Ah, well. I suppose I should be thankful I survived. The money should tide me over until I get back on my feet again.'

He took out some documents which we signed and Dr Ohira witnessed, formally handing over my trust fund assets to me. I noticed how business- like Darren became during this process. 'What do you do for a living?' I asked.

'I followed a career in the legal profession. I was the ABC's corporate solicitor until I retired recently.'

●

By the evening of Tuesday 30 Januri, I had gotten over my disappointment of losing 99% of my wealth. I have my ups and downs, but I don't stay down for long.

The staff threw a party for me in the canteen. By their standards, I think it was a big deal. They had a crate of beer and a flagon of riesling, which was bland and dry, but drinkable. With this, they toasted to my health, and wished me well in the big wide world outside. I put on my ocker voice and told them they were 'real dinky-di blokes and sheilas'. They laughed.

After we'd had a few nibblies (I called them 'horse duvers'), the others all lined up to help themselves to the steaming contents of the canteen's biggest wok.

I, however, was given a special dinner. Simon had done some historical research through old recipe books. So the chef was able to present me with – bless him – a hamburger with the lot, french fries and a sesame seed bun. Although the juices that dribbled down my chin had a more Asian flavour, I knew this was probably the closest thing I would get to a Big Mac in 2100.

After a desert of lychees, ice-cream and coffee, we got stuck into the beer – if you can call having two bottles of beer getting stuck into it. I thought of introducing everyone to the game of 'spin the bottle', but decided it might not go down too well. It was then that I noticed that Mara had disappeared. Rats, I wasn't going to have my way with her after all.

The party continued without her. My hosts soon lost interest in me and chatted about themselves. How were Simon's studies going? And Mr Chan's gall bladder? Should they subscribe to the Jernal of Applied Sikometry?

Having attracted everyone's attention, Dr Ohira made a short speech before presenting me with a suitcase. It was similar to the suitcases of my day, except that the plastic of which it was made was lighter and stronger. He suggested that it was time I tried it out.

So I went to my room to pack my few worldly goods: two or three robes, my hat, a spare pair of sandals, and the calendar Simon had given me.

I was beginning to feel excited about tomorrow when I saw Mara standing in the doorway. She had replaced her nurse's uniform for a loose- fitting blouse and tight slacks. With a quiet smile on her face, she asked me if I would care to join her in the holovision room.

I had mixed feelings about that room. What new terrors were they planning for me? With some trepidation, I followed her there.

The room was empty, save for a few cushions and a silky rug. The floor was soft and warm, like sand on a beach. A gentle breeze caressed my skin. There was a faint scent, a hint of warm, sea air. I could hear the rollers breaking on a distant beach. The walls of the room came to life with images of gently waving palms.

Mara closed the door behind us. 'I did say I might make it up to you someday, James,' she said as she started to undo the buttons on her blouse.

CHAPTER EIGHT

WILLOW

Next morning, Wensday 31 Januri, I felt pleasantly stiff and sore. I didn't need a regulator to put a smile on my face that day.

I was given my last meal in the canteen: fish and chips and a can of beer. They're not the sort of things I would usually have for breakfast, but I hadn't the heart to tell the hospital staff that.

At around 09:70, Ron Bushell arrived to pick me up. His car was an open, two-seater convertible. Ron wasn't driving it: in fact, no one was.

I shook hands with Dr Ohira, gave Mara one last, lingering kiss, and piled myself and my suitcase into the car. Ron said, 'Home'. I waved goodbye to the staff as the car drove us out into the big, wide world of 2100.

Although there were self-driving cars around in my day, I still found it strange that there was no driver. 'This would be great for parties.'

'Isn't it a bit small?'

'What I mean is, you wouldn't have to worry about the breathalyser.'

'The what? Oh, yes, for blood alcohol readings. We haven't had them for fifty years.'

That filled my heart with joy.

'Traffic accidents are rare these days,' Dr Bushell went on. 'Now that the human factor has been removed. Besides, there isn't as much traffic on the road as in your day.'

The road was indeed quiet. The only traffic we passed were a couple of cyclists, shortly before we saw a sign for North Canberra. We should by then have reached the suburbs. But all I could see were clumps of forest with a few rooftops, almost camouflaged, amongst the trees.

The car pulled off the main road and into a side street. We cruised alongside a park, about the size of a suburban street block. Halfway along, we stopped at an open gate with the sign: Willow Community.

Barely wide enough for two cars, the community's driveway was bordered by hedges. It was about fifteen metres long, and opened out into an area containing a few carports. The car slowed, hesitated, then turned into one of them.

'Here we are,' said Ron.

'What drives these things? Batteries?'

'Of course. Solar fuel cells in the carport roof collect enough energy to recharge them for regular use.' He opened up the car bonnet. I expected to see an array of large Eveready batteries. Instead, there was a box containing a series of opaque sheets that seemed to be made of plastic.

'Capacitors?'

Ron nodded. 'They may not look very big, but they're made of a complex organo-crystalline structure that can absorb large amounts of energy.'

'Next, where is the radar system?'

'In the bumper bars.'

I wanted to ask more questions because I enjoy tinkering with cars, and, of course, energy efficiency is my business, but at that moment there arrived a slim lady, dark-haired, with Eurasian features. She gave Ron a hug.

'James, I'd like you to meet my wife, Lena.'

'Welcome, James.' Lena gave me a hug as well. Despite her slight, wiry frame, she had a strong grip.

'Did you have a pleasant journey?' she asked. Her voice reminded me of Dr Ohira's: slightly clipped with a touch of Aussie drawl.

'Fine thanks.'

The walk to the Bushells' house was all of twenty metres: it was just on the other side of the carports. Their house block was tiny, ten metres wide and twelve metres long. Most of it was covered with small trees and shrubs, with the odd patch of lawn.

A narrow road, about three metres wide, curved round from the back of the carports, then curved again where it reached the corner of the park, some forty or fifty metres away. I could see another six house blocks following the curve of the road.

The Bushells' house itself was little more than a cottage, about seven metres square, with a porch reaching almost to the driveway. The sides of the house and its slightly raised roof had the same mottled appearance as some of the greenhouses at the hospital. I asked if they contained solar micros, and was told that they did.

We walked up the porch and through a pair of sliding windows into the house. Inside, it was large and airy, and refreshingly cool after the heat of the morning. Half of the room consisted of a lounge-cum-dining room and a kitchen. The other half was partitioned into sections. 'Are they the bedrooms?'

Ron laughed. 'No. That contains the mini-holovision, the main terminal, my hardcopy library, and some of Lena's artwork.' He led me past the partitions and down a set of steps. The area downstairs, which was just as large as that upstairs, was divided into the bathroom and three bedrooms.

'The one on the left is yours. Lena's put the kettle on. So come upstairs when you're ready.'

A moment later, I was standing in the room that was to be my bedroom for the next few months. Being partly underground, it was dark and cool, but well-ventilated.

It was not well-furnished: a bed, a chest of drawers with a mirror, a chair, a wardrobe, and a computer terminal set in a recess in the wall. There was an area on the wall, about 100 cm by 50 cm, that lit up when I touched it, and displayed the Macrosoft logo.

I was startled when a voice spoke out of nowhere, asking me what colour I wanted the screen to be. By now, I was used to what were called 'active walls'. There were no light bulbs in the rooms of 2100. The walls would glow to produce enough light to see by. I worked on a system like that at Climate Changers.

As I wandered back upstairs, I could smell the aroma of freshly brewed coffee. I sat down at the table with Lena and Ron, enjoyed my coffee, and looked around the room. It had a comfortable, lived-in feeling about it. Although the roof was dark, the windows were clear: I had a good view of the surrounding foliage.

On the walls, there were several paintings, aboriginal in style. When I said how nice they were, it was Lena who accepted the compliment. 'Do you paint?' I asked her.

'Mm. Mainly landscapes and wildlife.'

I looked at Ron. 'And you're a historian with the ABC?'

'Actually, I'm a consultant historian. But the ABC is one of my clients.'

'I saw your program about the arrival of the First Fleet. I didn't understand a lot of the dialogue. Still, it was very interesting.'

There was a wry smile on Ron's face. 'Many people have said that to me. The Creative History Unit aims for authenticity rather than popularity.'

'Tell it like it is.'

'Precisely. Popular or not, extensive research went into the making of the program, I and my bank balance are pleased to say.'

It was my turn for a wry smile. I looked around me while trying to find a new topic of conversation. What I saw was a mixture of the familiar and the unfamiliar. 'Canberra's changed a lot. Is this a typical house?'

'Typical for a suburban megacity. What you will find different is the neighbourhood. Come, I'll show you the park.'

Putting on our hats and sunglasses, we went out into the morning glare. We walked along the narrow road that went past the Bushells' house. There were a dozen houses in a neat curved row in what I worked out was the southeast corner of the park. They were all the same size, all with porches out the front, and trees, lawn and shrubs on the rest of their little blocks.

'These are all family houses,' Ron explained. 'It's good to stroll around here on summer evenings. By the time you've stopped and chatted to people on their porches, it can take half the evening to get around the park.'

The park was aligned east-west, about two hundred metres long and a hundred wide. Houses extended in a semi-circle from the southeastern corner to the southwestern. They would have made a monotonous row but for a kink in the middle. Here, where the road bulged inwards for a few metres, an area the size of a house block was covered with mounds, bushes and trees.

Up to then, I had not turned my attention inwards. I was aware that there was a small embankment on the other side of the road, but it was at this point that I saw the weeping willows.

Towards the southwestern corner, the embankment dipped away to a large lawn, and the fence of a swimming pool. The pool extended eastwards, between the willows, into an ill-defined area of grassy humps and hollows.

We reached the middle of the western side of the park, where there was another narrow driveway, some more carports and a kiosk. A narrow path ran up the centre of the park, which appeared to slope up gently from west to east. This may have been an optical illusion caused by the rising height of the embankment on the northern side of the park, and its rows of trees.

The central area was divided into four roughly equal quadrants: the swimming pool in the southwest, greenhouses and flower beds in the southeast, a large lawn in the northwest, and some fruit trees and a large building in the northeast.

'What's the building?' I asked.

'Our community centre. We hold all of our community meetings and social functions there. We also have our laundry and a large holovision room.' He turned my attention to the northwest corner of the park, where I could see a two-storey block of flats.

'We won't do the full circuit just now unless you're very keen. Over there is a block of flats for singles and young couples. Along the northern side, we have our vegetable gardens, and in the northeast corner we have some more houses and apartments for older people.'

'Neat.'

Ron pointed to a house in the corner around which we had walked. 'When this community was founded about forty years ago, a couple expecting their first child moved into that house. Their children grew up there before going out into the world.

'Some years later, their daughter returned with a partner. So the parents moved to the retirement village in the opposite corner of the park. Now, their daughter's son is studying at the ANU, and has moved into one of the flats over here.' He pointed to the flats in the northwest corner. 'Thus, we have three generations of the same family in this community, close to each other, yet far enough apart to live their own lives.'

We walked up the central path, to sit on a bench under the shade of the largest willow tree. I fondled some of its fronds. 'So this is why you call this place Willow Community.'

'That's right. Each community tries to create its own distinctive environment.'

'How many people live here?'

'About one hundred and twenty, in fifty dwellings, on two hectares of land. In your day, in the quarter-acre blocks of suburbia, the population density was about forty per hectare. Here, it is about fifty percent greater. Yet we are self-sufficient in vegetables, have our own little park and swimming hole, and a sense of belonging.'

'How did you manage it?'

'This place may look spacious, but every part of it is carefully planned. The major difference is transport. In your day, a typical house might have a driveway and garage taking up one-fifth of the land. Here, we have one internal road-cum-walkway taking up ten percent, plus two sets of carports.'

'Where do you fit all the cars?'

'That's the other major difference. There are only a dozen auto cars on the property, and most of them are owned by the community. The only private vehicles are owned by people who need to use them regularly because of the nature of their work; trades people, for example.'

'So what happens if someone wants to go for a drive?'

'They borrow one of the community's cars. It is rare that they would all be out at the one time.' Ron went on, 'Individually, we are about half as wealthy as people at the turn of the millennium.'

'And about one-third as much since I went into cryosleep.'

'Yet, through our communities, we can rationalise our resources and have as many of the good things in life as you did – and more.'

'Rationalisation, eh?'

'It has been said that the history of the twenty-first century can be summed up as a constant process of rationalisation.'

He didn't explain this remark. In the summer heat, I wasn't inclined to ask him what he meant by it. In fact, neither of us said anything for a while. Ron sat quietly and meditated. I had seen a few people at the medical centre doing that. Everyone was generally quiet and calm. There were no transistors blaring, no lawnmowers mowing. It was an eerie quiet.

Then I started to hear things: bird calls, the rustling of a branch, or peoples' voices in the distance. Even without my regulator, I felt a great sense of calm, which was unnerving.

Ron got up abruptly. 'Time for lunch.'

I was startled out of my reverie. As we walked along the path, I asked, 'Is it always so quiet?'

'Quiet? Didn't you hear the birds?'

'Yes. But what about traffic noises and things like that?'

'Unless you're an autocar enthusiast, who wants to hear traffic noises?'

A thought struck me. 'You know, it occurs to me that I haven't seen anybody on a smart phone or an iPad or any other mobile device. In my day, people were texting each other a lot of the time.'

'Hmm. Curious.' Ron thought about this as we approached his house. 'We do have such devices, but the bills are fairly high. Maybe it's one example of where being only one-third as affluent has affected our behaviour.'

We arrived back in time for lunch, which was set out on a wooden trestle on the porch. It was plain fare – wholemeal bread rolls, plenty of red and green salads, and fruit juice. We ate and drank from earthenware plates and cups. They were the sort of things one might buy from a craft shop in a small country town trying to lure the trendy tourist.

There were four of us at lunch. We were joined by a petite lass with Lena's Eurasian features, a cheeky expression and close-cropped hair. She looked to be about thirteen.

Lena introduced her. 'This is Tami, our child.'

'So this is the man Ron's been talking about?' She was wide-eyed as she shook my hand. 'Are you really a hundred years old?'

'Almost. But as far as I'm concerned, I'm only in my thirties.'

I was surprised that she didn't groan 'in your thirties'. When I was her age, I thought of thirty as being middle-aged. As I approached it, I changed my perspectives.

'So I'm still a young man,' I added.

She seemed to accept this. After all, she could expect to live to be ninety.

Later on though, she did surprise me with a question. Out of the blue, she asked, 'Did you have a carbon footprint? We're studying early twenty- first century this year.'

'Erm … to some extent. But when I set up a company to deal with climate change, I drove an electric car.'

'Oh. I didn't think you people believed climate change was happening.'

'At first, many of us were sceptical. But after the bad fires of 2019–20, I don't think many of us were left in any doubt.'

Tami seemed taken aback. 'It was horrible way back then, wasn't it? All those wars and pollution you people caused.'

'Tami.' For once, Lena reproached her, then smiled at me. 'You may find our ways a little strange at times. We like to pretend that the people who lived before Gaia's curse were different from us.'

I was surprised by her frankness. 'Because of wars and pollution and chopping down trees?' I looked straight at Tami, hoping to confound her by being equally direct.

'Well, it was your fault,' she insisted.

Ron put his hand on Tami's shoulder and rubbed it gently. 'That's not entirely fair, Tami. It was also the people of James's generation that warned about the dangers of climate change and developed the Gaia concept.'

'We even gave up using aerosol spray cans,' I added.

'What are they?'

'Well, if you wanted to spray a fly, or your hair.'

'Why would you want to spray a fly? Were you painting them?'

Ron laughed, while Tami was irritated. 'I should explain,' the historian said, 'that flies are biologically controlled these days. They are not the pests they used to be.'

I looked around: a typical Australian summer day, plenty of food and drink on the table, but no flies. 'I thought there was something missing.'

Ron laughed and Lena smiled. Tami lapsed into silence.

After a while, she asked, 'Did you say hair?'

'Mm?' I looked up from my salad.

'You said you sprayed hair.'

I nodded. 'To set it in place. To make it look prettier. Women did, anyway.'

'Prettier? How?'

'Remember those old pictures I showed you?' Lena reminded her. 'With the fancy hair arrangements?'

'Oh, yes. Is that how they did it?'

Tami now seemed less disenchanted with early 21st century. If anything, she was now a shade envious. She leant over the table to ask me quietly, 'Was it exciting?'

My mind wandered off into a reverie about my erotic adventure with Mara the previous night. 'What?'

'Earlier this century. Did you fly in a spaceship, or meet David Attenborough?'

'No.' I settled back in my chair. 'I watched it all on television.'

CHAPTER NINE

THE TAMING OF THE BEES

After lunch, I was sleepy: it was one of those contented, lazy afternoons that were part of the Australian summer. I retired to my room, plonked down on the bed, and fell asleep.

When I woke up in my cool room a couple of hours later, I felt refreshed. I wandered upstairs, where it was also cool. Lena was sitting at a terminal, plotting ornate designs on a 3D screen. Ron was reading a book on 21st-century social history. He looked up, saw me, and asked if I wanted a drink.

'Not just now, thanks,' I replied. 'I want to go for a walk. Just to clear my head.'

'Fine.' Ron went back to his book. 'Don't forget your hat and sunglasses.'

I was glad he didn't offer to come with me. My real reason for going walking was that everywhere I had been in the last month, there was always someone else around. I wanted a breath of freedom – to wander wherever I pleased.

I walked past the garages near the Bushells' place, then out of the driveway into the street. The grass was bare and the street trees were stunted. Only when I looked back into the community park could I see patches of green.

I soon realised that my new freedom meant little in itself. It was good to feel free, but free to do what? When I got to the end of the street, I couldn't decide which way to go. I took the tame option of going for a walk round the block that contained the community.

I meant to have a look at the community's vegetable gardens as I passed them, but I became wrapped up in my thoughts.

If I could go anywhere, then where would I go? I couldn't go back to my own time, nor was I sure how I could fit into the world of 2100.

Almost without realising it, I went round the block and came back to the driveway. As I walked towards the garages, I felt I was being followed. I looked around. There was an empty car crawling along the drive behind me. I stopped: the car stopped. I started moving again: so, slowly, did the car. I played a game of stop-start with it all the way to the garages. Then I stepped aside to watch it park itself in one of the carports.

I was about to head back to the Bushells' house when I saw a man changing a tire on one of the other cars.

'Need a hand?' I asked.

He was a tall man, middle-aged: sweat was glistening on his pink, balding head. 'Thank you,' he said, and offered me his large, flabby hand to shake. He spoke in a refined, English voice. 'Roderick Bray.'

'I'm James Lawson. A friend of the Bushells.'

For me, it was like old times. My first job was in a garage, and I always seemed to be around motors. Technology may have changed, but a jack was still a jack, hubcaps were still hubcaps, and there were still four sets of nuts and bolts to loosen and tighten.

One difference I did notice was that the tires were thin. They reminded me of those on pre-war vintage cars. I hadn't seen much rubber about the place.

'I'm afraid tires aren't what they used to be,' Roderick apologised. 'Composites are so expensive, and all the rubber trees in Malaysia died while you were asleep.'

'What? This afternoon?'

'No,' Roderick laughed. 'While you were hibernating.'

'Then you know about me?'

'Of course. Everyone in Willow has heard about you. There's a party in your honour on Saturday night, I believe.'

'First I heard of it,' I remarked as we wheeled the old tire into a shed. There were some other old ones there, and twenty or thirty bicycles.

'Oh? Well, perhaps I've made a mistake with the dates. My work takes me overseas quite often, so I'm not always au fait with what is happening here.'

'What sort of work do you do?'

'I'm a trade commissioner,' he said nonchalantly. 'I make all of my contributions to the community in cash rather than kind. But it's nice to do the odd community job when I'm here, just to keep my hand in, so to speak.'

I said goodbye to him and went back to the Bushells' house feeling pleased with myself. For once, I had been useful to someone.

●

In the cool of the evening, we had dinner, again on the porch. This time, we had a chicken casserole, and, of course, plenty of salads.

We ate in virtual silence as we listened to the evening birdsongs and the chirping crickets. As the orange-red of the western sky merged into the deep blue of the vault above, we met the first of the evening promenaders.

I recognised the tall silhouette of Roderick the trade commissioner. He was walking with his lady friend, Patricia. Like him, she was English. Early middle-age, she was plump, but attractive.

'So you're the man from long ago,' she said with obvious interest as we shook hands. 'You must come to visit us soon.'

She gave me a seductive smile: there was a refined, yet earthy quality about her. I said I would very much like to visit them.

Apart from Roderick and Patricia, we saw only one or two other promenaders that evening. Tami went indoors to do her homework, leaving Ron, Lena and I with the porch to ourselves.

A solitary moth buzzed around the patio light before it lost interest and went somewhere else. Lena explained that moths, like flies, were biologically controlled to keep their numbers down.

I asked what was happening on Saturday night.

Ron had produced a pipe which he was packing with tobacco. 'We're arranging a party at the community centre. It will be an opportunity to formally introduce you to the rest of the community. About fifty people maybe?'

'More like a hundred,' said Lena. 'Does that worry you, James?'

'No. Not at all. In fact …' I played with my drink.

Ron lit his pipe. 'Is something troubling you?'

I felt embarrassed. 'Well, it's just … I know this may sound big-headed, but—'

'Big-headed?' Lena queried. Ron thought for a moment. 'Ah. High ego.'

'Yeah. High ego.' I decided that I liked that expression. 'I was asleep for over sixty years. It must be some sort of record.'

'I believe so,' Ron said guardedly.

'I thought there would be more of a fuss. You know, HV cameras and press interviews and things like that.'

'Hmm.' Ron sucked on his pipe, and blew an unsuccessful smoke ring. 'Novelty value.'

'What? Er, yeah.'

'People have been coming out of hibernation since the middle of the century.' Ron explained. 'However, it's only been in recent years, with a better understanding of how the emotional regulator works, that doctors have been able to treat patients like yourself.'

That struck a responsive chord in me. A thought that had been nagging me, deep down, came to the surface. I muttered, 'Something somebody said.'

'Pardon?'

'I remember now. It was you. When we were talking about regulators, in the hospital, you said that you resisted having one for years after they came on the market.'

'That's right.'

'Which means that they must have been around for years before they used one to wake me up.'

Ron nodded his head. 'True. And because yours was an unusual case, Doctor Ohira waited until he was sure the regulator would work on you, and convinced your nephew that it was time for you to be revived.'

This explanation gave me a sense of relief and satisfaction. Even though I was happy when I retired to my bedroom, I decided to enhance the effect by putting on my regulator. But it had been a long day: all I did was fall asleep.

●

When I woke up next morning, Th01022100, I felt refreshed and relaxed. Ron suggested a swim before breakfast. We all walked down to the swimming pool.

It was only when I went inside the enclosure that I realised how big the pool was. The main part, at the western end, was a roughly circular pond about twenty metres in diameter. It narrowed into a channel, which went between the willows into a smaller pond. From there, it headed off into the grassy humps and hollows at the eastern end.

The water hole was a busy place: early morning swimming was a community activity. Everyone – young, old and in-between – arrived in robes which they took off, and swum au naturel. The Bushells did likewise.

Had it not been for my experiences in the hospital swimming pool, I might have been surprised at this. As it was, I tried to act natural. I was soon distracted by some of the attractive shapes in the water.

As it was in the hospital, so it was in the community: my introduction to many of my new companions was in the altogether, in a series of vigorous water fights. Splashing someone seemed to be a traditional way for people to meet each other.

This continued for perhaps half an hour, and may have involved up to thirty or forty people. For the most part, their skin was neither white nor brown, but a coppery colour. Many also had Asian features.

When people got out of the pool, they quickly donned their robes, not out of modesty, but out of a lifetime's aversion to bright sunlight and the ultraviolet.

'You must think it strange,' said Ron, as we put on our robes, 'that we are so careful with water in some ways and so extravagant with it here.'

I had not found it at all strange because my mind was elsewhere. There was a stunningly attractive dusky brunette on the far side of the pool.

'All of the water here is purified and recycled,' Ron explained. 'Swimming is our way of, as you would say, letting our hair down.'

'I know.' The brunette was ringing out her long, sleek hair.

'Time for breakfast, James.' Lena squeezed my arm. 'You can play with her another day.'

●

After breakfast, Ron used one of the cars to go to a meeting at the ANU, while Tami went to school. Lena invited me to come with her while she did her 'rounds'. As we left the house, I asked, 'Shouldn't we lock up?'

'Why?'

'Burglars.'

'Burglars?' Lena was shocked. 'We're not living in your day – oh, sorry.'

'That's all right.'

'Everyone around here knows everyone else, or would know if there were strangers. Besides, why should anyone want to steal anything?'

'What about the holovision? Or the computers? That sort of thing.'

'But they are an integral part of the house. You might as well try removing the plumbing. Besides, most houses and apartments have HV and computers in them already.'

'What about cash and jewellery and things like that?'

Lena thought for a moment. 'I don't think we own anything worth stealing.'

'Oh? I thought you people were well off.'

'I don't nexus. Well off what?'

'Financially. I mean, Ron's a professor, and you're an artist. You've only got one kid to support, and you've got your own home.'

'We don't actually own our home,' Lena explained. 'The community does. Although we have a long-term lease on it.'

'Who owns the community?'

'All of us. Everyone who lives here. We have an equity stake in it. We pay our body corporate fees and contribute our labour, which is why I am doing "rounds".'

We went to a small building near the community centre. Inside, there were several machines quietly humming. I recognised one of them as a compressor. There was also the Control Room which contained several monitors. It was from here that the flow of water into the pool and the gardens was regulated.

Lena sat at a terminal, and asked the computer for some details on temperature, oxygen content and water levels, which she wrote in a book.

'Why not store the data on computer?' I asked.

'We do. But writing it in the book helps us to store it in our minds as well.'

'Why bother to remember it?'

Lena paused for a moment. 'Because that way, we are always aware that we are monitoring a system.'

'Is that important?'

Lena nodded. 'When you have lived with us a while, you will understand why. You could say that we are a backup for the computer systems.'

'In case they fail?'

'Yes. Also, because human beings are holistic thinkers, we can sometimes nexus data in ways that computers cannot. And do artistic things with natural systems that computers cannot. These data are part of what Ron calls our "collective culture".'

Lena issued some instructions to the terminal. On the monitors, I saw two sprinklers shut down, while others started up.

'If you like,' I offered, 'I could make up a program so you could automate the sprinkler system.'

She thought for a moment. 'But what if we wanted to vary it? In fact, we do. We don't water as much in winter as we do in summer.'

'What I can do is to write a series of default programs – one for each season if you like. You can personally intervene on any day if you want to vary the program.'

Lena seemed to be disconcerted by my suggestion. She was used to doing things her way. 'Let me think about that.'

Her second task was extraordinary. She brought up the monitor for a beehive. She also called up a Solar Cordinats Program. 'Could you give me the cordinats book, please?'

I looked around for another book, then realised that she was talking to the terminal. It produced a schematic diagram of the park, with latitude and longitude co-ordinates to a fraction of a second.

'Close up on the rose garden,' ordered Lena.

One area of the map, where there were diagrams of bushes, expanded to fill the screen. 'Match monitors.' On the monitors, we could see the actual rose bushes, waving gently in a breeze. 'Transmit cordinats to hive.'

'What's going on?'

'The cordinats of the rose garden will be modulated into a scout bee's sun dance. A detachment of bees will soon arrive to work there.'

I felt uncomfortable. 'You mean, you control the bees?'

'Of course. Bees are simple creatures and easy to program. We have a lease-share agreement on the hive in the next community.'

'I don't nexus. Why not just let the bees do their own thing?'

'I don't nexus,' Lena retorted.

'Well, bees being bees, they're going to do your roses sooner or later, aren't they?'

'Yes, but if we program the order in which they operate, we get better results with plant propagation – and honey yields.'

I felt like saying that it was 'agin nature'. But then, what right had I, a man from the early 21st century, to complain about a little tinkering with the natural world?

Lena's third task was to take readings of atmospheric variables – temperature, humidity and UV radiation, which she also wrote in a book. 'The UV's up three points today.'

'Does it change much?'

'It fluctuates from day to day. It's higher in summer, of course.'

'What about over the last few years?'

Lena spoke to her terminal. 'UV trends, please.'

Responding to further commands from Lena, the terminal screen showed that in the previous decade, average annual UV radiation had trended downwards, but with the occasional upward spike. 'The ozone layer is slowly recovering,' she assured me. 'The last CFCs went into the stratosphere about sixty years ago. They are breaking down.

'Those spikes you can see are caused when sulphur aerosols are released into the upper atmosphere. They reflect the sun's energy into space, but they also affect the ozone layer.'

'Is that to prevent global warming?'

'Well, to try and keep it under control at any rate. Globally, the temperature has increased by about two degrees. Apparently, we are right on the cusp when it comes to preventing major climate change, which is why the aerosols are used from time to time. But it's a delicate balancing act.'

'So no more coal-fired power stations?'

Lena shook her head. 'The human race seems to have a flair for doing just enough in the nick of time. Perhaps.'

Her last task took us outside, with a pair of binoculars and a notebook. I asked what we were looking for.

'Birds. We must update the bird count.'

Although my interest in birds was mainly in the unfeathered variety, I did notice that most of the birds were locals: galahs, mynahs, magpies and cockatoos. When we approached them, the cockatoos performed some of their acrobatics. Yet they didn't squawk much. Perhaps they had been programmed not to.

Some familiar species were missing. 'What about rosellas and parrots?'

'The Indian mynahs forced them out of their natural habitats.'

'Oh.' I felt a strange sense of loss. There had always been rosellas in Canberra. I had never really taken much notice of them, but now that they were missing …

'You can see some rosellas and parrots in a large aviary in one of the communities near the markets when we go there on Saturday. There's even a few sparrows.

'We don't see many migratory birds in Australia these days,' Lena went on. 'The UV radiation, storms and air pollution have made bird navigation hazardous. Besides, many of their natural habitats in other countries have been destroyed.

'Australia is now the last refuge for many species of wildlife. Did you know there are more elephants in Australia than in any other country in the world?'

'African or Indian?' I asked flippantly.

'Both. There are big nature reserves near Perth, where the conditions of the Serengeti can be reproduced. We can replicate other natural habitats as well. There's a big gorilla sanctuary in a rainforest in Queensland.'

'What about lions and tigers and giraffes?'

'Yes. And rhinoceri – African and Indian, hippopotami, antelopes, wildebeest, and our own animals of course. It was all part of a giant rescue operation. Overseas, natural habitats were being destroyed because of the population explosion.'

'Australia,' I said grandly, 'zoo capital of the world. Must be great for the tourist trade.'

'There are even herds of yaks and llamas in the Snowy Mountains.'

'What? No yetis?'

Lena managed a wry, forced smile.

CHAPTER TEN

FLIGHT OF FANTASY

That afternoon, I had a different experience of life in the 21st century. Tami came home for lunch with Lena and myself, and then invited me to her school. Her classmates were eager to talk to the man from nearly seventy years ago. She said that it was appropriate for me to meet them that afternoon because it was their history seminar.

Even though I hadn't been to school since my teens, the word still had unpleasant connotations. Yet, I went with Tami.

The school was two blocks away from where we lived, on another community. No one seemed surprised at an adult turning up for the class. I was surprised though, when the kids called the teacher by her given name, Shauna. With a name like that, I might have expected her to be a young colleen with long, black hair: she was middle-aged and grey-haired.

At first, I didn't realise I was in a classroom. It was in a small dome with a sunken garden, which reminded me of the hospital's garden. There were a dozen students, mainly about Tami's age, sitting on chairs or benches strewn casually around the place.

After introducing me to the class, Shauna asked me if I would like to give a talk or field questions.

I was embarrassed. I gave Tami a black look because she had obviously set me up. Tami seemed puzzled by my reaction. 'Er, well, I never was a teacher,' I explained. 'I suppose I could tell you what it was like when I went to school.'

As I spoke, memories came flooding back of a time I thought I had forgotten; a time of classrooms and asphalt yards, of skateboards and chemistry labs. I didn't want to talk about the school excursions that Kylie and I couldn't go on because we were too poor.

I remembered some of my teachers and classmates, and their idiosyncrasies. I realised that I had outlived all of them.

My flood of nostalgia continued unabated for a good half-hour. The students were surprised when I told them that I used to ride a bike to school. They thought that everyone in my day went everywhere by car.

When I finished, the class was quiet, even when Shauna thanked me and asked if they had any questions. Tami, for whom I was obviously a school project, decided that she'd better start the ball rolling. 'What sort of things did you study at school?'

'English, history, science, maths. If you were one of the top students, you studied languages. I did commerce.'

A very serious, studious lad named Steven asked if I had studied human relations. I asked him what he meant by that. He was taken aback, as if I had asked what legs were.

'How people learn to live with each other. It's a compulsory subject from kindergarten to senior high school.'

I shook my head. 'We didn't have such a subject.'

This caused the students to mutter among themselves. I overheard one lass, Angela, say something like 'no wonder people in his time were so unhappy'. When I looked straight at her, she asked, 'Were you happy at school?'

'It was all right, I suppose. I was glad to get out of it, though.'

'Why?'

'Didn't like homework.'

The students laughed. Angela continued her line of enquiry. 'What did you do outside of school hours?'

'Mucked around with my friends. Played cricket and footy. Watched TV. Much the same as kids do these days, I suppose.'

After that, questions flowed thick and fast. Did I fight much? Sometimes. Did I know about ecology? A bit – it was always in the news. The most intriguing question was: 'Did I fly?'

'Fly? No, I couldn't afford it.'

Shauna cleared her throat. 'Flying means something different now, James. Perhaps some of the class could arrange a flight for you.' She looked straight at Tami, who nodded.

They left me in suspense about what they meant by flying. Instead, they pressed me with questions about the current affairs of my time, most of which they seemed to know more about than I did.

I had to explain that I had never personally met Patrick White, David Attenborough or Julia Gillard. But I had met Alan Border once. This drew another blank look from my audience.

'It was a big thrill for a kid of my age,' I insisted.

'What do you mean by "kid"?' Angela demanded.

'Well, kids are, you know … children.'

'The term is obsolete,' Shauna insisted. 'Unless you are talking about goats. Referring to children by such a demeaning term as "kids" is considered now to be a form of ageism.'

I didn't want to argue the toss on that one. Instead, I went on the attack. 'Do you kids, er, children, fight much?'

That caused a ripple of murmurs until Angela took it upon herself to answer on behalf of the class. 'No. Not really. Sometimes we quarrel and there might be a bit of pushing and shoving, but we never hit each other, or shoot each other.'

I was disturbed by her last comment. Did she assume that shooting each other was routine in my day? The students were surprised when I told them that I never saw a murder, except on TV. I didn't tell them about my slug gun, and the time I nearly took a pot shot at the kid next door after an argument. Dad had belted me behind the ear and taken the gun away.

I heard a whisper in the class about 'aggro centres'. I sensed that it was a taboo subject because Shauna quickly cut in to ask me what I did when I left school.

'Firstly, I worked as a mechanic in a garage. Then I thought of following in my father's footsteps by becoming a bus driver.'

The students were as curious about this as I was about the fact that I hadn't seen many buses in Canberra.

Because people had bicycles and programmable autocars, and did most of their paid work on terminals at home, there wasn't much need for scheduled bus services. You could charter a bus from your home terminal, program its destination, and pay for it by community credit card.

Returning to my life story, I had decided that there was more future in accounting and computing. So I had studied for my Bachelor of Commerce degree. I explained my first job was working for a solar panel company until I got retrenched.

'What does retrenched mean?' asked Steven.

'Laid off ... sacked.' Another blank look from the class. 'I lost my job.'

Steven was puzzled. 'How could you lose your job?'

'The company went through a bad period due to competition. It wasn't making enough money to justify our salaries, so some of us had to be dismissed. Including me.'

'Couldn't you have done other work?' Steven insisted. 'In the company's food gardens or their workshops?'

'They didn't have anything like that. All they had was a small office and warehouse space.'

The class was horrified by this. In the Australian corporate sector of 2100, companies were required to diversify their activities to ensure that even in lean times, there was still enough work for their staff.

When I suggested that it was surely up to management to decide whether their workers should be redeployed or retrenched, I was told that all companies had profit-sharing schemes and worker participation in management. Many companies were now owned by their employees.

Well, I could relate to that. I explained that after working for other businesses, I set up my own company, Climate Changers, which I eventually sold to a consortium that included my employees. The students seemed impressed.

Steven asked, 'Why did you come to our time?'

I explained about the brain tumour and the sixty-five years in Cryosleep. He seemed puzzled. 'But they've been using nanites to cure cancer and tumours for forty years.'

'There were problems with reviving people from Cryosleep. I know most of them were successfully revived over twenty years ago using the regulator, but mine was an unusual case, because of the tumour.' Even as I said that, it sounded odd.

Young Steven, who seemed destined not for a career in the Diplomatic Corps, wanted to continue his line of questioning. Shauna intervened: 'I'm sure there are other things James would like to talk about. Did you have a, er, girlfriend?'

The class tittered. 'Or are you gay?'

'I am not gay,' I asserted. 'I did have a girlfriend, Janet. I'm not sure if she's still around. She must be over ninety.' I remembered Darren's vague answer when I asked him about her. Was he being deliberately evasive, or did he genuinely not know? I began to feel distinctly uneasy. 'I'd prefer not to discuss personal matters at this stage.'

'Well,' responded Steven, 'how can we nexus with you if we don't ask personal questions?'

I was stuck for an answer. Mercifully, Shauna looked at the time. 'I think that's enough for today. We don't want to tire our guest. Perhaps James will answer some more of our questions some other time.'

The class applauded me for coming, and Tami for bringing me. Emotionally drained, I left the classroom.

As I headed back towards the community, questions were running around in my head. Why had it taken them another twenty years to attempt to revive me? Was it just the tumour, or was it something else? And why had Darren been so evasive about Janet?

I hadn't worn my regulator to the school. Most of the time, I didn't seem to need it. I hadn't seen many people in the community wear them. Perhaps I had stopped noticing, just as in my day, I often couldn't remember if someone wore glasses.

When I got back to my room, I put the regulator on straight away. It soothed me … relaxed me. My questions soon went away.

●

I wore my regulator that night at dinner. The Bushells were quiet; even Tami wasn't her usual bubbly self. Then I noticed that she was wearing her regulator. As a sort of peace offering, I smiled at her. She smiled back.

After dinner, Tami disappeared with her mother, leaving me on the porch with Ron, and two cans of beer.

He waited until he had lit his pipe and blown another unsuccessful smoke ring before he asked about my visit to the school.

'It was certainly different from when I went to school.' I explained. 'And I'd rather they didn't ask me personal questions.'

'In a community, it's likely that people will be interested in each other's private lives. And you can't blame children of that age for being curious.' Ron transferred his interest from his pipe to his beer. 'Has it occurred to you that they might have been paying you a compliment? In our society, if someone asks personal questions, it means that they care enough about you to be interested in your problems.'

'I'm not used to that sort of thing. In my day, people didn't ask personal questions unless they were really close to you.'

'That's something you'll have to get used to in modern society,' Ron said uncompromisingly. 'But why should you object to other people knowing about your personal problems? They might be able to help.

'By the way, the usual method of indicating that you are displeased is to place your hand on your regulator, or the place behind the ear where it sits.'

'Thank you. I'll remember that.'

Ron seemed undecided between his beer and his pipe. All around us, in the night, the crickets were chirping their heads off. 'I believe you played cricket.'

'Yeah. Opening bat. Slow-medium bowler. I played mainly in second grade. Who knows? If I had trained harder, got a few more runs—'

'A team game,' Ron said abruptly.

'A team game, as you say. I had some good mates.'

'Tell me about your mates. What did you do?'

'We were a team, see. On the field, we backed each other up. You got a blast from the captain if you didn't.'

'And off the field?'

'Well, I was something of a nerd, so I didn't have that much in common with them. There wasn't much that we could talk about.'

'And Janet? Did you talk with her much?'

'Janet? I meant to ask you about her. Is she still around?'

Ron seemed uneasy. 'If she is, she'd be quite old. Would you want to see her after all these years?'

'Well, of course. I told her to save the planet until I returned.'

'Hmm. Well, I'll make some enquiries and see what we can do.'

●

Next morning, Fr02022100, at breakfast, I was subdued. My regulator was working overtime. I knew that I was unhappy about some things, but I did not feel unhappy: I was placid. Tami, however, was very secretive. Eventually, she said, 'We've got a surprise for you.'

'Who are "we"?' 'The class.'

Sure enough, members of her class were gathering outside. Most had smiles or grins on their faces.

'What are they doing here?'

'Come and see,' Tami insisted.

Lena nodded. Reluctantly, I went outside and allowed myself to be led across to a neighbouring community. The kids (sorry, children) had an air of suppressed excitement about them. They led me into a small building with white walls. I recognised it immediately as a holovision room. Suspended from the ceiling was a contraption that reminded me of a hang glider.

'You don't want me to fly that, do you?'

'In a way,' Tami replied.

Even with my regulator on, I was alarmed. If this was some form of revenge, then I wasn't impressed. Against my better judgment, I allowed myself to be strapped in.

Giggling, Tami and her friends left the room. Then it was plunged into darkness. I fumed, but didn't dare try to unstrap myself. Kids were as malicious now as in my day.

The music started: a soft, irregular rhythm that slowly built in intensity. The lights came on. I gasped. I was hovering on the edge of a cliff. I plunged with the music, then soared with it, high over the cliff tops. For forty minutes I swooped and soared over cliffs and reefs, or above the majestic cloud tops in the afternoon light.

I became part of a storm – I was thunder and I was lightning. Then I was on a long, slow glide at dusk by a tranquil sea. As I soared, so did my spirits. The music, which started so gently, became fierce, proud, uncompromising, relentless, exultant. Twice, as it reached a climax, I cried out in joy, and thought of my night of passion with Mara.

When the music ended with three triumphant chords, I wanted to punch the air with joy as if I had kicked the winning goal in a football grand final. There were tears running down my cheeks when the children came to unstrap me.

'That was fantastic,' I exclaimed as I hugged Tami. 'Who wrote the music?'

Steven said nonchalantly, 'Symphony number two in D-major, opus forty-three, by Sibelius.'

'Never heard of that group,' I replied. 'When were they around?'

'Sibelius wrote it about two hundred years ago.'

●

'So you enjoyed the flight fantasy?' Ron asked when I returned, obviously in a better frame of mind.

'Yeah. It was terrific.'

'It's one of our classic holo fantasies,' he said. 'Very popular with people of Tami's age, especially boys. It's an effective outlet for their aggression, and appeals to their growing sexual awareness.'

I thought of Mara, then commented, 'I notice the kids don't seem to fight much.'

'No. Aggression therapy is an important part of their personal development courses. Learning to recognise their feelings and using them constructively. That is one reason why our crime rate is so low. The other reason is that most people belong to a community.'

I nodded. 'I heard somebody whisper something yesterday about "aggro centres".'

Ron nodded. 'There are places you can go to vent your frustration.'

'Beat up rubber dummies and play war games and things like that?'

'If you want to. There are martial arts classes as well. When aggro centres were established, they were as controversial as sex shops were in the twentieth century.

'They came about at a time when the level of violence in our society was steadily rising. They were inspired by a rock group called "Aggro" whose song "Battery Rat" was so rhythmically irritating that it inspired riots wherever it was played. Three of the group members were killed.

'As for the Aggro Centres, there were debates about whether they stimulated people to commit violent acts, or provided a healthy outlet for their aggressions. Evidence suggests that they did both.'

'Both?'

'Some people did become more violent. Others became healthier and less frustrated. A classic case, perhaps, of "one man's meat is another one's poison".'

CHAPTER ELEVEN

TO MARKET

That evening, we watched holovision at home. Home holovision sets were much smaller than the ones I had seen at the hospital, or where I had the flight fantasy that morning. The Bushells' set covered part of one wall, and projected only about two metres into the room. It was like watching a performance on a mini stage.

There were four channels to which we had direct access, and we watched one program on each. We began with the ABC News. The theme music was electronic, yet bore a strange resemblance to the well-known theme of my time. Even though the news reader wore a blue caftan, she still had that conservative, knowledgeable ABC manner.

The news was presented in a very different way from what I was used to. Instead of starting with dramatic headlines, it had a low-key, systematic format, beginning with a review of the global weather – 'the state of Gaia's health' as Lena put it. So I learnt about the effect El Niño was having on our rainfall, and the rate at which the tundra was melting in Siberia.

Much of the news that followed was about the Eastern Zone. The Great Hydrogen Pipeline, which extracted hydrogen from the methane released from the rotting vegetation exposed by the melting tundra, now extended all the way from Vladivostok to Mumbai. We saw an Indian housewife using Siberian hydrogen gas to boil fresh, cool Siberian meltwater.

We were told that India's population of nearly two billion was about to level off. We also saw a report on how the pipeline was helping industrial production in China.

Finally, we reached Australia, via the state visit of the Japanese Prime Minister to discuss his nation's trade problems. Much of the Australian news was about the weather and the environment. There was a drought in the west. We saw an elephant, outside Perth, dusting itself.

The second show we watched, on an education channel, was for Tami's benefit. I didn't understand much of it because it was in Japanese. I worked out it was a program about growing organic microcomputers in Kyoto. There were some elaborate diagrams of long-chain organic molecules.

The only bit that I could understand was a computer program with English characters. By using mathematical equations, it showed how to make a series of self-replicating nanites out of carbon and silicon chains, each being a variation on the one before.

I wished we'd had something like that when I was running Climate Changers. I knew that the micros in the roof of the Bushells' house regulated the temperature, but without an electron microscope, there wasn't a lot to see.

After a coffee break, we switched to a channel run by a local co-operative of business and media people, for some community information news. Community associations of various kinds permeated the whole of Canberra, and, as far as I could make out, just about everywhere else as well. There were advertisements for community markets to be held on the weekend, including one in our own suburb.

'We'll be going there tomorrow,' said Ron. 'Would you like to help us?'

'Sure. Sounds interesting.'

Finally, we switched to a subscription service to watch a classic movie from the 2050s called The Enchanted Forest. It was a melodrama set at the turn of the millennium, or at least, what the people of 2100 thought life was like back then. There were goodies and baddies. The goodies were green, and were trying to save their pristine valley from the wicked developers. Though they didn't wear white and black hats, it was easy to tell the good guys from the bad guys: the villains dropped litter everywhere.

There was some conflict, and at one stage it looked like the goodies and the baddies were going to have a punch up. In a scene that might have been straight out of High Noon, the heroine tried to persuade the hero, a reformed lumberjack, that violence wasn't the answer. 'Have faith in Gaia,' she insisted about fifty times during the movie. Unlike Gary Cooper, he agreed not to fight.

A film like that had to have a happy ending. The turning point came when the bad guys got lost in the forest. Here, by mysterious means that seemed to involve guest appearances by about half the animal kingdom, Gaia worked her magic on the developers. They emerged from the forest converted to the green cause. Then they got together with the greenies to work out some environmentally sustainable economic activities for everyone, and they all lived happily ever after.

I was amazed to see the normally cool, hard-headed Lena wiping tears from her eyes. Then Ron explained to me that while 1he Enchanted Forest might look like a cheap melodrama, it was actually a cinematic masterpiece in which everything was of deep symbolic significance.

I hate symbolism. I like to watch a good movie plot unfold without wondering whether each scene has a thousand different meanings.

On Ron's advice, I set my regulator to wake me up at 06:00. We would have breakfast early because it was market day and we had much to do.

●

Next morning, Sa03022100, Ron called the garage to ask truck number one to prepare for its 'market routine'. Meanwhile, Tami and Lena wrapped three bark paintings and a hologram of a family of gorillas that lived in the Queensland rainforests. It had a logo for the World Wildlife Fund, for which Lena was a commission agent.

The truck, which was little more than a glorified utility, crawled up the road to stop outside what I now regarded as 'our place'.

'Shall we start loading?' I asked.

'No. We'll have to work out the optimum loading strategy first.' Ron climbed inside the cab of the truck to check its computer. On its screen, there was a manifest of goods to be picked up from each property. He pressed a comlink button to send a message to everyone, reminding them that the truck would be programmed for loading by 08:00.

Meanwhile, I was examining the tray of the truck. I could feel lines on its seemingly uniform metal floor. 'Organo-metallic micros,' Ron explained. 'You'll soon see what they are for.'

We went back inside to help Lena and Tami with the packaging. There were several jars of conserves and two potted ferns from the nearby conservatory. Tami keyed the details into the computer.

At 07:99, Ron told me to look at the floor of the tray. One metric minute later – 100 metric seconds or 36 seconds on my time scale – I saw the tray change from an even, dull grey to a patchwork of lighter and darker areas, each with a white number. Our place happened to be number 1. Space number 1 was at the front of the tray, so that was where we stacked Lena's paintings and other goodies.

When Ron banged the cabin with his palm, the truck went on to the next house, while Ron and I stayed in the tray. From there on, it was loading by numbers. It was a good way of meeting people because at least half the community had goods to send to the market. I met so many people that I forget them unless they were young and female.

There was one in particular that I was looking out for – the brunette whom I had seen at the pool. We met her at a house in the southwest corner. Her name was Ramona Perez. At close quarters, her sultry Latin- American beauty made me think of moonlit nights on tropical beaches.

I was just about to kiss her hand with exaggerated gallantry when a large, hearty man with fair hair came up alongside her, carrying a box of artichokes. Ron introduced him as Harry Carpenter, Ramona's husband.

'How d'you do, James?' Harry had a vigorous handshake, and the closest thing that I had heard to the good old-fashioned Aussie accent. He had been rostered to help us. So he hopped on the tray and we continued our journey round the park.

I had guessed that Harry and Ramona were about thirty. I revised this estimate when we stopped at the block of flats in the northwest corner of the park. Here, I met their teenage son, Julio Perez Carpenter.

We continued along the north side of the park. The road did a couple of s-bends through the mounds and troughs of the vegetable gardens. Half a dozen people were waiting to load crates of produce onto an area of the truck marked with a 'V'.

In the northeast corner of the community, there was a set of cottages around a neat little square. It looked like a retirement village. Sure enough, it was here that I met an elderly, weather-beaten couple, Eduardo and Ignacia Perez. So this was the family of three generations that Ron had told me about.

We didn't have much time to chat, however. It was nearly 08:90 and we had to get to the market. When we completed our circuit of the park, I saw that most of the cars had already left the garage.

Our drive through the streets to the marketplace was one of the few times that I saw much traffic on Canberra's roads. Vehicles converged on a large rectangular park surrounded by pine trees.

The park was divided into large playing fields, and a mixture of gardens, trees, shops, offices, and apartments. They were all linked by pathways to a square surrounded by old buildings.

I felt a pang of nostalgia. 'I used to come to markets here when I was young,' I told Ron and Harry.

All around us, there was the apparent confusion of people and vehicles going hither and yon. Produce was being unloaded, trestles and awnings set up, children running everywhere, and everybody greeting each other.

The market was a great social occasion. People had shed their normally drab robes for multi-coloured ones, and colourful hats as well. There was entertainment: jugglers, clowns, musicians – many of them Asian. I came across one group making a dragon for the Chinese New Year.

Somehow, like a well-trained workhorse, our truck wended its way through the confusion to the shaded place where our community was setting up its stalls. Lena and Tami were waiting for us, among others. Patricia was there.

After we had unloaded the truck, I helped the Bushells to set up their private stall in an impromptu outdoor art gallery. Ron and Tami then went hunting for fruit and vegetables. It was while Lena and I were minding the stall that Patricia started to set up hers directly opposite.

'Well, hello,' said Patricia in a husky voice.

'Hello,' I said. 'How do you do?'

'Do what?'

'It's just an old expression. How are you?'

She laughed. 'How quaint. You must visit us sometime and tell us all about yourself. We live in number seventeen, although Roderick has had to go to Tokyo at short notice. Lena, why have you been keeping him from us?'

'He's only been with us for three days,' Lena protested. 'He hasn't had time to orientate himself. Besides, you can talk to him at tonight's party.'

'I shall look forward to that.' There was a roguish look in Patricia's eyes. 'Would you like to see my etchings?'

I raised my eyebrows and my hopes. Then I discovered that Patricia did indeed have some etchings, which she was unpacking and displaying on her stall.

I also sensed that there was rivalry between Lena and Patricia. It was veiled, of course; the cats still had their claws sheathed. So I was surprised when Lena came over to help Patricia set up, and sent me off to look for Ron and Tami.

They were inside a supermarket, which was unlike the ones I had known in my day. At first, I was disappointed: the shop had a 19th-century quality about it. The shelves contained no goodies in bright shiny wrappers or brightly coloured cartons. Most things were in jars, barrels, or plain, reusable wrappers. Ron and Tami even brought some wrappers with them. It occurred to me that I never saw much litter in the streets of 2100. Canberra was, as ever, a clean city.

Most of what Ron and Tami bought were things they couldn't get in the markets – coffee, tea, sugar, chocolate, meat, wine and beer. With the Austral 'pocket money' that Ron had given me, I bought a can of beer. Maybe there was something symbolic about the fact that the first thing I bought in this strange new world was a can of beer: maybe I was just hot and thirsty.

I sat down at a table in the small square beside the shops and drank slowly. The flavour, or lack of it, took some getting used to. I was confident, though, that with time and a bit of perseverance, I would acquire the taste. When I had finished the beer, I went to drop it in a rubbish bin. Instead of a single bin, I found a whole array of brightly coloured ones.

I wandered amongst the stalls, watched a fire-eater and some acrobats in medieval gear, then went back to help the Bushells on their stall. I was left in charge while they chatted with some friends. I didn't have any problems – the prices were clearly labelled and the Austral currency was decimal – until somebody gave me some Yen. Lena said that was all right. The Yen was easily convertible into Australs and was legal tender throughout the whole of the Eastern Zone.

By early afternoon, the market was winding down. It was time to load up the truck with all of the things we had bought or bartered. The Bushells had been buying, not just for themselves, but for the whole of the community because it was their turn on the buying roster.

We had to make two trips. The first load went into storage near the kiosk of our community. I was already starting to think of 'my community' even though I had only been there since Wensday. When we returned to the market, Lena and Patricia were helping each other pack up their stalls. Perhaps I had misjudged their rivalry.

Eventually, we had the truck and several other of our community's vehicles loaded up. We headed back home in convoy.

Lunch was a frugal, hurried affair. We had to prepare for the evening party at the community centre, which had a kitchen and a large meeting- cum-eating hall. However, tonight's dinner was to be outside, a smorgasbord in the cool of the evening.

Lena and I laid out tables, tablecloths and cutlery. Ron and Tami busied themselves in the kitchen. Ron was a very good chef. He spent much of the afternoon at the kitchen console, programming the large solar oven and the hot plates to produce succulent, juicy, roast beef and vegetables.

While Tami tossed salads, Lena and I put up the decorations, including a large banner saying 'Welcome James'.

The guests started arriving around 20:00. They were dressed casually, having changed their robes for shorts and batik shirts or skirts and blouses. Some were wearing sarongs or saris. Harry turned up wearing a sarong and carrying a carton of beer. This so distracted me that for a moment I didn't realise that Ramona, who had also arrived, was wearing an outfit with one breast exposed.

Soon, just about everyone in the community arrived. There were over a hundred people, spread out from the community centre onto the lawn and near the pool.

Ron plied them with a delicious assortment of non-alcoholic fruit cocktails that he had devised. Lena gave me two plates of hors d'oeuvres to take to the multitude, which gave me a good opportunity to meet everyone. They seemed a friendly bunch. I managed to avoid staring too long at Ramona, but when Patricia made her entrance, it was a different matter.

She was wearing golden sandals and an elegant, loose flowing, almost translucent robe, split along the thighs. When she stood between me and the setting sun, with her robe billowing gently in the breeze, I realised that was all she was wearing.

I nearly dropped the petits-fours. 'Oh, la la.'

'Thank you, James,' she said in a husky voice as she smiled. There was more than a hint of perfume.

Any further social intercourse was interrupted by Lena announcing, rather loudly next to my ear, that dinner was served. She took my arm and led me away to sit between her and Ron, at the head of the largest table, as guest of honour.

'I'll ask you later to give a short talk about life in your times,' she said, smiling sweetly. 'You won't mind, will you?'

'As long as they don't want to ask me too many personal questions. About my love life, or whatever.'

'Oh, I don't know James, you might get a few offers.' Her smile was now more mischievous.

I hadn't thought of that before. Maybe that's why I had some success with the lovely Mara. Hmm. When was I due for a check-up at the hospital?

My thoughts were interrupted by the aroma of roast beef. Ron had neatly divided the roast into a hundred thin slices with a laser scalpel. About three-quarters of the guests helped themselves to a slice of beef. I was given the honour of a second slice. Enough remained for Sunday leftovers. I later learnt that the roast cost about one hundred Australs. No wonder a quarter of the guests were vegetarians. I meant to ask whether it was real or synthetic beef.

Even though there was a large smorgasbord of salads, as well as baked potatoes and stir-fried vegetables, the guests chose sparingly. They were not big eaters, and I couldn't remember seeing any fat people. My plate was piled twice as I high as anyone else's, but I can eat a lot without putting on much weight.

After the main course came a modest desert of fruit, jelly and ice-cream, along with some of the best ground coffee I had ever tasted.

Lena tapped her cup with a spoon to call everyone to order. Then she rose to speak. 'My friends, members of Willow Community, we welcome into our midst a man who was born in 2000, and who lived for thirty or so years, until he went into hibernation. As Convenor of Willow Community, it gives me great pleasure to introduce James Lawson, who will tell us what life was like in Canberra in the first third of this century.'

I spoke for a long time, much longer than I had intended: about catching buses, playing cricket, buying petrol for my car until I got an electric one, my favourite TV shows, poker machines, the price of beer, Climate Changers, Janet, our flat, the ozone layer, spray cans, and Cryosleep – roughly in that order.

There were one or two questions about Climate Changers, and I explained the energy efficiency systems we had developed, and how handy it would have been to have clusters of micros back then. They were still at the developmental stage when I went into hibernation.

Ron remarked that I had lived at the point of nexus between the old ways and the new, 'at the dawn of the age of Gaia', as he put it. This somehow led to a discussion about where the community's next mulch pile should be, and what vegetables we should plant for the winter. Soil, nutrition and economics were the main factors.

This grew into a debate between Lena and Patricia about what they should do with the community's new glasshouse. Lena wanted to grow legumes, which were nutritious, but which didn't thrive outside because of the ultraviolet. Patricia wanted to grow begonias for the international market to improve the community's cash flow.

Ron explained to me on the quiet that Patricia was likely to challenge Lena for the Convenorship of the community when elections were held at the end of the month. Now I understood the reason for their rivalry.

I soon realised that the community was no longer interested in me, but in the power struggle between the two women. I went for a stroll in the cool night air. The moon had risen, and was casting its eerie light across the trees and the flower beds. It was a night for romance, if only I had someone to be romantic with.

A while later, I returned to the party to discover that a legume-begonia compromise had been worked out, mainly to the benefit of the legumes. Lena and Patricia were sitting together, drinking coffee and discussing batik designs.

Sensing that they wanted to be left alone, I joined Ron and the Perez- Carpenter clan, who were gathering up the leftovers and doing the dishes. Afterwards, we drank some of Harry's beer and played soccer by the moonlight on the village green.

Meanwhile, as I later found out, Lena and Patricia had been having a 'heart-to-heart' talk. Lena had won the debate, and with it probably the Convenorship. It was a community custom, however, that the winner and loser would then have a private chat so that the loser could air their frustration.

They had evidently reconciled their differences by the time we returned. Lena gave Patricia a matronly peck on the cheek, and then invited me over to join them.

'James,' she said, 'Patricia has some floral shirt designs that might interest you.'

'I'm not really into—' I caught Lena's wink just in time. 'Floral shirts, you say?'

'Yes, James. But I shall need your measurements.' Patricia took my arm and led me away into the night. 'We'll go the long way round, I think.'

By the time we stopped at a small grassy nook, set in a grove of trees, I felt a strongly growing desire in my loins. She told me to bend down and feel the grass. 'It's a special variety that is grown for its sensual texture.'

It did indeed have a smooth, silky feeling. I looked up just as Patricia undid the clasp on her robe. She stood before me in the shadows and the moonlight, naked and mysterious.

CHAPTER TWELVE

THE FOUR ZONES

Late the next morning, Su04022100, when I arrived back at the Bushells' house, nobody said anything about my absence the night before. Given Lena's collusion in what happened last night, I wondered if I was some sort of consolation prize for Patricia missing out on the Convenorship.

Lena and Tami were busy decking themselves out in green and floral costumes.

'We're going to a Gaia service,' Lena explained. 'Want to join us?'

'No thanks. I'm not into religion.'

Nor was Ron. 'Lena and Tami take part every Sunday,' he explained after they left. 'I go sometimes, but only for the season festivals. Everyone is involved in them.'

When we sat on the porch to have lunch, Ron was quieter than usual. As he chewed thoughtfully on a bread roll, there was obviously something on his mind. At length, he remarked, 'I suppose you are curious, James, about what has happened in the world while you were in hibernation. Why are things as they are today?'

'Some things,' I replied. 'At the time, there were about eight billion people in the world. The effects of climate change were really starting to bite, and lots of people in the Third World had food shortages.'

Ron nodded. 'The future was not looking rosy.'

'True,' I conceded. 'So what did happen? I mean, you didn't all die in a pandemic or get zapped by radiation or burnt up by global warming.'

'Most of us, no,' Ron agreed. 'But we've been through some difficult times. The economy was a bit shaky back then, wasn't it?'

'Oh, the impending Second Global Financial Meltdown. Governments were gearing up for a round of quantitative easing to try and forestall it. I know that it worked for a while, but it led to runaway inflation, and in the end the financial systems did collapse.'

Ron nodded. 'But not necessarily because of quantitative easing. Much of the inflation was caused by resource shortages. What it boiled down to was that too many people wanted too many resources, and the rate of capital formation was not able to keep up. Many countries that had borrowed heavily to upgrade their infrastructure defaulted on their loans. The world's financial system teetered on the brink.'

'And it collapsed?'

'Not immediately. Denied further credit, many countries could not maintain their infrastructure, including health services. We all paid the price for that.'

'How?' I was puzzled. 'Surely that would have been their problem?'

'Soon after you went into hibernation, there were outbreaks of a virulent form of influenza that appeared sporadically along the banks of the Ganges. Then, one year, with the Indian health service in crisis, Ganges Fever spread throughout the whole of the country and beyond. Unlike the COVID-19 pandemic two decades earlier, the world lacked the resources to contain it. Plus, they were complacent after a couple of pandemic scares that turned out to be false alarms.'

'I remember the COVID-19 outbreak. I was in my last year at uni. That was when I developed my first app. We did have a pandemic alarm a few years later, and governments started closing borders until the whole thing fizzled out.'

Ron nodded. 'In seven years, Ganges Fever claimed half a billion lives worldwide, directly or indirectly, before it burnt itself out. With world trade disrupted by the pandemic and bad weather, the financial system teetered on the brink, and in 2042 it crashed. Trillions of dollars of savings were wiped out—'

'Including most of mine,' I interrupted.

'Untold millions of people were thrown out of work, and many governments went bankrupt.' Ron helped himself to some salad. 'It was the disaster that saved the world.'

I did a double take. 'Did you say it saved the world?'

'That's right. Ganges Fever, the host of little wars that broke out when the economies crashed, and financial uncertainty all combined to slow world population growth so that it levelled out at a much lower figure than it might have done.

'Also, world industrial production fell sharply, and so did greenhouse emissions. It gave the environment the breathing space it needed. Even when economies did recover, a decade later, people realised that things would never be the same again. For one thing, we would never have the resource base that people in your time had.'

'My generation squandered the world's inheritance?' I suggested uncomfortably.

Ron nodded. 'That's one way of putting it. When it had recovered from the Second Great Depression, the western world became more generous helping in poorer countries, because it realised that it ignored their problems at its peril. The creation of the four-zone world economic order, and the building of modular megacities, improved people's living standards worldwide and reduced the birth rate.'

I wanted to ask about 'modular megacities', but my host immediately went on to explain how the world had become divided into four major economic zones.

'The Northern Zone,' Ron continued, 'already existed in your day. Despite ups and downs, the European Economic Community eventually expanded to form an economic zone that stretched "from Reykjavik to Vladivostok" as the saying goes.'

'But we live in the Eastern Zone?'

'Correct. Containing half the world's population, it stretches from China and the Indian subcontinent through Southeast Asia and Oceania, although China seems to be going through another isolationist phase.

'The Western Zone is the Americas, and the Southern Zone is Africa and the Middle East.'

I helped myself to some salad. 'What do these zones mean? They're sort of common markets, aren't they?'

'Well, there are few trade barriers within each zone, although there are agreements about who produces what. There is some competition, and a lot of haggling at zone meetings. On the whole, there is enough flexibility in the system to ensure that every country gets a fair deal.'

'What about between the zones?'

'Oh, the usual endless round of tariff discussions and bilateral agreements, usually zone to zone. Individual countries are discouraged from having direct negotiations with other zones. There's strength in unity, you see.

'So, in practice, the "one common world" that the idealists of your day hoped for is, in fact, four worlds; five if you regard China as separate. Economically and politically they are virtually self-contained, but on environmental matters they usually co-operate with each other.

'It also means that, psychologically, the human race is starting to feel that the world is under control. The zone system means that we can tackle the major problems of our region, if not those of the whole world. We have survived our Rite of Passage, but at the price of many people being forced to live in the regimented societies of the megacities.'

'Rite of Passage?'

'We were children of nature, in the grip of superstition until we developed science and technology, which enabled us to use the laws of nature for our own ends. But we used them in a piecemeal and selfish fashion. Our Rite of Passage has been to learn how to, as the saying goes, "have our cake and eat it too".'

'You mean, to learn how to use science and technology for our benefit, without destroying the environment?'

'Well put, James.'

'And we have passed our Rite of Passage?'

'In a sense.' Ron looked away for a moment. 'The human race is in a state of siege. We are retreating from the land we have damaged into the megacities. While the population stabilises and falls, governments are rejuvenating the deserted countryside. Perhaps, in a century or two, our less numerous descendants will move out to reclaim the land, and hopefully use it wisely. Meanwhile, we bide our time by improving human relations while we weather the worst effects of climate change and other environmental upheavals.'

●

As we took our plates and bowls back inside, and loaded the dishwasher, I asked, 'So what has been happening in Australia all this time?'

'Australia has become hotter, and rainfall is less predictable. When we do have droughts, however, they can be very severe. And bushfires, of course.'

I thought back to the droughts and bad fires we had earlier in this century. 'Has Canberra's climate changed much?'

'Did you ever go skiing?'

'Sometimes. At Perisher. Perhaps one or two weekends each winter.'

'There's very little snow these days. Just a bit in the Snowy Mountains. Unless there's a freak storm somewhere.'

'That's sad.' I had fond memories of the weekends that Janet and I had spent in cabins in the snow.

'Another problem we've had to deal with is erosion. It's been a long battle to protect the soil.'

'There was a big fuss about soil conservation in my time,' I recalled. 'People arguing about pesticides and fertilisers.'

'Agriculture has changed a lot since then,' Ron explained. 'The image of the farmer riding his tractor around the waving fields of wheat in the blazing sun is not so common now. His grandchildren are more likely to be in fish farming or hydroponics.'

'Don't they grow wheat anymore?'

'Of course. But the days of monoculture – of vast fields of the same crop – are all but over. Diversity and drip feed irrigation are more important now. We've learnt from our past. Slowly, the semi-arid lands are starting to bloom again.

'But agriculture is an expensive business. It must be carefully planned to make maximum use of limited resources. That's why we have so many glasshouses and vegetable gardens in the cities, where the soil is often fertile, and transport and storage costs can be minimised. That's also why we no longer have so many sheep and cattle, and why meat and beer are expensive.'

We sat down for a fruit juice.

'There are over thirty million people in this country,' Ron said sagely. 'Our population stopped growing when the world's population stabilised. We now rely on immigration to maintain our population because our birth rate had already fallen below replacement level in your time.'

'Why bother with immigration? If we're short of food and everything.'

'We are not short of food. Despite the droughts, we still produce more than we consume.' Ron toyed with his glass. 'Like most countries in the affluent world, whose populations are declining, we have international agreements to take immigrants from poorer countries – partly for humanitarian reasons, partly because of intra-zonal agreements, but mainly for economic requirements.

'You see, capitalist economies were geared to growth. The levelling off in population and per-capita demand for goods and services means that we have had to adjust to steady-state or declining economic activity. Maintaining a stable population, or allowing it to decline only slowly, gives us time to adjust.'

'These immigrants. Mostly Asian, I suppose?'

'Yes. Especially Indonesian. Have you heard about the Kimberley region?'

I shook my head. I dimly knew that it was in the northwestern part of Australia.

'Kimberley became separate from Western Australia about the time we switched to regional government. During the Indonesian civil war, it was taken over by refugees. Most of them arrived by boat on the coast between Broome and Derby.'

I remembered all the fuss about boat people in my time. 'Couldn't we have turned them away?'

Ron looked shocked. 'There was nowhere we could send them to. And we couldn't turn them all away. Not several hundred thousand of them. Besides, Australia became involved in the conflict in Indonesia. Our agreeing to settle the refugees was part of the peace plan that helped to stabilise the new Indonesian Federation.'

Now it was my turn to be shocked. 'You mean, we were invaded by hordes of Indonesians?'

'Half-starved, unarmed Indonesians,' Ron explained. 'They adapted to their strange new environment, and the north is starting to flourish. As with all immigrants, they are moving out and becoming part of the wider community.'

I thought about this for a while. 'Do they speak English?'

'Most of them. Although Kimberley is Australia's only official bilingual region.'

'Hmm.' I sighed. Australia had certainly changed a lot since my time. 'What about the aborigines? – since one of them is President.'

'Population geneticists estimate that now, between five and ten percent of the population has some indigenous ancestry.'

'I haven't seen too many around.'

Ron said quietly, 'Mara.'

'How did you know about her?'

'Does it trouble you that I know?'

'No. I guess not. I'm just a bit surprised, that's all. About five or ten percent, you say?'

'It depends. People tend to emphasise that part of their ancestry that is fashionable at the time. Some years ago, there was as much kudos in claiming to be part indigenous as there used to be about having convict ancestors. Especially in the art world and the Gaia movement.'

'And now?'

It was Ron's turn to sigh. 'We are doing some soul-searching, coming to terms with the environment. But where do we go from here?'

●

I wandered out onto the porch to look over the community park. Not much was stirring in the summer heat. I could see a few people, clad from head to toe, working in the nearby flower gardens. Ron came out to join me.

'Tell me, Ron, how did this all come about? The community, I mean.'

He leant on the railing of his porch. 'We've come a long way from – what were they called in your time? – quarter-acre blocks in suburbia.'

'Yeah. Everyone wanted a house, car, garage, lawn, video, colour tele. You didn't notice your neighbours unless they annoyed you. I couldn't imagine working in a veggie garden with them, or sharing a swimming pool.'

Ron toyed with the idea of lighting his pipe. 'Not everyone had those things, did they?'

'No. But they wanted them. What are you getting at?'

'That if you can't own things individually, you can own them collectively.' He decided to light his pipe. 'Tell me, what percentage of the time would you use all of these wonderful things that everyone wanted?'

'Er, well, I used the car a lot, for business reasons. I often went out to visit clients. Plus, Janet and I drove to and from work every day.'

'What did the car do while you were in the office?'

'Nothing, I hope. Parking cost a bloody fortune though.'

'In this community of over one hundred people, we manage perfectly well with twelve cars. Even they are idle much of the time.'

'So what? You live a different lifestyle from us. People in my day sometimes organised car pools, or borrowed each other's lawnmowers, but we weren't really into community television or swimming pools.'

'And yet, that is what has come to pass.'

'Why?'

'Economics,' Ron said grimly. He puffed vigorously on his pipe. Clouds of smoke drifted lazily into the summer haze.

'In the Second Great Depression, even in an affluent country like Australia, millions of people were out of work, and state and local governments went bankrupt. Only the national government had the resources to keep going. As an expediency, it organised the regional governments that we have today.

'People were thrown back on their own resources. With the shortage of land and money, they created communities like this one, where many people can live comfortably and creatively in a small area.'

'But wouldn't there have been fights, quarrels?' I objected. 'In my experience, people don't live well in communities.'

'People had to learn to live with each other because it was only by co-operation that they could survive. We had to pool our resources, and live in the most cost-effective and energy-efficient way we could find. After a while, people realised there were other advantages to community-based lifestyles. They offered something that was lacking in suburbia and its affluence.'

'What was that?'

'A sense of community. A feeling of belonging. An awareness that each person had a part to play and was in some way important. And the realisation that one had a support group in times of need.'

Ron continued relentlessly on his theme. 'Australia went through a painful transition period. We became experts in energy conservation and micro technology. There were many people unemployed or underemployed. It was then that organisations like local community associations and the Gaia groups came to the fore.'

'Gaia has become a sort of religious thing that Lena and Tami go to, is it?'

'Yes. They're probably the best people to tell you how the Gaia groups became organised, and the part they played in turning self-help groups into viable communities. Gaia has often fused with other religions, so you have Christian Gaians and Muslim Gaians, for example. Women have usually been the prominent figures in the Gaia movements, although many men have been involved as well.'

'Including you?'

'Only to a limited extent. People in the Gaia movement usually have emotional involvement as well as ideological commitment.' Ron paused to puff on his pipe. 'I find it a convenient paradigm to regard the world as if it were a single self-regulating organism as the Gaia theory postulates. Yet many devout Gaians believe that the Earth actually is a living being, a manifestation of a cosmic life force of which we are all part.'

I thought of Helen at the hospital. 'But you don't believe in that sort of stuff?'

'Do you? Were you a believer in any faith?'

'Oh. Sort of. Not really. I went to Sunday school when I was a kid. I s'pose I sort of believed that something had to be running the show. But I never had any mystical experiences or anything like that.'

'Neither have I. Or if I have, my rational analytical mind has interpreted them in a more worldly way.'

'How do you mean?'

'Take love, for instance. Lena sees it as a mystical thing: a harmonising of two parts of the life force. I see it as a pleasant feeling I often have when she enters the room, and I know that I'd rather not live without her.'

Who should come walking up the path but Lena and Tami.

●

After greeting them, I went to my room, because I had to do some soul-searching of my own. Putting on my regulator, I found that I could see things more clearly. I had grown up with attitudes about quarter-acre blocks in suburbia, the importance of test cricket, and the right to own and drive my own car.

I had already had the shock of seeing that test cricket wasn't what it used to be. I couldn't find anyone with much interest in the game. Ron saw it as a historical curiosity.

As for suburbia, I was getting used to the community park. It seemed to have the right mix of privacy and togetherness. Even so, as with test cricket, I had a sense of loss. My career, my whole life, had been geared towards making lots of money so that I could own a good home with a garage, wife, colour tele, two children and a dog. What could I aim for now? It was too soon to work out how I could make money in this place. I probably couldn't even get a car of my own unless I dipped into my meagre assets, but I wanted to save them for capital investment.

It wouldn't be so bad if there were some clubs where I could have a few beers and let off steam. I never realised before how important that was to me.

I laughed. In a way, I had cheated death. I wasn't sure if I was happy about living beyond my time or not. From what Ron had told me, Australia had been through some rough times while I was in hibernation.

Gradually, my mood improved. Pragmatic is as pragmatic does. I might find it hard to accept all of the things in this strange new world. But I would make the best of it.

CHAPTER THIRTEEN

DUST TO DUST

Feburi, as it was now called, was a month of dry, relentless heat. The temperature often climbed above 38 degrees Celsius, or 100 degrees Fahrenheit. Ron told me that because of climate change, when it was hot and dry in Australia, it was really hot and dry.

And dusty. The ground, except for areas tended by the communities, was bone dry. Scorching northerlies and westerlies often blew dust along the roads.

Ironically, this helped me to settle into Willow Community. Sophisticated as they were, the cars' radar systems were baffled by dust clouds. The cars would grind to a halt. The dust clogged their delicate sensors, or worked its way in under the bonnets to grit itself to the battery terminals.

As a former mechanic, I was therefore able to find a niche in the Community. I soon learnt how to service and repair the cars; how to pull them apart and reassemble them. For all their plastic, semi-organic technology, they still responded to wrench and spanner (and the occasional well-aimed kick). I learnt how to recharge the batteries from the power storage plant. I also learnt how to program the computers that synchronised the Community's wind/solar generators. It was like old times.

For all of this, the Community credited me with 12 hours' work per week, at ten Australs per hour. Half of this was deducted as my contribution to the Community's food buying fund, leaving me with 60 Australs of pocket money. Some of this went on beer. Ron, Harry and I formed a syndicate to buy cartons of beer at discount rates from the supermarket. But it still worked out at only one or two cans a day.

Fortunately, I had the lovely Patricia for consolation. I suspected that her relationship with Roderick was more platonic than physical. While he was away in Beijing or Mumbai or wherever, I made the most of my opportunities – and so did Patricia.

She had a passion for fornicating in unlikely places – the grassy bower where we had our midnight tryst, the village green in the dead of night, and the secluded reedy hollows near the swimming pool in broad daylight.

We enjoyed about two weeks of pure, unadulterated lust. Then she tried to interest me in art. She enjoyed art and talking about art – canvas or fabric, music or the culinary arts. I always got a good feed at her place. I feigned interest in her artwork, of course. But it became clear to her that I would sooner feel her texture than that of the fabric she was working with.

One evening, after failing to arouse my interest in Gaian impressionist art, she challenged me. 'Why don't you do something artistic for a change?'

'Me? What? I can't paint or do sculpture. And the only culinary art I know is called cooking for survival.'

'I don't care,' she replied. 'I didn't realise that people from your time were so boring. Just do something creative, or original. Something different, at least.'

It was clear from the tone of her voice that if we were to continue our lustful relationship, I would have to do something artistic. I thought about this for a while.

When I was reprogramming the cars, I had a spark of creative genius – the one magic moment that the people of Willow Community would always remember me for. I planned it to happen the following Saturday evening, when the Community was having one of its parties. For a couple of days beforehand, I was deliberately mysterious, hinting that I had arranged something special.

While everyone was spread out between the community centre and the village green, I went to the eastern garage with a remote control unit. On my signal, the cars left their carports and followed me Indian file round to the western carport, whence the cars parked there joined the file.

As I marched up the central path by the lawn and the community centre, the cars followed me in stately procession. I pressed another button on the remote. I had adjusted the pitches on the car horns and programmed a sequence so that on my signal, the cars beeped 'Colonel Bogey' as we paraded before the party.

'Company … halt!' I commanded. The cars stopped. 'Left … wheel!' Again, they obeyed. 'By the right … number!' One by one, in correct sequence, they beeped their horns.

It was Eduardo's birthday. On my command, he was treated to a cacophonous version of 'Happy Birthday', which my audience joined in with great merriment.

To my dismay, Patricia just stood there as if turned to stone. It wasn't her idea of art. She glared at me and walked away in a huff.

To my surprise, Lena, whom I didn't think had a sense of humour, fell about in hysterics. Between gasps, she told me it was the funniest thing she had ever seen. I was given three cheers by the assembled multitude.

Next morning, Roderick returned from Kathmandu.

●

A few days later, I asked Ron about an ideological problem I had encountered on the Saturday night. I had planned to make a short announcement to introduce my automotive orchestra, when it occurred to me that I didn't know how to address my fellow community members. The only word I could think of, which I decided not to use, was 'communists', the derivation of which I had never thought about. In my day, I had associated it with some vague 'evil empire' of Russian and Chinese dictators, and a crumbling, discredited political system.

I explained my quandary to Ron.

'We have a four-sector economy,' he told me. Taking me over to a computer terminal, he spoke to it like a lord to his slave. 'Cordinat grid, please. No scale. Overlap quadrants by ten percent.'

A horizontal and a vertical line appeared on the screen. 'Top left quadrant red.' The quadrant was filled by a red square, which overlapped into the other three quadrants by about ten percent. 'Ten percent is an arbitrary figure,' Ron explained. 'The actual amount of overlap is probably much greater, but not easily quantified.

'Let us say that the top quadrants represent large scale, and the lower ones small scale. Let us also say that left means shared or collective ownership, and right means private ownership: if you like, socialism and capitalism.

'Top left therefore means large scale collective ownership – the government sector: mainly infrastructure, defence, education, public health, macro-ecological management, that sort of thing.'

'The Public Service?' I asked.

Nodding, Ron spoke again to his computer. 'Top right quadrant gold.'

Gold filled this quadrant and overlapped into the others, forming a translucent orange strip where it meshed with the red. 'We'll make the corporate sector gold because, traditionally, that is the sector with all the gold. This is large-scale private ownership – national and zonal corporations that provide everything from farm produce to microcomputers.

'As you can see by the orange strip, it overlaps with the government sector. The government may contract private companies to construct capital works, or go into joint ventures such as the Great Hydrogen Pipeline. Closer to home, we have the high-speed Austrail network around the continent.'

Ron made the bottom right quadrant blue. 'This is the small business sector. From sole traders, freelance professionals and artists to small- and medium-sized companies. Again, it overlaps with the other sectors. Many small firms are sub-contractors.'

Finally, he made the bottom left quadrant green. 'This is small-scale collective ownership: the community sector. Many people now devote much of their time to their local communities. Like Willow, for instance.'

'Is that where you fit in?'

'I fit into all sectors. I lecture at the ANU. I'm a history consultant for the ABC and several private corporations. Lena and I work for the community, and she sells her paintings. So make of that what you will.'

●

Next day was unbearably hot. The temperature rose to above 40 degrees Celsius. No one worked in the gardens or the glasshouses. No bird sang nor creature stirred. Apart from the shimmering heat, everything was dead calm, silent.

The scorching wind started to blow: looming up in the sky to the northwest was an eerie orange cloud. The smell of dust got into our nostrils. Lena told us that a dust storm had hit Wagga, and was heading our way.

Suddenly, it was action stations. People ran hither and yon in a seemingly random fashion. Yet, there was method in their madness. They shouted orders to each other as they did the heavy physical work of hauling up barriers, and covering vegetable gardens and glasshouses with tarpaulins. They were like sailors manning the riggings in a storm.

Overhead, a great cloud of dust loomed towards us like a giant wave. As the wind reached a howling pitch, Ron shouted to me to go to the eastern garage. I saw that one of the carports was empty.

Roderick was inside the garage. Beads of sweat pouring from his forehead, he was on the car intercom. 'Patricia, can you hear me?'

An indistinct voice came over the intercom. 'You're breaking up,' he shouted. 'Listen. There are gale force winds in West Belconnen. Can you get back here in time?' Again the voice was indistinct. Something about 'beating the storm'.

'Right,' he shouted. 'Carport three will be open.' He looked up and saw me. 'She's been out delivering flowers,' he explained. 'If she can't get here in five minutes, she'll just have to seal the car windows and weather the storm. Come, we must hurry.' Picking up a lug wrench, he bounded past me, and headed for the generator plant with surprising speed.

'The windmill,' he gasped. 'We've got to disconnect the driveshaft from the flywheel or the whole thing will go.'

We clambered up onto the roof of the generator plant. The wind was already strong and the windmill blades where whirring around at a great rate of knots.

'The flywheel controls the speed of the blades,' he explained between breaths as he undid the cowling that housed the driveshaft.

'That regulates the power input. But in a wind like this, we've got to disconnect it. Grab the spindle, will you?'

He stood dangerously close to the rotating blades while he reached inside with the wrench to work on the restraining bolt. I grabbed the rotating spindle. But try as I might, I couldn't hold it and it burnt my hands.

'Hang on,' he snapped. 'Or we'll lose the blades.'

I grabbed it again. 'I can't … can't …'

The knuckles on his large, seemingly flabby hands turned white as he strained on the wrench. The bolt started to give. With a grunt and a sharp snap of the wrist—

'… can't hold it!' I cried. The spindle flew out into space. With the agility of a panther, Roderick shot out his hands and grabbed the spindle. For a moment, man and rotor blades hung dangerously on the edge of the building. Like a man wrestling with an umbrella in a gale, he did an ungainly dance along the side of the roof, until he flung the blades into some rhododendrons. 'Soft landing,' he breathed.

I picked up the wrench he had dropped in order to do up the cowling. But my hands were too shaky.

'There isn't time,' he shouted. 'Look.'

I could feel the blood drain from my face as I saw, just up the road from us, a great wave of grey, brown and white sweeping over everything. I also saw two car lights just in advance of it.

We scrambled down the side of the generator plant and sprinted across to the garage. The sky was turning to twilight and the dust was stinging our backs when we reached the shelter of the carports.

As we did so, the car swung into the drive and into the dust. With its radar confused, its engine cut out. Only its momentum carried it as far as the garage. We pushed it inside and closed the door. Darkness descended around us.

A dusty figure clambered out of the car. 'Gosh, that was exciting.'

Without further ado, Patricia took off her robe, underneath which she wasn't wearing anything. She shook out some of the dust in her robe and her hair. Then she hugged Roderick.

Normally, the site of an unclad Patricia would arouse my interest. But at that moment, erotic feelings were the furthest thing from my mind. I had always thought of myself as pretty tough. Not exactly a macho man, but one who showed true grit in a crisis. Yet I felt I had failed at a critical time.

'And you know what I'm like when I get excited,' Patricia said in a throaty voice that was soft, but loud enough for me to hear. Roderick gave her a lingering kiss as he put his arm around her. When they looked at me, I felt myself turn red. Were they inviting me to join in, or saying 'excuse us'? I felt as bad as if I'd dropped a simple catch with all my teammates watching.

Mercifully, it was only a glance. Roderick led her away to the adjoining storeroom. I sat alone, stunned. Just a few minutes earlier, I had rushed out full of bravado to the garage to help Roderick. Now he had proven himself to be the stronger man, and what's more, judging by the rhythmic sounds coming from the storeroom, Patricia obviously preferred him.

'Ooh, that's much better,' she moaned.

Much better than me, or than being out in a dust storm? I wanted to escape. Should I chance it in the storm? Looking out of the window, I saw the strangest thing I have ever seen – a dense orange-brown swirling 'fog'. Visibility: about zero.

I was trapped. It wouldn't have been so bad up on that generator roof if I hadn't been so damned useless. If only there was something I could do to take my mind off things, especially windmills.

There was one thing I could do. I set to work cleaning the dust-ridden car in carport three: first the exterior, then the upholstery, and finally the gritty business of cleaning under the bonnet. I decided to take the engine apart to clean everything properly.

I became so absorbed in what I was doing that I forgot all about Patricia and Roderick until I heard his voice in my ear: 'Storm's clearing up, old boy.'

I grunted in acknowledgment while I ran some tests on the capacitors. I didn't realise that he and Patricia had gone out and reassembled the windmill until he returned with the lug wrench.

'All fixed,' he said. 'We don't usually get winds that strong, but the blades are undamaged and I think the rhododendrons will recover.'

'Fine.'

He looked as though he wanted to say something else. 'Yes, well, I'll leave you to it.'

●

I worked all afternoon on that car. I reassembled the engine, recharged the batteries, and ran a few test programs on its computer. Then I gave it a really good wash and polish. It was a sporty little number.

After a swim in the murky pool in the late afternoon, I decided to take the car for a spin. I told it to go to the Mount Ainslie lookout. Despite its little motor, it chugged its way slowly but steadily up the steep winding road, scarcely missing a beat. I and the computer had tuned it well.

In the cool of the evening, I stood on the mountain top. Below me were the suburbs of North Canberra. All I could see was a forest and a few pale street lights. Beyond them, the sun was setting in a blaze of red glory. Never had I seen such a magnificent sunset.

I felt as though I was back at square one, which was where I wanted to be at that moment. Many years earlier, I could have stood on the same spot and seen much the same scene. It was as though nothing had changed. Nothing, except that the last time I was in this place, Janet was with me.

Janet? Was she still around? No one I had spoken to, Dr Ohira, nephew Darren or Ron, seemed to know. I worked out that she would be at least ninety. I would like to catch up with her if she was still alive, or at least find out how life had worked out for her.

Remembering the good times we had made me feel nostalgic. I remembered driving my own (electric) car, living in my own little kingdom, running my own business, playing cricket, eating Big Macs and french fries, and drinking beer that didn't cost an arm and a leg.

I patted the bonnet of my sporty little energy-efficient, environmentally friendly, hi-tech, low-tech runabout. I felt a sudden yearning for the smell of petrol, the roar of the engine, and the satisfying strobe that told me I had done a good job of tuning it.

I had worked with computers for much of my life, but I didn't want a computer digital readout to tell me I had tuned the engine; I didn't want a computer to tell me where I could drive; and I certainly didn't want a computer to do the driving for me. The only good thing about that was that I could get as drunk as I liked, and the car could drive me home.

Then I realised that the computer might be useful after all. I asked it, 'Are there any pubs in Canberra?'

The computer's voice, although a definite improvement on those in my time, sounded flat and mechanical: 'Explain pubs.'

'Er, public houses … taverns. Hotels.'

When it displayed a list of hotels in Canberra, I saw that one of my old watering holes was still operating. I told the computer to take me there.

'Do you wish to make a reservation?'

'No. Just take me there.'

'It is not sequential to go to a hotel without making a reservation.'

'I don't care.' I decided I would have to do something about this computer when I got back to the Community. 'Does it have a saloon bar?'

The computer showed me a list of the hotel facilities. 'It has a restaurant with bar service,' it answered helpfully.

'That'll do.'

'Do you wish to make a reservation for dinner?'

'No. Just take me there.'

'It is not sequential to—'

'Listen, pal,' I snapped. 'Let's get one thing straight. When I give you an order, I expect it to be obeyed. If I want your opinion I'll ask for it.'

No response: I swear the damn thing was sulking. To my relief, Ermingtrude (as I now affectionately called 'my car') pulled out of the car park and drove back down the mountain. I would like to think that she did it of her own accord, not at the command of a grudging computer.

The hotel, with its curious cone-shaped roof, resembled the one that had stood there in my day. I expected to walk straight into the bar. Instead, I was greeted by a doorman, who asked me where I had come from, whether I'd had a pleasant journey, and was I expecting to stay in Canberra long?

'Why do you ask?'

'Well,' explained the doorman, 'if you're staying for more than a few days, I can arrange for a greeting committee to show you the sights of the city and arrange longer term accommodation for you.'

'No, thanks. I'm just passing through.'

'I don't nexus. Passing through what?'

'I just want to have a few drinks at the bar. I used to drink at this pub long ago.'

The doorman frowned for a moment. Then his eyes lit up. 'Ah. You must be the man who's come out of hibernation.'

'How did you know that?'

'Your speech mode.'

'But how did you know about me. I haven't been on HV.'

'Everyone in Canberra knows about you, sir. On the informal network.'

'The what?'

'The, er, grapevine, I believe it is called.' With that, he ushered me into the restaurant.

All I wanted to do was to prop myself on a barstool and have a couple of beers. But a waiter insisted on showing me to a table and brought drinks to me. When I asked how much they cost, he insisted that I was their guest.

A few people said good evening to me, or pointed me out to their dining partners. I felt ill at ease. This wasn't the anonymity I had been hoping for. I just wanted to wander into a bar, have a few drinks, and make friends with total strangers without having to worry about who or what any of us were.

After three beers, the waiter was reluctant to give me any more. I thanked him and the doorman for the hospitality and went out to Ermingtrude. Her computer adopted a more friendly tone than before. 'Where to, sir?'

'Call me James,' I insisted. 'Somewhere wild. Is there a nightclub in town?'

The term 'nightclub' did not compute. By accessing a database, I found there were several dance academies in Canberra, but no nightclub. It seemed that the wildest thing people did in 2100 was to have water fights in their community swimming pools.

'We might as well go back,' I said ruefully.

'Home, James?'

'And don't spare the horses.'

CHAPTER FOURTEEN

AGRESHN THERAPY

Next morning, I went over to the garage, where I found Ron, Roderick and Patricia examining 'my car'.

'Something the matter?'

They seemed a bit uneasy. 'Erm, did you notice anything unusual about the car's computer system last night?' Ron asked.

'Not really. Apart from its arrogance.'

'Arrogance?'

I explained the little run-in I had with the computer, and how I had ordered it to do as it was told, and not to tell me what to do.

'Ah, that explains it,' said Patricia.

'Explains what?'

'You've upset the poor thing,' Roderick explained indignantly.

'Upset it? How can you upset a computer?'

Ron came over and put a fatherly arm on my shoulder. 'Without meaning to, you set up a contradiction in its logic circuits. You see, computers are designed to help us, which was what it was trying to do. When you were aggressive to it in return, it became confused between its intentions and your reactions. It was caught in a logic trap from which it couldn't escape. As a result, it went round and round in circles, frantically scanning its algorithms for answers to a contradiction that it couldn't resolve. In the end, it broke down.'

'Broke down?' I protested. 'But it was all right when I drove home last night.'

Ron nodded. 'It would have been a gradual process. At first, only a few circuits would have been involved. In time, the dilemma would have spread until the major functional circuits were affected.'

'You must speak nicely to your computer,' Patricia purred as she stroked Ermingtrude's bonnet.

'In your day,' Ron added, 'computers were very good at the mechanics of calculating things, but they were intellectually inept. Now, they think better, but they have the mental stability of immature children, and they must be treated with love and kindness.'

'I know that computers are stupid,' I snapped. 'As far as I'm concerned, a computer's job is to obey. We've got to make it clear to them right from the start who is the boss.'

The others were shocked by this. Roderick dabbed his sweaty brow with a silk handkerchief. 'Perhaps what James needs is a computer with fuzzier logic.'

Patricia smiled. 'And a woman's voice, I suspect.' The rest of us looked at her. 'The gentle touch is needed with computers. James is more likely to learn it from a woman than a man.'

'Fair enough,' I agreed. 'Ermingtrude is a woman after all.'

After the others had left, Roderick stayed behind because he wanted to talk to me. 'About yesterday,' he began awkwardly.

I gave him a sharp look, and he squirmed. 'I feel I should apologise.'

'Why?'

'The windmill. I didn't mean to expose us to such danger. Truth to tell, I should have attended to it before the winds picked up, but

I was so worried about Patricia that I stayed near the intercom instead.'

I was relieved to hear him say that. Fancy him apologizing to me when I couldn't look him in the eye after yesterday's fiasco. 'That's OK.' I responded. 'Sorry I got into a tangle with the driveshaft. Still, we'll both be more experienced next time.'

With that, we shook hands, and became friends.

●

The stifling summer heat continued throughout Feburi. The eastern end of our pond dried out, and cracks appeared in the mud. Mercifully, we were spared from more dust storms.

Towards the end of the month, I could feel the tension rising in Willow Community in general, and in the Bushell household in particular. Part of this tension was due to the air gradually becoming more humid. The other part was due to the forthcoming community elections. Normally a quiet person anyway, Lena now became somewhat withdrawn. She started wearing her regulator.

●

When I awoke on the morning of Th29022100, I realised that I was one hundred years old.

That evening, we had a small get-together for my birthday, because we would have a bigger one the following night, following on from the Annual General Meeting.

Darren turned up for my birthday party, and presented me with a 100th birthday card.

Ron said that he had a surprise for me. On the family holovision, he projected some two-dimensional footage, extracts from the newsreels from 29 Feburi 2000. There was also footage, taken in the hospital, of the proud young parents with their new baby.

As I stared at myself on the screen, I imagined the screen image of myself staring back at me, over a chasm of one hundred years. It was like that scene from the movie 2001, where the old man and the baby stare at each other.

'Full circle', I muttered quietly to myself.

'Pardon?' asked Lena, who was sitting next to me.

I also looked at the images of my parents. Dad had a full head of hair back then, while mum was dark-haired. When I last saw them, on the day I went into cryosleep, Dad's hair was in retreat and Mum's had turned grey. At that time, Kylie had the dizzy blonde look, while ten-year-old Darren had tousled, dark hair. My eyes moistened, and Lena gave me a tissue.

I looked at Darren now: dignified, mid-seventies, with thinning white hair.

Although there were conversations going on all around me, I soon lapsed into a reverie. I kept seeing images of my infant self, my youthful parents, Kylie and young Darren. And Janet. What had become of her? I sensed Darren knew more than he was willing to tell me.

I was never into poetry at school: I had no use for it. But now, one line of verse kept running through my head.

In my beginning, is my end.

●

Willow Community held its Annual General Meeting on the night of Friday 30 Feburi. Nearly everyone turned up for the dinner and meeting at our community centre: about one hundred and twenty people in all. Lena and Patricia both wore large pendant earrings to hide their regulators.

I have never found Annual General Meetings exciting, but this one was a real anti-climax. Lena gave a speech in which she said that despite the drought, the community was managing reasonably well, but we might have to tighten our budget if the drought continued much longer. She referred to me as 'our Centenarian' and praised my efforts with my automotive orchestra. This raised a titter or two from the audience.

The financial statement was then read: the community ran on an annual budget of a quarter of a million Australs, and had assets worth nearly five million – about 40,000 Australs per man, woman and child.

All seven committee positions were then declared vacant, and nominations were called for. Lena diffidently accepted the nomination for Convenor again. Patricia was also asked, but she declined because she wanted to concentrate on her artistic work. This broke the tension: Lena was visibly relieved. Apart from her, three of the outgoing committee were re-elected, along with three new members who were dragooned because it was 'their turn'.

During the cocktail party that followed the meeting, I saw Lena quietly taking off her regulator. She gave me a guilty look when she realised I had seen her.

The highlight of the party was a birthday cake with '100' printed on the icing. There were cheers as I blew out the candles. Then, the bubbly was produced and they toasted my health. I gave a speech in which I insisted that I didn't feel a day over thirty-five, which was true.

●

The election eased some tensions, but not others. The languid summer heat that had held us in a contented torpor now became humid and oppressive. Insulated though the houses were, they were too uncomfortable to sleep in at night. Throughout the community, everybody moved outdoors to sleep under the stars.

I was feeling tense for other reasons. I had seen little of Patricia since Roderick's return, and it seemed to me that every other reasonably attractive female was 'spoken for'. This made me restless: I yearned, if not for female company, then at least for some sort of action and excitement.

So, one afternoon, I set out in Ermingtrude and drove north. Once clear of the city limits, I told her to go faster. She increased speed to 100 kilometres per hour. 'Faster,' I demanded.

'But James,' Ermingtrude protested sweetly, 'I am not designed to go much faster.'

'Faster,' I insisted. She struggled up to 120. 'James, my engine is overheating.'

I had the top of the car pulled back, and was enjoying the cool air rushing past me. 'Faster, dammit, faster!'

'I can't,' she wailed, 'I'm overheating.'

I looked at the temperature gauge. It was up to 130. 'Bloody wimpy cars.'

'My tires are …' – Ermingtrude skidded around a curve and raised dust by the edge of the road – '… not designed for this.'

'All right, all right, I get the point. Slow down to one hundred.'

I soon told Ermingtrude to pull over to a clearing at the side of the road. She cooled down while I took a walk. The scrub around me didn't look any different from what it had before my hibernation. It was, like much of the Australian landscape, dull and boring.

I didn't have my regulator on and I was feeling aggro. Aggro? When that word popped into my mind, I remembered that Ron or somebody had said something about 'Aggro Centres'.

Scanning Ermingtrude's directory, I found that there was such a centre in a part of town that had, in my day, been the home of adult book shops and massage parlours. I told her to drive me there.

From the outside, it looked like an adult bookshop, but was much bigger.

Its windows were blacked in, and it called itself the Centre For Agreshn Therapy.

I walked inside, feeling as nervous as I did the first time I went into an adult bookshop when I was just old enough to pass for eighteen. I entered a small waiting room. I could hear the ritual grunts of a martial arts class in progress. There wasn't much in the way of decor – just a few signs pointing to the Dummy Room, the Fantasy Room and the Martial Arts Room.

I was about to take a peek in the Martial Arts Room when a man walked in through a door I hadn't previously noticed. He was a big man, with a beaming face like a Buddha, and wearing a blue robe. He bowed. 'Good evening. What is your pleasure?'

'Is this the Aggro Centre?'

'It is.' He bowed again.

'What sort of things do you do here? Apart from Martial Arts?'

'In what way would you like to express your aggression?' The smile never left his face. 'Wrestling, beating dummies, or do you prefer sado- masochism?'

'Erm … not really. I want something wild. Actually, I'd like to get drunk.'

The beaming Buddha looked uneasy. 'Tell me your fantasy.'

'I just want to let my hair down. You know, have a few drinks, go for a burn down the highway. Go to a nightclub. Chat up a girl.'

Buddha was getting more worried by the minute. Then his face lit up. 'Ah. You must be the man from hibernation.'

'Yes. I'm the man from hibernation,' I said wryly. 'And I don't want something aggro like smashing someone's face in. That isn't my style. I want something wild and exciting.'

Worry lines appeared all over Buddha's face as he contemplated deeply.

'Something wild and exciting for the man from long ago … Ah, yes. You like racing cars?'

'You bet. I went to watch the Grand Prix twice.'

'We have an old fantasy,' he explained as he opened the door to the Fantasy Room. 'It does not mean much to us because cars drive themselves. But you might appreciate it.'

The Fantasy Room was made up of several virtual reality booths. He told me to wait in one while he went to the storeroom. While I was waiting, a young lady in a kimono gave me a glass of beer and some peanuts.

Buddha soon returned with a crash helmet, a leather jacket, and a steering wheel, which he clamped to the console in front of me. The helmet was a size too small and the jacket was a size too large, yet they fitted well enough for the purpose. I found the situation so ridiculous that I burst out laughing.

But not for long. The lights dimmed: the screens around me lit up. Suddenly, I was off and racing. I'm not sure how many cars there were in the race, nor could I recognise the circuit. We shot down the main straight past the grandstands, into the chicane, then down the back straight to the hairpin.

After three laps, I had left the other cars behind, yet all I had done was grip the steering wheel. It was then that the computer asked, 'Do you want an interactive fantasy?'

I accepted like a shot. There was a glove on the consul. When I put it on, I found I could interact by changing gears. Up into the straight, down into the chicane, a bit of left wheel, and I was burning down the back straight.

It was exhilarating: the roar of the engine, the smell of leather, hot oil and burning tires. I was alive and at one with a machine that was thundering down the straight … towards the hairpin.

I changed down gears, but it was too late. The wall of the hairpin was looming up fast. I put my foot on the brake. The car squealed and skidded. With lightning reflexes, I did the only thing I could do – swing the car sharp left so that the rear end struck the wall.

I swung so sharply that I hit the floor with a thud and went rolling around in the booth.

A worried Buddha and his kimonoed assistant rushed in to help me up. Thanks to the crash helmet and the leather jacket, I wasn't hurt. They took me off to the locker room for a shower and a rub down. I was caked in sweat.

After a nice, relaxing massage, and some more beer, I felt much better. Then it occurred to me that I wasn't sure how I was going to pay for this adventure.

When I asked about payment, my host said he wouldn't dream of accepting any. Maybe he was embarrassed by my little accident, or perhaps he thought it was a great privilege to have a celebrity like me in his establishment.

I didn't argue. I told Ermingtrude to drive home at a nice, leisurely pace so that I could enjoy the evening air. Feeling in an expansive mood, I wished I had a cigar in one hand and a glass of sparkling in the other.

As we drove through the streets of North Canberra, I heard a curious sound … something vaguely familiar … coming closer. Horse's hooves?

Ermingtrude slowed right down and pulled over to the side of the road. On her computer screen, the word INTERCEPT flashed in red letters.

Out of the gathering dusk came a strange sight – a white, pulsating object suspended a metre or two in the air. It was close before I realised it was a white uniform, worn by a black man riding a dark horse. A traffic cop?

He pulled up alongside, towering over me. 'Good evening. Mr James Lawson, I presume.'

'Good evening, officer,' I replied. 'Yes. How do you know my name?'

'I inferred it,' was the reply. 'You must be the man from hibernation.'

The constable dismounted, walked over and touched a button on Ermingtrude's computer. The INTERCEPT sign went out. He reached into his pocket to pull out a pamphlet which he gave to me.

'What's this?' I asked.

'The Highway Code. It may have changed during your hibernation, sir.'

'Er … have I done something wrong?'

He nodded. 'An offence called a one-twenty because that was the speed that was recorded. The speed limit throughout Australia is one hundred kilometres per hour.'

'Recorded?' I thought back to earlier when I had taken Ermingtrude for a burn. 'How?'

'You were recorded by Road Traffic Control passing through successive grid points in time intervals indicative of that speed, sir.'

Why do cops always call you 'sir' when they're going to book you? That was something which hadn't changed. 'So,' I asked tentatively, 'what happens now? Do you want to see my license?'

'You don't need a license now, as long as you allow your vehicle to operate within program limits.'

I decided to move to a different tack. I figured the longer we talked, the less likely he was to book me. 'How did you know it was me?'

'A logical inference, sir. Speeding violations are rare these days. But for people in your day it was commonplace to exceed speed limits by about twenty percent or more. And since you are the only such person in town, it seemed logical that you were the driver.

'Road Traffic Control tracked you to the Aggro Centre, but rather than spoil your pleasure, I thought it more polite to wait until you returned, before pointing out the error of your ways.'

'All right, I get the point.' I affectionately patted the dashboard. 'I promise never to be cruel to Ermingtrude again.'

'Thank you, James,' her soft voice purred.

The constable nodded approvingly. 'In that case, sir, I don't think we need to take this matter any further.'

Relieved, I looked up into his dark face. 'Thank you, er …'

'Jack. Constable Jack Wilberforce.' He offered his hand, which I shook.

It occurred to me that I had just been told off by, and shaken hands with, an aboriginal policeman whose ancestors may well have been black trackers, but who kept tabs on me by means of a traffic computer.

'Tell me, er, Jack, what would your ancestors have made of all of this? Everybody fenced in, and knowing where everyone else is.'

He scratched his head. 'I don't suppose I've ever thought about it, James. With the horse, I have a lot more freedom to go where I want to than people in cars have. As for everybody knowing everyone else's location, one way or another, my ancestors did that anyway.'

●

After being let off with a friendly warning from Constable Wilberforce, I went home and put on my regulator. At first, far from calming me or deadening my chastened feelings, it caused me to feel a whole range of emotions. Gradually, though, it did cheer me up.

Which was more than I could say for the weather. The air was becoming electric, and the clouds appeared low on the horizon. Apart from the dust storm, they were the first ones I could recall seeing in nearly three months in 2100.

On the morning of Fr14032100, the air was almost unbearable. Dark clouds with massive thunderheads were looming. Steam was oozing out of everything, the air was heady with the scent of damp earth, and it was impossible to get dry or cool.

Far from being depressed, the members of Willow Community were hard at work, aerating the soil in the gardens and the village green.

By mid-afternoon, we heard hear the distant rumbling, growing ever closer. From time to time we glanced nervously at the sky.

Roderick and I checked the garages to make sure that all of the cars were home. Then we went to the generator plant to remove the windmill blade and to hoist the lightning conductors. There was no panic this time, just orderly, if exhausting and sweaty, work.

Yet we had scarcely finished when we were dazzled by a great flash of light. Seconds later, we heard the sky exploding. Everyone downed tools and ran for cover.

From the window of the Bushells' house, I watched the spectacle unfold as the lighting flashed amid the great thunderheads. Thunder shook the house to its foundations.

Gradually, the aerial sound and light show moved further away, leaving in its wake a black sky and still, muggy air. One final bolt of lightning zipped across the sky as if slitting the clouds open.

It seemed like all the water in the clouds fell out of the sky at once. Great curtains of rain swept in across the park. To my astonishment, everyone rushed outside, in various states of undress.

We danced in the rain, to a chant of 'Gaia be praised. Gaia be praised.'

CHAPTER FIFTEEN

BLACK FRIDAY AND GREEN MUNDAY

The rain that was greeted with so much enthusiasm soon became a curse: it rained and it rained and it rained. It looked as though Canberra was going to get a year's rainfall in one month.

The dust turned to mud, and the mud became a quagmire. Our lovely swimming pool filled and flooded its banks. We had to put up barricades to protect the flower beds.

Our cars had as many problems with the rain and the mud as they'd had with the dust. They bogged in the driveways or the verges of the roads. When they got onto the roads, they often stopped because heavy rain fooled their radar braking systems. This was probably just as well. They weren't very sturdy vehicles, and their thin tires lacked the grip needed for slippery roads.

The rain did ease the tension, but after a couple of weeks, it started to build up again. Our Community was getting excited about the forthcoming Gaia festival, which had taken the place of Easter for most people.

The women and children were more excited about it at first, but as we drew closer to Friday 28th, the men were also affected.

The weekly market was moved forward to Thersday 27th, and many stalls did a roaring trade in black and green bunting. Also sold on a day of hectic trading were paintings, holograms and strange plastic globes of our planet, and large quantities of fruit, vegetables and preserves.

We spent much of the afternoon at the Bushell household decorating the place in black streamers. All around the park, black wreaths were hung on front doors. Willow Community, like other communities around Canberra, around Australia, around the world, went into mourning.

That night, we ate tea in a funereal silence. After tea, I asked Ron, 'Why is everybody so glum?'

'Glum?' For all his historical knowledge, Ron didn't know the word.

'Er, depressed, sad.'

'Tomorrow is Black Friday, when we lament for what has happened to the Earth.'

'Well, it's still here.'

'It has survived,' Ron said grimly, 'along with ten billion people. But at a price.' He assured me that I would find out more tomorrow. In the meantime, he gave me a robe, which was black on one side and green on the other. 'You're under no obligation, of course, but we would appreciate it if you wore it black side out tomorrow.'

'OK.' I said reluctantly. I didn't fancy going around dressed in black robes, but if that was the done thing, I wasn't going to argue.

Next morning, I was about to get my normal clothes when I remembered the black robe. I put it on, felt a bit silly, and went up for breakfast. I didn't wear my regulator. It wasn't the done thing either at Easter.

I should have felt reassured by seeing Ron, Lena and Tami also in black. Instead, it was strange: the normally mundane routine of breakfast took on the air of a mystic rite.

Nobody spoke much. After a frugal breakfast, we cleaned up and went outside. By the swimming pool I saw a bizarre sight – a gathering of black- hooded brethren. As we got closer, they looked even weirder. Many of them had painted their faces a motley mix of black and white.

'Sackcloth and ashes,' Ron told me.

When the hundred-odd (that day, very odd) residents of Willow Community had gathered near the pool, Lena led us in procession, single file, towards the community centre. People wept and uttered strange cries. As we filed towards the centre, they broke into a weird chant. By the time we got there, some were just about in hysterics.

Inside, it was dark and sombre: dimly lit lanterns cast shadows on black bunting. By then, I was close to hysterics myself: I felt like laughing my head off.

As soon as we filed into the holovision room, however, everyone was silent.

The doors closed behind us, the lights went out: we were in pitch darkness.

The holovision came on. Over our heads floated a globe of the Earth; a beautiful, pristine, blue, white and ochre world. Around it was a shifting pattern of images – sunsets, green valleys, fresh-flowing streams, dolphins in the deep … In my day, these splendid visions would have been part of an advert for air fresheners, beverages, or holiday cruises.

But then more holovisions floated before our eyes – oil spills, choking birds and seals, whale hunting, city smog, sewage drifting along the coast, famines, wars and wrecked cars.

Accompanying this was a relentless piece of music, a march in slow- time. I later found out it was the Te Deum from the Mass by Berlioz. The globe above our heads was changing from a vision of beauty into something ghastly: the seas turned to grey, and the land and the swirling clouds into an angry mass of red and black.

The world burst into flames. Everyone gasped and had hysterics. Surrounded by all these gasping, weeping people in an enclosed room I felt claustrophobic.

Our burning planet withered away into the blackness until there was nothing left except a crowd of people wailing in the dark. The irritatingly rational citizens of the brave new world of 2100 were blowing their collective mind.

More shocks were to follow. The doors opened, and we all went out into the fresh air and sunlight. There was a strange, yet familiar aroma … gum leaves? … smoke!

The citizens of Willow Community spread themselves on the lawns. Many were sobbing uncontrollably, and had to be helped by their loved ones and neighbours. I stood in the middle of it all, confused and numb.

Some of the children started fighting. It was just a bit of pushing and shoving at first, until Angela and Steven resorted to calling each other names. They were obviously rivals for leader of the pack.

Angela hit Steven on the nose. It might have been accidental; she may have just been trying to fend him off. With blood coming out of his nostrils and steam out of his ears, Steven got stuck into her. How pleasing it was to see the budding young social workers, who had grilled me in the classroom about human relations, laying into each other for all they were worth.

To my surprise, none of the parents showed any signs of wanting to break up the fight. They took little notice of the fracas.

I let things go until Angela started crying. Her tears appealed to my gallantry. Grabbing Steven by the scruff of the neck, I pulled him away. 'Enough is enough.'

Steven glared at me. 'Listen, pal,' I told him, 'you don't hit a lady.'

'Mind your own business,' he retorted, and put up his dukes.

Fancy Steven telling someone to mind his own business! 'Cool it,' I snapped.

Folding my arms, I stood between him and the sobbing Angela. He retreated to a safe distance while Angela's friends thanked me and comforted her.

This drama was brought to a sudden end by the arrival of Harry, Eduardo and Julio with a load of wood. Immediately, there were cries of 'the globe, the globe'.

These were the magic words that brought everyone to their feet with renewed enthusiasm. Ron and Roderick raced into the community centre. They rolled out a large, red, black and grey plastic globe of the earth. It was like a ghastly fitball.

Everyone formed a circle around a pile of logs on which the globe was soon hoisted. They chanted, 'Burn, burn, burn.'

Ron tied a piece of cloth over a wooden stave, dipped it in oil, and set a light to it. The chant increased to fever pitch: 'Burn, burn, burn.'

Ron walked over to me. 'Would you care to do the honours?'

I looked about me: plumes of smoke and similar chants were rising up from communities all around us. The air hung heavy with the pungent smell of burnt plastic. One hundred blood-crazed savages looked at me expectantly.

'No,' I protested. 'This is silly.'

'After what your generation did to the world,' Harry retorted, 'you call this silly?'

'It is a great honour,' Ron insisted.

I shook my head. 'This is crazy.'

Ron turned and hurled the blazing stave onto the wood pile. Eduardo and Julio, who had been pouring oil all over the 'funeral pyre', leapt out of the way just in time.

Up she went: flames swept across Africa, scorched through Europe, and ignited the North Pole. The globe crumpled, melting into thick, black pungent smoke that hung in the air ominously. All the time, the chant of 'burn, burn, burn' became louder and louder.

I felt very uncomfortable. I had upset them by not 'doing the honours'. In their present frame of mind, would they put me on the pyre next? I slunk away, retreating to the safety of the Bushells' house.

When the Bushells came back an hour later, they were not in a good mood. 'How could you refuse?' Lena berated me. 'Being asked to torch the globe is a great honour.'

'Well, I didn't know that,' I protested.

'And why didn't he know that?' Lena demanded of Ron.

'Because I didn't tell him beforehand,' Ron snapped.

I had never seen Ron and Lena behave like this before. Had everyone gone crazy?

More craziness was to follow. They later had a row because Ron chose to have a shave in the middle of the day and left his beard trimmings in the washbasin.

I thought of going for a walk, but a thick pall of smoke hung in the air over a city gone mad. Later, on the holonews, I found the same thing happening throughout the country.

Dinner, which was unusually unappetising, was eaten in silence. The Bushells were moody. When I asked what was going on, I was curtly told that all would be revealed on Green Munday.

'In the meantime,' Ron told me, 'wear ordinary clothes for the next two days, but don't wear your regulator.'

Despite his orders, I did wear my regulator to bed that night. It didn't make me feel any better, but I slept soundly. In the morning, I was in a state of bland neutrality. So, it seemed, was everyone else. Nobody spoke much: they were cordial, but not friendly.

This continued for two days. We ate unappetizing food, and did lots of spring cleaning. On Saturday, everyone cleaned out their houses or flats. On Sunday, we cleaned out the community centre, the garage, and the muck in the swimming pool.

When we reported for working bees on Sunday morning, everything was organised in a matter-of-fact way. Nobody smiled or laughed or said much. Yet as the day wore on, I could feel a rising sense of excitement, of expectation, among the community members.

Tea that night was still plain fare, but it was eaten in an atmosphere of suppressed excitement. Tami didn't eat at all. 'I want to save myself up for tomorrow,' she explained.

'Why?' I queried. 'What happens tomorrow? Or shouldn't I ask?'

The three Bushells looked at each other. 'Not yet,' Ron replied. 'Tomorrow at breakfast is the appropriate time to ask such questions. I know you may be puzzled by what you have experienced these last three days, but in the morning all will be revealed.

'By the way, it is our custom to go to bed early tonight. We have a long day ahead of us tomorrow. In the morning, don't forget to wear that special robe I gave you, green side out.'

I actually went to bed feeling quite happy: the burning fitball of Black Friday had given me an idea, which could have commercial possibilities.

●

Mu01042100 'Green Munday': next morning, I dreamt of elephants. They were trumpeting and shouting in a shrill voice, 'Happy Green Munday!'

I staggered to the door. Tami was running up and down the corridor, blowing a trumpet. 'Happy Green Munday!' She jumped on me and gave me a hug. 'Don't forget to wear the green.'

A short time later, greenly attired and bleary eyed, I wandered into the bathroom. It was already occupied: Lena was giving Ron a shave. I staggered upstairs into the sunroom. The grey light of dawn was giving way to a brighter light in the east.

Remembering the reason why I wanted to go to the bathroom, I went outside and was about to water the geraniums when a green elf went prancing by, still blowing her trumpet. 'Did you want to use the bathroom?' she asked. 'Sorry, should have warned you. Lena always gives Ron a shave on Green Munday morning.'

'Why?'

'For the same reason Ron always leaves his hairs in the washbasin on Black Friday.'

Ask a silly question …

Later, relieved and showered, I sat down to breakfast with the Bushells. Tami kept jumping up to blow her trumpet at passers-by, while Ron and Lena were as lovey-dovey as could be. I watched them all suspiciously.

Ron looked at me, and chuckled.

'What's wrong?' I demanded.

'You.' Lena giggled. 'You look so worried.'

'Cheer up,' cried Tami, 'the best is yet to come.'

I frowned. 'Have you been at the jungle juice or something?' They laughed.

'Poor James,' said Lena, still smiling. 'I suppose we do owe you an explanation.'

'It would be appreciated,' I replied.

Tami attempted to blow a fanfare on her trumpet. 'And now, the explanation!'

'As you've probably noticed,' Ron began, 'most of the time we are peaceful, responsible citizens who care for the world and each other as best we can.'

'Mm. I'll buy that.'

'However, it would be foolish to pretend that human beings do not have aggressive tendencies, that it isn't easy being nice to each other all of the time.'

'True.'

'So once in a while, we need to – how would you say? – "let off steam". As the Easter Gaia festival became more important over the years, people felt that this was the time when we should remember the world we have lost, in its good and bad aspects.

'Thus, on Black Friday, we are deliberately unpleasant towards each other. It gives us a chance to air any grievances that we may have, but in a context in which, in effect, we give each other permission to do so. If you have a longstanding complaint against someone, that is the day to tell them, as bluntly and rudely as you wish.'

'Doesn't that upset them?'

'Of course. But it is the day on which you are allowed, even expected, to be upset. That is why you are discouraged from wearing your regulator. At the back of your mind, of course, is the thought that in three days' time, all will be reconciled, so it doesn't matter.'

'And this business with burning the globe?'

'A deliberate act of pollution by people to whom such a thing is anathema. In your time, it would be like having a day on which everyone burnt money.'

I thought about that. It didn't sound as though it would be a popular day.

'The next two days are days of neutrality,' Ron went on, 'when we think about what happened on Black Fri—'

Tami blew her trumpet and rushed outside to hug somebody.

'—day. We deliberately don't discuss it with anyone. We allow our emotions free reign internally while we, physically, get our house and community in order. We wear bland clothes, eat bland food, and treat each other with ritualised cordiality.'

'So that's what it was,' I remarked, wondering about the events of the past two days. 'And today's the day when you fix it all up again?'

'We already have.' Ron put his hand affectionately on Lena's arm. I remembered the business about Ron leaving hair in the washbasin on Friday, and Lena shaving him this morning. Their annual ritual was apparently their way of reaffirming their love for each other.

'The wonderful time,' Lena said, almost with tears in her eyes, 'is Sunday evening. When we each work out in our own minds how we are going to make our peace with other people, and they with us. It's like Christmas Eve when you're a child, and you wonder what presents you are going to get.' She did break into tears. 'I'm so happy.' She wrapped her arms around Ron.

They were getting lovey-dovey again. As they fondled each other, it was obvious they were eager to get back to the bedroom.

'I think I'll take a walk,' I announced as I got up from the table. I winked at them. 'A long walk.'

●

I set out for a leisurely walk around the park. It was an embarrassing experience. Green-clad brethren came up to me to apologise for putting me on the spot about lighting the plastic globe on Black Friday. I in turn apologised for not lighting it. Then they'd say, 'You must find our ways rather strange.' I replied that I did, but that Lena and Ron had explained it to me. Then they'd give me a hug.

From time to time, I was 'buzzed' by a little green pixie blowing her trumpet. I was tempted to snatch it away from her, not because it annoyed me, but just to see what would happen. Would there be tears on Green Munday?

I didn't, though. Why spoil a good party? Instead, I sat down on a quiet bench by a shady bower to contemplate the meaning of life. I remembered the exercise that Ron and I had practiced on my first ever walk around the Community.

I sat very still, sensed a gentle breeze on my face, smelt the fragrance of newly mown lawn, and listened to the twittering of the birds and the fun- and-games in the bushes behind me. A female voice giggled. Patricia? No. The voice was too young.

I'm not into voyeurism, but I couldn't help taking a peek through the curtain of bushes into the shady bower beyond. Two young bodies were writhing and rolling over each other on the lawn of the sensuous texture.

A slight movement on my part must have disturbed them. They stopped and looked up: Angela and Steven were 'reconciling' their differences.

'Oh, sorry,' I said involuntarily. They didn't seem in the least embarrassed.

●

I arrived home in time for lunch. It was a frugal affair because we had to save ourselves for that night's feast. We didn't speak much. Tami was worn out from her trumpet blowing, while Lena and Ron were worn out for other reasons. I didn't speak because I had things on my mind.

Over coffee, Lena asked, 'Is there something wrong, James?'

I decided that this was not the time to discuss late-21st century morality. Yet there was something else I wanted to ask them. 'Do you blame me for what happened?'

Ron frowned. 'In what sense?'

'Wrecking the planet and everything.'

The Bushells looked uneasily at each other. 'Well,' Ron hedged, 'the planet's environmental situation is the result of a long and complex process—'

'No. Me. For what I did, or didn't do. Or do you blame everyone from my time?'

Ron squirmed a bit. Lena also looked uncomfortable. Tami merely raised an eyebrow. 'Actually,' Ron replied, 'there were people in your time who warned about the environment and climate change. And yours was the first generation that really did anything about it – recycling, experiments with solar power, carbon credits and monitoring the ozone layer.'

'I know,' I protested. 'I ran a company that developed and sold energy- saving systems.'

Lena looked straight at me and asked, 'Do you feel guilty about what happened?'

'Do you?' I retorted.

Silence. Even Tami was perturbed. Lena wrung her hands. Ron cleared his throat. 'I suppose we feel guilty about what happened to the world in the same way that people in your time felt guilty about the treatment of indigenous people.'

'But …' I was about to say that while I regretted how our ancestors had treated them, I didn't feel guilty about the indigenous people. I held my tongue because I realised I could make a fool of myself. 'It doesn't matter.'

Another silence. Lena smiled. 'You could say we feel guilty on your behalf.'

I had the uncomfortable feeling that I was being patronised, or in this case, matronised.

'Put it this way,' Ron intervened. 'Yours was a time for action. Ours is a time for reflection. It's easy to look back at the past and say what should or should not have been done. But we weren't living then, and it's hypothetical to discuss how we would have behaved if we had. So we've no right to judge.'

This seemed a good point at which to close the conversation, but Ron went on. 'Each generation is more critical of its forebears than perhaps it ought to be, for an obvious reason. Any generation is likely to do some things that will benefit their descendants, and other things that will harm them. The benefits tend to be taken for granted by future generations, while they are preoccupied with solving the problems they have inherited.

'Where, for example, would we be today without the computers that people in your time developed?'

That was a fair enough answer. I was happy to let the subject rest there. Yet it was Tami who surprised me by having the last word. She had become increasingly serious during the conversation, an expression that I had not seen on her face before. A trifle self-consciously, she quoted:

'The evil that men do lives after them,

The good is oft interred with their bones.'

CHAPTER SIXTEEN

RECONCILIATION

After lunch, Ermingtrude took me for a drive. I told her to go at a leisurely pace to the Mount Ainslie lookout.

It was a warm, sunny afternoon. Below me, the city had changed from the mottled browns of summer to lush greenery. In a few more weeks, when the early frosts nipped the leaves, Canberra would be a riot of red and gold.

I had the top down, and lay back in my seat tunelessly humming an old song: 'I wanna know what love is.' I stroked the dashboard affectionately. 'Do you know what love is, Ermingtrude?'

'Yes, James,' she replied huskily. 'It's a human emotion.'

'Are there any other kinds?' I asked wryly.

'Of course. Animals have emotions too.'

'And machines? Do cars have emotions?'

'No. We are not programmed for them.'

'Hmm. I'm not so sure about that.' I had taken off my sunglasses, and was twirling them in my hand. 'Remember when I told you to drive fast, and you told me it was dangerous. You got upset then, didn't you?'

'I … your request was contrary to my standard operating procedures. My circuits became heated.' Ermingtrude's voice was just a trifle strained. I noticed that the heat gauge flickered a tad.

'Think of other times,' I suggested. 'Like, when everything is going smoothly. You know exactly where you are and you are on schedule.'

'Yes,' she purred. 'When there is no dysfunction between my programmed instructions and my operating parameters.'

'Well, maybe that's what love is. Although that's the least romantic description of it that I've ever heard.'

Ermingtrude was unfazed. 'Thank you, James.'

I yawned and stretched. 'Home, my dear. I have to get ready for tonight's fun and games.'

We wound our way back down the road into town. There was hardly any traffic about; Ermingtrude was dawdling along. We reached the point on the road where we had been stopped by the constabulary on the evening I had been to the Aggro Centre.

'James. We have a Request Stop.'

'A Request Stop? What does that mean?'

'It means that it is not mandatory.'

'Who from?' I looked up the road. 'Oh, no.'

As a familiar figure trotted towards us, I told Ermingtrude to pull over. In my experience, a polite request from the law means an order.

'Happy Green Munday.' Constable Jack Wilberforce dismounted and walked over to us. He handed me a twig with leaves on it.

'What's this for?'

'An olive branch. On Green Munday, I like to contact the people I had to deal with during the year. To see how they are going and to assure them that my actions were not motivated by malice.'

I was taken aback. I could see by the expression on his face that it was important for him to have a reconciliation. 'Er, thanks very much.' I extended my hand. 'As we would say when I was young, "No hard feelings."'

He shook my hand and smiled. 'No hard feelings.'

After that, we had a friendly chat about the weather, the Gaia festival, and his horse. Jack and I got on a first names basis. Then I remembered the lunchtime discussion with the Bushells. I asked him if he knew much history.

'A bit. Why?'

'I just wondered if you thought … if you felt angry about the way us whitefellers treated your people in the past.'

He knitted his brow. I don't think he'd ever been asked that question. At length, he said, 'I don't nexus. What's the point?'

'The Bushells said that I ought to feel guilty about the way we treated the aborigines and the environment. But they felt guilty on my behalf.'

When I mentioned the word 'environment', there was a hint of anger in Jack's eyes. 'In my experience,' he said coldly, 'there is little nexus between crime and guilt.'

We parted company on that point. Ermingtrude continued on her way back to Willow Community. We were nearly there when we had to slow down because there were some girls and boys playing on the road. They waved to me and I waved back. We wished each other 'Happy Green Munday'.

On impulse, I got out of the car and walked slowly down the road. Once or twice, I turned around sharply to see if Ermingtrude was following me: she was, hesitantly. The children found this amusing. Then I stood in front of her, turned part of my robe into a cape, and shouted, 'Toro! Toro!'

My audience laughed. But Ermingtrude just stood there, her silicon circuits nonplussed. A lad of about ten looked at her dashboard. 'Ermingtrude's computer is overheating again.'

'Oh. Sorry, Ermingtrude.' The children laughed at this. I hopped in and patted her dashboard. 'Come on. Back to base.'

Ermingtrude was relieved. Her heat sensors dropped back to normal as she ambled back to our community. The kids waved after us and shouted, 'Toro! Toro!'

It was only as we pulled into the driveway that I realised the significance of what the young lad had said: 'Ermingtrude's computer is overheating again.' These children lived several blocks away from Willow. So how did they know what I called the car, and how did they know about the previous incident with her computer?

No wonder policemen were so friendly. With everyone knowing what everyone else was up to, the crime rate must be just about zero.

It was time to prepare for the Gaia festival. Ron, Harry and I hopped on the market truck to drive around the Community. We collected synthetic holly and mistletoe, genuine ferns, and rolls of green bunting from houses along the way. There was a lot of cooking going on; delicious aromas wafted into our nostrils from just about every place we visited or passed.

Part way round, we were joined by a band of green pixies, or leprechauns as I dubbed them. Blowing her trumpet, Tami led her merry band and the truck on a raucous procession around the park.

The community centre was a hive of frenetic activity. People were running hither and yon, setting up woks and other cooking utensils, laying out tables, putting up the bunting and other bits of greenery that we had collected, and generally having a great time.

Harry and I went to the storeroom to collect a speaker system and long leads of cabling to set up on the lawn. Then he walked up and down the village green, testing sound levels while I adjusted the speakers. It was an intricate business: we had to get the sound levels just right.

Afterwards, when we went back inside the community centre, I felt there was something odd. At first, I couldn't work out what it was because we were all busy preparing a mountain of salads. We were also being driven mad by the aromas of meat and delicacies that were being ferried over from the houses.

Then I realised that 'we' were all males: men, lads, young boys. There were no females to be seen.

'Where are all the women?' I asked.

Everyone laughed. Harry patted me on the back. 'Don't worry. They'll be here soon enough.' More laughter.

When we had finished preparing the food, we all went outside. We lounged around chatting, while we each drank a can of beer. We talked about cars and computers, soccer and globall.

It was the closest I got to 'going out with the lads' during the whole of my stay at Willow. I told them about the good old days of one-day cricket and the Big Bash, of coloured uniforms, exciting run-chases and the flags with the boxing kangaroo.

'Does anyone know who won the test series?' I asked.

'It was drawn,' Ron replied.

The sun was low on the horizon. We were thinking of opening some more cans – well I was, anyway – when we heard the blast of a trumpet.

'They're coming,' said Harry.

The women and girls came, in stately procession, out of the west. They were dressed in green, white and black, which were Willow's colours. Some wore tunics, while others were in a shimmering translucency of veils. The effect was not so much erotic as mysterious.

Harry threw a switch by the wall to start the music.

Everyone stood quietly for a few moments while a solo flute played. Then, as the other instruments of the orchestra came in, the dancers started to move, slowly, gracefully, silhouetted against the red disk of the setting sun.

An ethereal chant drifted out of the speakers and across the park. The music picked up its tempo, and so did the dancers. The ones in tunics stood in the middle, moving in the precise, deliberate manner of Tai-Chi performers. Those dressed in veils swirled around them.

As the music welled up to a crescendo, the males chanted 'Gaia, Gaia' while the females danced in circles, sometimes expanding, sometimes contracting. They seemed to be in an ecstatic trance that transformed them. The wrinkled, weather-beaten face of Ignacia Perez became almost beautiful. Eduardo had tears in his eyes.

The performance went on for about a quarter of an old hour. By the time it was finished, and the performers sank exhausted to the ground, the sun had set.

After that, it was time for us to prepare the feast, while the dancers went off to change. Eduardo and I filled a punch bowl with fruit and fruit juices.

'A non-alcoholic punch?' I asked.

'Not quite.' He grinned, and produced a few bottles. 'We add some tequila.'

Then, Ron dimmed the lights. 'It's traditional to use non-electrical lighting on occasions like this,' he explained.

It was dark when the women and girls returned, in single file, carrying candles. They presented them to us as 'love tokens from Gaia' that symbolised the flame of life.

Lena recited a verse, giving thanks to Gaia for her bountifulness, while acknowledging that we had a role to perform of stewardship over the land. When she finished, I inadvertently said 'Amen'.

Then we ravenously devoured Gaia's bounty: slices of roast beef, tender breast of chicken, roast potatoes, spring onions, mushrooms, stir-fried rice with everything else chopped up and mixed in with it, and masses of salad – all washed down with tankards of something that tasted like mead. It reminded me of a medieval banquet.

Afterwards, on the village green, we played the children's games: blind man's bluff, piggy-back races and, with the aid of an ancient bat that Harry had found in the back of a storeroom, French cricket.

A spectacular fireworks display brought our sporting activities to an end. Shooting up around us in the night sky were 'Gaia globes', rockets that exploded in such a way as to create large, shimmering images of our world made anew. When they finished, the children had grown tired enough to be packed off to bed.

Then, it was time for the adult games. These involved, among other things, dancing, and getting stuck into Eduardo's punch.

The punch seemed pretty mild to me, but it was affecting everyone else. Young and not-so-young couples chased each other around the dance floor, or out into the shrubbery. For some, the combination of a big meal and Eduardo's punch was too much. 'The trouble with the modern generation is that they can't hold their liquor,' I said for the umpteenth time as somebody else threw up.

It wasn't affecting me at all … I can remember complaining that the punch didn't have enough punch in it … I can also remember doing Greek dancing on the Village Green in the middle of the night … I can also vaguely remember floating on my back about a metre off the ground, with Ron holding my shoulders and Eduardo my legs as we headed towards home … Eduardo thrusting two thick, gnarled fingers down my throat to make me throw up in the toilet … and then giving me some weird concoction of herbs that tasted like nothing on earth.

●

When I woke up next afternoon, my stomach felt as though it wasn't there, and my head felt just as numb. I was aware that my regulator was humming, and was warm to the touch. It had been working overtime to counter the effects of the mother of all hangovers.

I decided to cancel the rest of the day, which I later found out was often called Hangover Tuesday, and went back to sleep.

CHAPTER SEVENTEEN

DECISIONS

A few days later, I walked into the living room to find that Ron had a visitor. It was his assistant, Imogen Smith. She was the same as when I first met her – classically beautiful and as cold as marble. Yet she seemed chuffed when I told her that I enjoyed the First Fleet thing she was in with Ron. He suggested that she explain what the Creative History Unit did.

'It should really be called re-creative history,' Imogen began. 'We try to simulate as accurately as we can, what conditions were really like in the past. From the colour and patterns of interior decor, to the feel of leather upholstery, the taste of hamburgers and beer, and the smell of petrol.'

I felt like suggesting that she join a gang of bikies, but something told me that it might be wise to be nice to her. 'Like that First Fleet re-enactment?'

'Yes. I realise that to you it may have seemed, as you would say, "low key", but we think that was the way it really happened.'

I nodded. 'I thought there would have been, you know, some sort of dramatic music, or something.'

'But it was a very low-key affair: a band of travel-weary soldiers and convicts meeting a group of indigenes going about their everyday business. It's hard to say which group was the more bewildered.'

'Mm.' I put my hands behind my head. 'And we've been a laid-back society ever since.'

Ron managed a quiet smile, but Imogen looked very serious. 'Not always, James. Australia has been through some tough times while you were asleep: the breakdown in the world economic and ecological order, the search for new meaning and purpose in life, and the creation of a new world in harmony with nature and with each other.'

Her eyes glazed over as she spoke about the creation of a new world. Was she another Gaia freak? I smiled. 'I'm sorry I missed all the fun.'

'Fun?' She frowned. 'It wasn't much fun. You don't seem to realise that many people suffered and worked very hard to create the world we take for granted today.'

It was my turn to frown. Did she think that life in my day was a picnic? 'Things weren't so easy in my time, you know. I was out of work for six months at one stage.'

'Really?' For once, her eyes widened. She looked at me as an animal lover might look at a distressed pet. Perhaps her coldness towards humans was matched by her compassion for lame dogs and stray cats. 'You must tell me about it someday.' She turned to Ron. 'We could interview him here, of course, but would it be possible to take him to Sydney?'

'That's up to James.' He glanced at me. 'As an Australian citizen, he's free to come and go as he pleases. Why don't you tell him about the script?'

So there was an ulterior motive to Imogen's visit. 'What script?' I asked.

Imogen's lily-white face turned the faintest shade of pink. 'It's a work of fiction, actually. Sometimes it's easier to explain what things were like in the past by telling a story.'

Ron went over to his bookcase. Even in the electronic world of 2100, some people still had bookcases, and books. Ron had a set of the *Encyclopædia Britannica* (1875 edition), the *Bicentenary History of Australia*, several of Lena's art books, an Atlas, the *Concise Oxford Dikshnry*, a book of quotations, the Holy Bible, and the complete works of William Shakespeare. He picked up this last volume, thumbed through the index, turned to page 941, and handed the book to me.

'*Hamlet?*'

Imogen nodded. 'Do you know it?'

I thought for a moment. 'Neither a borrower, nor a lender be.' They looked at me, surprised. 'We studied Hamlet at school.'

Imogen turned to Ron. 'He could be useful to us, after all.'

'Useful?' I echoed dryly.

'The fact that you already know the play means there are many things the production team won't have to explain to you.'

'Production team? You're not planning to audition me, are you?'

'No. We want you as an adviser on contemporary settings.'

I laughed. 'Listen, darling, I'm not that old. Hamlet was hundreds of years ago.'

'But we've updated it, you see. To turn-of-the-millennium Australia.'

Imogen's face had come to life. 'In this version, Hamlet is an executive with a large Australian company. He is haunted by the environmental damage the company is causing. He must decide whether to accept this, or to rebel against it. His famous soliloquy begins with "To change or not to change, that is the question".'

'And where do I fit in?'

'As an adviser,' Ron explained. 'What sort of things would this latter- day Hamlet talk about with his mates in the pub?'

'Well, I wasn't born until 2000. But I would guess maybe work, women and computers.'

'That's precisely the sort of thing we need to know,' Imogen said enthusiastically. 'And what sort of beer they would have drunk.'

'If it was lunchtime, they might have stuck to the light beers.'

'Very good.' For once, she smiled. It was an enigmatic smile. There was something in her eyes that … hmm.

She looked at Ron. 'What do you think?'

'That's entirely up to James.' They both looked at me.

'Thinking is something that takes me a while to do,' I said warily.

'That's fine,' said Imogen. 'We won't be starting the project until May.'

●

From our lonely vantage point, Ermingtrude and I looked down on the city in the late afternoon. Because of global warming, Canberra did not have frosts at the end of April. The deciduous trees did not assume their mantles of red and gold. The best their leaves could manage was to slowly turn yellow.

Over the previous two weeks, I was restless. Even my regulator wasn't much help: it could calm me down, but it couldn't make my decisions for me. Part of me wanted to stay with my friends in Willow, while another part of me wanted to go to Sydney. Had it changed much since my day?

'To change, or not to change, that is the question.' I patted the dashboard. 'Ermingtrude, would you miss me?'

'I am programmed not to hit people, James,' she assured me.

'No, what I mean is, if I went away from here, would you be lonely?'

'What is lonely?'

'It's … being on your own. Having no one to talk to. No one to have good times with.'

'I am never lonely,' Ermingtrude explained. 'I can link to the entire metropolitan traffic network.'

'Wow,' I said dryly. 'You're not having an affair on the quiet with the central traffic computer, are you?'

'Question not understood, James.'

'Never mind.' I got out of the car and paced up and down a bit, like Hamlet in his soliloquy.

I leant against the railing to stare out over the tranquil city as the sun dipped behind the mountains. Almost as soon as it did so, I heard a rustling and a stirring of leaves. The first cool winds of winter blew through my open shirt.

'That does it,' I snapped as I got back into the car. 'Home, Ermingtrude. I have some packing to do.'

I couldn't get Imogen's smile out of my mind.

CHAPTER EIGHTEEN

SYDNEY

e01052100 'May Day': three months since I arrived at Willow Community, I said goodbye to it – for three months at least.

I signed a contract to work as a consultant with a company called Historitek, of which Ron was one of the principal partners. Their pay offer wasn't very good, only 1,500 Australs a month.

'You should be able to live reasonably well on that,' Ron assured me. 'It's close to average monthly wages.'

'Yes, but I'm a consultant,' I reminded him. 'What about on-costs?'

'On-costs?'

'If you have employees, then there are additional expenses like superannuation and pro-rata costing for furniture, equipment, stationery, floor space, rental and power. As a consultant, I would normally add another sixty-five percent to cover them.'

'For most people,' Ron replied, 'superannuation has been replaced by their stake in a community. Once they settle in one, their aged-care needs are met, by virtue of their being part of the community. If you have any spare cash, you might purchase an annuity, but that has to be paid out of your wages.

'As for the other costs, since you will be working in the studio, they will be covered anyway.'

Hmm. I signed the contract for 1500 Australs a month, even though I felt I was being ripped off. Still, it would be good work experience.

To tide me over until I had settled in Sydney, I was paid an upfront bonus for giving some advice on the type of car that our latter-day Hamlet would have driven. We settled for a company Volvo.

I was embarrassed, and touched, by the fact that nearly everyone in the community was there to see me off. Our entire fleet of vehicles was used to transport about half the Community to the railway station. There were more tearful farewells, even though I was only going for three months.

Imogen, Ron and I boarded the Very Fast Train, which glided on a magnetic field as it sped towards Sydney. We crossed the countryside that was mainly open, yet I didn't see many fields of wheat or herds of sheep and cattle. Now and again there were plantations made up of a variety of trees. I saw some greenhouses and hydroponics farms, and small clusters of domes and communities that reminded me of Willow.

Gradually, the domes and communities became more common, until we reached the Megacity of Liverpool, in the southwest of the metropolis. It was one of the twelve megacities that made up the Sydney Metropolitan Area, often called the Great Conurbation of Woollencastle. The megacities stretched, with a few breaks, from Wollongong in the south to Newcastle in the north. In total, they contained six million people, nearly one-fifth of the population of Australia.

Yet, when we arrived in Liverpool, it looked like a medium-sized city of perhaps a few thousand. I was surprised to learn that it was the centre of a megacity of half a million people. As our journey continued, we were surrounded by trees, parks, gardens of flowers and vegetables, more trees, and an occasional small cluster of domes.

'Where are all the people?' I asked.

'See those buildings?' Ron pointed through a gap in the trees to some high-roofed buildings in a park the size of Willow.

'They look like overgrown army barracks,' I commented.

'Those are houses,' Ron assured me. 'Soon, you may be living in one.'

'They're mighty big houses.'

We headed on, speeding past more megacities until at last we arrived at the Terminus in Central Sydney. From there, for my benefit, we went to the CentrePoint Tower for a panoramic view of the city.

I was excited. 'I remember coming here when I was a kid.'

We looked out over a panorama that was both familiar and different. The Harbour Bridge was still there. So was the Opera House. In front of it was an embankment to prevent flooding, a reminder of the effects of global warming.

The biggest surprise about Sydney Harbour was that most of the tall buildings, including the luxury apartments, were gone. So were many of the big city office blocks. In their places were many older style buildings, none more than six or seven stories high, with 19th-century facades and solar panels on their roofs. It reminded me more of what the city might have looked like in 1900, not what I imagined it would be in 2100. Apart from the tower itself, there were no gleaming buildings of concrete, metal and glass, or moving walkways, or strange craft flying from building to building. It didn't look very science-fictiony at all.

Indeed, the city had contracted. Although I could see the hydro ferries plying their way across the Harbour, I could also see that the city was surrounded by a sea of blue on the east coast, and a sea of green on land.

'There would be less than a hundred thousand people in the city by day,' Ron explained. 'And perhaps half that number by night. Mostly to see the sights, or to go to the Opera, Darling Harbour or Chinatown. We can appreciate the layout of the city better from the Bridge.'

So we walked to Circular Quay and climbed up onto the Bridge. The toll stations had gone, as had the mess of roads on the northern side. There was a steady flow of traffic across the Bridge, but nothing like it was in my day. I learnt that the tunnel under the Harbour had long since been closed, due to the lack of traffic.

From the Bridge, I could see what Ron meant about the layout of the city. The banks of the Harbour, all that prime real estate, were now open, or consisted of parks. Behind them, on either side of the Harbour, the buildings were arranged in neat rows. Those nearest the water were only one or two stories high, those behind them had an extra storey, as did those behind them, and so on back to the six- or seven-storey 'skyscrapers'. It was like standing in a great, long amphitheatre.

Once again, as I had done when at the hospital in Canberra, I felt the strange mixture of the familiar and the new: here was a city that I had known, but it was not as I had known it. I reached in my pocket for my regulator.

'Are you all right?' asked Imogen.

I nodded. 'I think so. It's still a bit of a shock.'

'As with any change, you'll get used to it in time.' Ron looked at the time on his smart phone, which didn't seem very different from the ones of my time. 'Speaking of which, Imogen's parents will be waiting for us.'

We spent the evening at their house in Cronulla. It was on one of the few good old-fashioned suburban quarter-acre blocks that were left, even in a relatively low population density country like Australia. Once again, I had the strange feeling of familiarity and newness.

Although Imogen's parents were a pleasant enough couple, I could see where she got her cold, scientific manner from. They were both scientists – he in structural engineering and she in medicine. I learnt that it was only because they were both on high incomes that they could afford a freestanding house in the suburbs. Imogen had a flat of her own, but came over to visit them on occasions.

Next morning, Ron, Imogen and I went to Bankstown Stolport to go on a scenic flight. 'We could just take the flight in the video room at the Turist Buro,' Ron explained, 'but actually flying over Sydney may make the experience more real for you.'

The aircraft in which we were to fly didn't look at all real to me. It was a short, squat, bug-shaped machine that was almost all cockpit. There was a propeller at the front, and two delta-shaped wings that were paper-thin. Sensing that this was some sort of joke, I frowned. 'Does this thing actually fly? It looks like its wings are about ready to fall off.'

Ron's response was extraordinary. He unleashed a judo chop at the flimsy trailing edge of one of the wings. His hand bounced straight off. The wing quivered for a moment or two, then was still. 'Living metal,' he explained.

We climbed into the cockpit and strapped ourselves in. The fuselage was almost entirely transparent, except for a dark area in line with where the sun was trying to shine through. 'Micros?' I asked.

'There are more micros per square centimetre in the skin of an aircraft,' Ron told me, 'than in almost any other invention bar one, which you will see later. The micros don't just regulate light and trap solar energy, they measure temperature, wind velocity, air currents, and of course, enable the aircraft to talk with each other and the tower.'

'Fine. Where's our pilot?'

Ron was sitting in the left-hand seat, which was normally the pilot's seat. There was a console in front of him, but no joystick or controls. He unstrapped himself and got out of the seat. 'You can fly it if you like.'

'Me? I don't have a pilot's license. I've never flown a plane.'

Ron and Imogen laughed. He produced a card which he handed to me. 'All you have to do is to insert this in the slot on the console, and follow a few simple instructions.'

Against my better judgment, Ron and I changed places. I inserted the card.

'Good morning,' said a well-modulated computer voice. 'Greetings from the Bankstown Aviation Coperative. Which scenic flight would you like today?' A screen lit up to show a set of twelve options. Ron suggested that we take option seven – a two-hour flight along the coast to Wollongong, then northwards along the western side of the conurbation, before heading back along the north coast.

'Excellent,' said the computer. 'One of my favourites. Please press the contact button when you are ready to commence the flight.'

A green button glowed on the console. I looked at Ron, who nodded. I pressed the button. The propeller whirred and we taxied out to the edge of a short runway. After a moment's hesitation, during which an image of a control tower on the console turned from red to green, we swung out onto the runway. The revs picked up, the propeller became a blur, and we were airborne.

As we banked, and headed for the coast, I saw a much larger, more familiar aeroplane landing at the nearby Sydney Airport. It was a type of airliner that had been in service for some decades. Apart from some improvements in fuel efficiency and noise reduction, the design of large aeroplanes had not changed much during the 21st century. In an age of zooming, higher fuel costs and lower incomes, fewer people went on long- distance flights, and so there had been little demand for improvements to airliners.

Below us, Sydney was spread out in a series of giant, irregular wheels, separated by expanses of natural terrain. Only on the edges of these wheels, especially along the coast, did I see the old familiar pattern of suburban streets and houses.

I felt something was wrong. Then I realised that the engine had stopped. 'Er, what do I do now?'

Ron and Imogen laughed. 'Nothing,' explained Ron. 'Look at the wings.'

To my amazement, the wings were changing shape. They were becoming narrower, longer, and more flexible. Ron leant over and pressed a button on the console. A data screen lit up to show a hologram in which arrows were flowing in different directions at different levels.

'Our plane is now a glider,' he explained. 'Based on the information it receives from its own sensors, and from other aircraft, it is picking up the best air currents available. Why waste fuel when nature will do the work for us?'

Throughout the remainder of our flight, the aircraft glided for much of the time, and used its engine only intermittently. Its wings changed shape as it soared and glided like a giant bird.

As we turned over Wollongong, Ron reminded me that I had once asked him about megacities. 'For the simplest version of a megacity,' he began, 'imagine a broad, flat, featureless plain. On this plain, imagine two concentric circles. The inner one has a diameter of five kilometres, and the outer one a diameter of fifteen kilometres.'

He pointed down to a large, almost circular area in the centre of Wollongong. 'The inner one is the city centre. It contains the major shops, offices, hospitals, government departments, parks, amusement centres and sporting stadia for a population of half a million people. This means that, strictly speaking, our cities are only half-megacities. In most countries overseas, however, they do contain a million people.'

Later, he pointed out to me a typical segment of a megacity. In a pure, regularly shaped megacity, there was a ring, ten kilometres wide, surrounding the city centre. The ring was divided into ten segments, or districts. Within each segment was a smaller district centre to serve the needs of fifty or a hundred thousand people.

There were also in each segment ten large circles, each a few hundred metres in diameter. Ron said they were called 'huburbs'. When we flew over Liverpool, we descended to three hundred metres to take a closer look at one of them. It was like a small-scale version of a megacity. There was a central circle, surrounded by a ring that was divided into ten segments, like slices of cake.

In each of these segments there were five buildings, set amidst a mixture of vegetable gardens, the odd greenhouse, and small groves of trees. 'Are they communities?' I asked.

Ron nodded. 'Like Willow, they cover two hectares of land. But they support about five hundred people instead of the hundred or so at Willow.'

'So each of those buildings is home for about a hundred people?'

'That's right.'

'Sounds very crowded.'

'In most megacities overseas, there would be just one building, five stories high, consisting of four connected towers. Within them would live a thousand people.'

'Whew. How do they survive?'

'Quite well,' Imogen said. 'You'll find out when you live in one.'

'There are ten communities,' Ron continued, 'and about five thousand people in a typical Australian huburb, which covers thirty hectares. There are ten huburbs in a district, each of which covers around five or six hundred hectares. So there's more room to move about than you think.'

'Are they self-sufficient?'

'Not entirely. They produce most of their own vegetables, fruit, fish and poultry. Much of the water is recycled.'

We swung round to the east and headed back along the coast. The thing that struck me, looking out over the city, was that for the most part it was like a forest with a few rooftops sticking up. We made a graceful touchdown at Bankstown Stolport, thanked our aeroplane, and went on our way.

Our next stop was the ABC studios. We walked into a studio that was completely bare. At first, I thought it was a holovision room. 'Where are the cameras?' I asked.

'Cameras?' Imogen queried. 'Oh, sensors. All around us, built into the walls of the studio.'

I touched the wall. 'It feels like wallpaper.' I thought back to the 'intelligent' wallpaper in the hospital.

'It's the most expensive wallpaper in the world,' Imogen told me. 'It contains visual, auditory, temperature and pressure micros that between them rival the human sensory system in their complexity. They enable us to simultaneously monitor a performance from many different angles and perspectives.'

She took me into an adjoining holobooth, where she replayed our visit to the studio. It was strange to watch ourselves standing, talking and moving around, as seen from each side, above, below, with different sound levels. No wonder holocasts were so real.

'Editing must be a nightmare,' I remarked. 'With so many angles to choose from.'

'It's a highly skilled art. Requiring years of study.'

A tall, slim, fair-haired young man wandered into the studio. He had a detached, absent-minded air about him as he paced to and fro reading from a script. He reminded me of Hamlet.

'To change or not to change,' he declaimed, 'whether it is nobler, in the world …'

'Who's he?' I asked.

'That's Nigel Campbell,' Imogen told me. 'One of Australia's finest actors.' She called out to him through the intercom.

Nigel looked up. 'Hark. What voice through yonder holobooth breaks? Imogen, Imogen, wherefore art thou Imogen?'

Imogen retorted with a time-honoured theatrical line: 'Thank you. We'll let you know.'

When I was introduced to Nigel Campbell, I found that, despite his frail features, he had a very strong grip. 'So you're the man from long ago who's going to teach me how to drive my Volvo?'

'I am?' I shot a glance at Imogen.

'In the simulator, of course. You won't actually get to drive a real one.'

●

Within an hour, Nigel, Ron, Imogen and I were in a real car. At least, as real a car as I ever allowed myself to think the cars of 2100 could ever be. I always felt there was something unreal about travelling in a car that drove itself. I yearned for a steering wheel because I like to be in control.

We drove out from the city centre, past the quaint old University, and into the Megacity of South Sydney. It happened that there was a vacant flat at the community house where Nigel was staying during the production. He might have been one of Australia's finest actors, but he didn't live on a superstar's salary.

However, he was one of the few people in the community that actually owned his own car. We parked it at the local shopping centre at Shakespeare Huburb, so-called because many actors lived in the area. We hadn't seen a lot of traffic on the road, and most of that was buses or, around the communities themselves, bicycles.

The community in which he lived, which was about the same size as Willow, was just a short walk up the road from the shops. In keeping with the name of the huburb it was whimsically dubbed the Hamlet Hamlet.

The house in which Nigel lived was one of five on the hamlet. Each house was a two-storey structure about fifty metres square. They were arranged in an irregular pattern amidst gardens, a pool, some groves of trees, and a playground with a small castle called Ellsinore.

'Is this where you got the idea for the play?' I asked Imogen.

Entering the house through an archway, we walked past some bicycle racks, and into a large, covered courtyard. There was a community kitchen, a laundry, a holoroom, a small artificial lawn on which the children played, and an open space that served as the community dining and meeting area.

I was introduced to the Housemaster, a large, jovial fellow named Ben, who took us upstairs to a corner flat. As in Willow Community, many of the permanent residents had a financial stake in the hamlet. But because this part of town had a high floating population of actors and other artists, there were usually some flats available for short-term rental.

My new residence was a one-bedroom apartment, about seven metres by five, with a small bathroom, a tiny kitchenette and a minuscule fridge. Ben explained to me that it was the custom these days for people to prepare only light meals in their own apartments. The evening meal was usually eaten downstairs with the rest of the community.

The fact that he bothered to explain this to me meant that he must have known in advance that I was from an earlier age. I felt as though I was being manipulated. Yet I signed a three-month rental contract – one hundred Australs a week plus an extra fifty for the community food fund, and two hours a week on the community work roster.

After that, they left me to it. Nigel went off to his flat down the hallway to study his lines, Imogen said she would see us at the studio on Munday morning, Ron headed back to Canberra, and Ben reminded me that dinner was at eight.

As I unpacked the suitcase that the hospital staff had given me, I had the strangest feeling. Throughout the four months since my revival, I had spent the whole of my time in or near the company of other people. Now, at last, I had a place of my own, from which I could come and go as I pleased.

Looking out of my window, I could see the miniature Ellsinore – a medieval structure viewed by a man who was also out of his time.

CHAPTER NINETEEN

GLOBALL

The apartment that I called my own was destined to be my home for three months. During this time, I settled into a new pattern, a new rhythm of life.

At first, I wasn't sure what to make of my new lifestyle. The only person I knew there was Nigel Campbell, whom I had just met. At dinner that night, he introduced me to the other members of my new community, which was called a 'house' or a 'lodge'. I learnt that lodges came into their own during the Second Great Depression earlier in the century. The old economic order had collapsed, unemployment reached over fifty percent and the social security system broke down.

In the battle for survival, people had banded together to pool their resources and form lodges or communities, usually of about a hundred people. In time, housing arrangements became built around these groups, and suburbia as I had known it all but died out.

I was surprised to learn that, even with the return of more affluent times after the four-zone structure was created, most people still preferred to live in their communities or lodges. (In most countries they had very little choice.) What people had lost in terms of personal freedoms and living space, they had more than made up for in their community life.

There was a big contrast between the lifestyle I had known in Canberra and the one I now encountered in Sydney. At Willow, the people had all worked together for probably a day or two a week, but lived in separate houses. At the Hamlet Hamlet, for much of the time, the five hundred people who lived there pursued their various occupations in the city, but got together with their other house members at meal times, or with the other hamlet members for the occasional working bee.

Soon, I looked forward to the evening meal at my new home. Everyone would get together, help prepare tea if they were on the roster, or otherwise sit around chatting to each other about the sort of day they'd had.

After tea and washing up, there would often be impromptu entertainment. People would tell jokes or stories, or play music or charades. Because many residents of our house were actors, musicians, artists or entertainers, life at Hamlet was never dull. With performers keen to try out new material, we saw many of the top live shows in Sydney, free of charge, in our own living room.

My contribution to the entertainment was to tell everyone what life was really like earlier in the century – that it wasn't half as melodramatic and dangerous as the old holomovies they watched used to make out.

In Hamlet, there weren't many children or elderly people. This was because ours was an 'open house': it had a high proportion of short- to medium-term renters. They were mainly young adults, going out into the big wide world to work full-time for perhaps ten years until they could afford to put down a stake in a community. During that time, they would usually find a partner with whom they would want to settle down. There were always romances breaking out or breaking up around us. They were an endless source of gossip.

I was on the lookout for my piece of the action. From the little I knew of the actors of my time, I thought there would be lots of wild parties, and maybe even the odd orgy. I discovered that for the theatrical people of 2100, there was a lot of work and not much play.

Until I started working on the production of Hamlet, I thought that life in this new age was laid back. Most of the time, the people of Willow did a moderate amount of work. It was only when there was a special event, like a storm or the Gaia festival that they put in a big effort.

In the big cities, people did work hard, especially the younger ones doing their ten-year stint. For actors, work was particularly gruelling. At the studio, once the production got into full swing, we often worked ten or twelve hours a day, six or seven days a week.

What made it really tough was that Imogen was a perfectionist who demanded that we re-create the early 21st century as accurately as possible. Her aim was to totally steep the viewers of 2100 in that world. She made the actors move as though they had been wearing the strange, tight-fitting clothes of my time all of their lives, and that the food they ate tasted and smelled exactly as it did back then.

On this last point, I was very glad that she did. I persuaded her that a scene in which Hamlet met the workers, the 'industrial cannon fodder', should take place at MacDonald's. This meant that our cook had to re- create Big Macs and french fries. With a bit of help from me, he almost got it right – close enough for me to appreciate it, anyway.

Unfortunately, the hamburgers were a bit rich for the actors of 2100, who were used to a bland, mainly vegetarian, Asian diet. Several of them became violently ill. Imogen decided to include that in the production as a commentary on how nasty and brutish life was in those days. I didn't think that was fair: a Big Mac never did me any harm.

In this updated version of Hamlet, our tragic hero was an executive for a big plastics company. The ghost, a subtle Gaian manifestation, consisted of nightmares Hamlet had about petrochemicals flowing into streams and destroying the wildlife, plastic bags choking seals and dolphins, and thick, pungent smoke from burning plastic rubbish.

The King (Company President) was a corporate raider who had imported a billion dollars to take over the company. The Queen was his secretary, a high-class bimbo who had betrayed his predecessor. Laertes and Horatio were other company executives. They were renamed Lawrence and Harold, but I called them Larry and Harry. Ophelia was a sweet young 'flower child' – a sort of early Gaian with whom the viewers of 2100 would sympathise.

Polonius, renamed Percy, was the devious, conniving Company Secretary and corporate yes-man. On the one hand, his speech about 'neither a borrower nor a lender be' became an appeal for maintaining a balance between energy input and output. (The company was paying lip service to the environment at the time.) On the other hand, he stitched up a deal with a Japanese woodchip company. Hamlet ran him over in his company Volvo.

In his 'to change or not to change' speech, Hamlet resolved to live a more environmentally friendly lifestyle. He also plotted the downfall of the company by leaking sensitive technical information to Greenpeace and the Conservation Foundation.

The Company President decided to get rid of him by sending him on a fact-finding mission with two charming hitmen named Ross and Gil. Hence, the meeting with the workers at MacDonald's. Hence also, a weird scene on top of Uluru where Hamlet was saved from his would-be assassins by a sudden and mysterious wind that swept them away. The viewers would see this as the work of Gaia.

The drama ended, not with a bloodbath, but with a chaotic Annual General Meeting. The company was plunged into liquidation, and the bankruptcy lawyers tied up its assets forever.

I could take all of this with a grain of salt because the more realistic Imogen tried to make it, the more unreal it seemed. Until we got to the bit where Hamlet broke up with Ophelia. At one of our numerous team meetings, Imogen said that she and the other writers had written themselves into a corner and needed my advice. 'The problem is, James,' she explained, 'that Ophelia is an early Gaian and Hamlet has become a convert to the environmental cause. Why then, does he reject her?'

'Erm.' I cleared my throat. 'Perhaps she snored.'

There was a titter from all the company assembled except Imogen. 'Seriously, James, why would an environmentally sensitive man reject her?'

I think I blushed. 'Maybe Ophelia was, you know, too environmental.'

'Too environmental?'

'Yes. What I mean is … I don't know if you still have words like "hobby horse", but supposing she was always going on about saving the planet. Supposing he wanted to make love to her, but all she wanted to do was talk about whales and dolphins and recycling food scraps.'

Everyone, including Imogen, found this amusing. I began to see the funny side of it myself. Nigel Campbell, our latter-day Hamlet, stretched languidly in his chair and put his hands behind his head. 'Why do you presume it was her fault? Maybe it was his. Something to do with his male ego.'

The others nodded approvingly. Imogen had a look of triumph in her eyes. 'Of course. That fits perfectly. Hamlet is still in a state of transition between the old ways and the new. His conscious rational mind can see the logic of environmentalism, but things are happening too rapidly for his male psyche to nexus with Gaia.

'He misinterprets Ophelia's concern for the environment as an attempt to dominate him. And the more compassion she feels for him and the planet, the more he rejects her.'

Inspired, she paced up and down. 'What a beautiful metaphor of the early twenty-first century. The interaction of Yin and Yang. Hamlet loves her and yet he fears that her compassion is a threat to his male ego. Now, if one equates male dominance with environmental destruction …'

'Then it's no wonder that both of them went balmy,' I interjected.

'No wonder indeed,' she retorted. 'Because the paradigm shift needed to reconcile the genders to each other and the environment had yet to happen at the psychological level. Thus, the tragedy of Hamlet is that he changes and yet he does not change.'

'What's a paradigm?' I asked.

Nigel stretched his arms and casually answered, 'A pattern or model. A scientific theory or world view.' He put his hand to his mouth to cover a yawn. He didn't care much for writers explaining things. All he wanted to do was act. 'But what does that mean in practice? Does she object when he wants to, um, hoon around in his car?'

'You didn't usually hoon around in a Volvo,' I objected. 'An old bomb maybe. But company executives didn't normally do that.'

We discussed other possibilities. Maybe she objected to Hamlet wanting to play a macho game like football. But our Hamlet was the wrong build for that anyway. Did he go out boozing with his mates? Probably not after his 'conversion'. Was he lax about sorting the garbage into separate bins for recycling? Not likely, and besides it was hardly grounds for divorce, nor the stuff that Shakespearean tragedies are made of.

Imogen decided that the fault did, in a sense, lie with Ophelia. In Shakespeare's play, it was she who initially started rejecting him. Our latter- day Ophelia feared that, being a man, Hamlet still hungered for power, and she didn't fancy being a company director's wife.

With this issue resolved, the production ran smoothly until Imogen decided she wanted to change the ending. 'It's too negative,' she complained to her writers. 'Too indecisive. I want a more positive ending.'

What she wanted was that the sacrifices of Hamlet and Ophelia would not be in vain – that as a result of their sufferings, the workers would take over the company to run it on an egalitarian and environmentally friendly basis. The writers felt that this was too much of a fairy tale ending, especially for the dark ages of the early 21st century.

Ron, on one of his numerous visits to Sydney, suggested a compromise. In the end, Hamlet becomes Company President, and implements a series of modest reforms. The company starts to produce some recyclable and biodegradable products, introduces new production methods to reduce the level of pollution, and gives the workers a share in the company profits.

In his dreams, Hamlet would be haunted from time to time by images of Ophelia. She had drowned when she was caught up in a large sheet of plastic while floating down the river, but was then symbolically transformed into some sort of water spirit.

I told Ron privately that I thought the ending was a bit corny. He agreed, but said that the people of 2100 would enjoy it for its symbolic content. Besides, this was Imogen's first major work as a producer. It was wise to give her some latitude, even if the story became a bit corny.

●

I spent a lot of time at the studio, and was therefore regarded as part of the company. Because I was the only 'authentic' person from that period, Imogen thought it might be nice to write me into the script. She made me a foreperson of the workers whom Hamlet met at MacDonald's.

The rest of the company, most of whom were members of Actors Equity, said that they didn't mind as long as I either joined the union, or had a part that was no more than three metric minutes long.

Imogen wanted me to be the real Ocker type. At my screen test, I walked onto our lifelike set, shook Hamlet's hand, and said, 'Giddaymate'owyergoin'orright?'

Hamlet was bewildered, and the rest of the company laughed. They hadn't understood a word I said. During my long sleep, the broad, flat Aussie accent had given way to the more precise, clipped, and clearly enunciated language of folk who had to communicate with people from many different countries, and with computers.

So I didn't get the part. I was glad, really, I don't think I could have stood being ordered around on set all day by Imogen. Instead, I was given two very short scenes as the company president's chauffeur.

Meanwhile, back at the Hamlet Hamlet, I had settled into a comfortable routine. By the time I had finished a long day at the studio, done my housework and enjoyed our long evening meals, I didn't have much spare time.

Yet I did rediscover the bicycle. I hadn't ridden one much since I was a kid, er, child. But our hamlet was typical for Sydney in that it had only a few cars for a community of five hundred. Instead, nearly everyone owned a bicycle. There were about 400,000 in the Megacity of South Sydney. So, on my days off, I cycled. Sometimes I went with other house members to explore the scenic attractions of the metropolis, or for a jolly picnic in one of the parks.

At other times, I just took off on my own, cycling aimlessly around the streets of Sydney, wherever my fancy took me. It gave me a greater sense of freedom than Ermingtrude had given me, because I was in control.

One evening, I got caught up in a large party of cyclists, most of whom were wearing blue and black or red and white scarves. My curiosity aroused, I followed them to the bike park outside an oblong building with a curved roof. As one of the cyclists dismounted, I asked him, 'Excuse me. What is this place?'

He looked at me as if I had just stepped out of another age. 'South Sydney Globall Stadium.'

I knew that Globall was a very popular sport. I had seen snippets of it on the holonews, but I had never been to a game. Having a few Australs in my pocket, and the evening to myself, I joined the queue, paid for my ticket, and went inside.

I entered a large auditorium that seated several thousand people. Many of them were wearing regulators. They evidently got nervous before a big game.

In the centre of the auditorium was a large court, at each end of which was a net of cyclone fencing, supported on metal uprights about two meters high and a crossbar about two metres wide. Around each net, marked out in the field of play, was a semi-circle with a radius of about three metres.

There was some polite applause as three khaki-clad umpires trotted out onto the court and jogged a lap or two for a warm-up. I discovered as the game progressed that they worked as a team, and alternated between the field umpire and two boundary umpire positions.

There was more vigorous applause, and some cheering, as the red and white team, the Tarantulas, ran out onto the court. There was an even louder reaction when the black and blue team, the Scorpions, made their appearance.

The teams encamped on benches, removed their tracksuits, took out their rackets, and trotted onto the court. The Tarantulas wore white shirts, interlaced with red spider web and a large, red tarantula. The Scorpions wore iridescent blue, with the stars of the constellation of Scorpio in white, linked by a black scorpion.

For a few minutes, both sides warmed up, each using half the court. Several globalls were produced which the players flicked from one to another. They were about the same size as tennis balls, but were seamless. Coated in gold or silver metallic paint, they flashed as they sailed through the air.

Soon, the preliminaries were over. The captains tossed for ends, which didn't mean very much in an indoor stadium. Four of the ten players on each team went off to warm the benches. The other six a side lined up in their own half like they do in ice hockey – three across the centre, two in defence and one in goal. The goalkeepers, dressed in grey, were the only players allowed in the goal zone – the semicircle within three metres of goal.

The field umpire blew her whistle; the game clock started. The captain of the Scorpions was a big, red-bearded gentleman, whom I dubbed Captain Redbeard. He casually dropped the globall onto his racket and flicked it out to his right wing.

During the next minute or two, not a lot happened: Scorpions and Tarantulas were equally tentative in their moves as they stalked each other. This gave me time to appreciate that the players were developing a rhythm as they flicked the ball around. I saw that with subtle cuts and glances off their rackets, they could make the ball swerve and spin.

Suddenly, Captain Redbeard played a long backspin cut out to his right. The ball propped, swung further to the right, wrong-footed the Tarantula defence and landed nicely in front of the racket of the advancing Scorpion wing. He charged up the court, tapping the globall in front of him. A Tarantula defender challenged him, and with their rackets they fought a duel for the ball.

The Scorpion broke free, fired a long pass to the left wing, who weaved and zig-zagged to within a few metres of goal, then laid off a neat little back pass to Captain Redbeard. He unleashed a thunderbolt. Sparks flew as the globall struck the crossbar. The ball described a high, fiery arc as it sailed deep into the stands. The crowd went 'ooh'.

While waiting for the ball to be returned to their keeper, the Tarantulas made a quick substitution. They interchanged on the sideline, bringing on a defender to tag the Scorpions' nimble left wing.

But the tagger's first job was to deceive the opposition by trapping the keeper's goal hit and racing upfield to try a quick (and wildly inaccurate) riposte. It had the desired effect; however, the Scorpion's next attack was more cautious.

Soon, the Tarantulas were guarding their goal, surrounded by Scorpions who passed the ball around, looking for an opening. When they lost the ball and the Tarantulas went on the counter-attack, the same thing happened in reverse. But neither side was really prepared to throw all of their players into an attack, in case the opposition stole the ball and made a quick breakaway.

So when the quarter-time siren sounded, the score was nil-all. It had been an absorbing, if cautious term, uninterrupted by those tedious time- outs that they have in sports like basketball.

The teams changed ends. In the second quarter, I discovered just how fast the game could be played. The Scorpions mounted a concerted attack in which they flicked the ball from player to player at amazing speed. I was mesmerised by the globall that criss-crossed the court. So were the Tarantulas: a subtle, barely detectable flick of the wrist by the Scorpion right wing sent the ball whizzing through the defence. In a reflex action, the keeper deflected the ball over the net: corner.

To meet the high cross from the corner, the great frame of Captain Redbeard launched itself into the air like a Saturn rocket. From a great height – the ball must have been all of four metres above the court, he brought the ball down. Like a bolt from Thor, it flashed and cracked into the net.

What an awesome goal! Before I knew it, I was on my feet, cheering and clapping with the rest of the fans. The black and blue supporters were ecstatic, and even the red and white fans applauded. It was like a towering six at the MCG.

Yet how often in sport does one see the opposition score an equaliser almost immediately. From the hit-off, the Tarantulas launched an attack down the left flank, drawing the Scorpions' attention in that direction. A quick flick across the court found the tagger, unguarded. She gently lobbed the ball past the keeper and into the net.

At half-time, it was one-all. One goal had stung like a bee, the other had floated like a butterfly.

I was beginning to think that Globall was a low-scoring game. For much of the third quarter, I held on to that impression. Both sides were making attacking moves, but not getting clear shots at goal.

Yet, slowly but surely, the Scorpions were getting on top. They were winning the one-on-one duels across the centre, and were launching more attacks. The tension was building. It was just a question of time before the Tarantula defence cracked. And crack it did. The Scorpions put on a dazzling display, slamming home three goals in as many minutes.

The crowd went as berserk as their regulators would allow. The players also wore regulators, which, given the fast and fiery nature of the game, was hardly surprising.

The Tarantulas launched an all-out attack early in the final term. They forced the Scorpion defence into committing an obstruction foul in front of the goal. From the resultant penalty, the Tarantula centre unleashed a powerful serve and 'aced' the keeper: 4 – 2.

From there on, the Tarantulas launched attack after attack, but the Scorpion defence held firm as a series of shots were parried or went wide. Even the Tarantula keeper was thrown into the attack. The Scorpions bided their time, waited for gaps in the Tarantula backline to open up, then swept downfield to run into an unguarded goal.

After that, the game petered out into some tired, half-hearted forward moves from both sides until the final siren sounded: Scorpions 5 – Tarantulas 2.

Even though I wasn't a supporter of either side, I went home exhausted, with a hoarse throat. But I had found an exciting outlet for my aggression.

FAREWELL

By the middle of July, the production of Hamlet was winding down. There was now little need for my services. I felt they were only keeping me employed on the off-chance that there was some minor point to do with clothing, cars or lifestyle that needed sorting out.

Ron and Imogen found some other work for me to do. I was interviewed for ABC Radio about life in the early 21st century. I rehashed what I had told the children at Tami's school. I also did a segment on how to drive a car for an HV series on the history of transport.

I could see the work was petering out. I wondered what to do next. Should I stay on in Sydney and look for other work? Should I go back to Willow?

I lay awake in my flat one night thinking about this problem. Up to then I had regarded myself as a tourist that was visiting another time instead of another place. But I had to come to terms with the fact that I really was living in 2100. Whatever my past had been, I had to look to the future. Could I set up a business for myself in this new world that was both strange and familiar? I had an idea that involved fitballs, but I would need to research it first.

And could I find myself a partner, settle down in Willow or some other community and raise a family? Did I really want to?

I came up with more questions than answers. I put on my regulator, but that didn't help. I had a feeling of loss, as if part of me was missing, anaesthetised.

●

When I woke up next morning, it was still dark outside. I lay in bed trying to sort out my feelings. I thought back to the flat I had lived in years earlier.From all that long ago, I had bought with me a feeling that haunted me, a vague, evasive feeling of loneliness.

Yes, that was it. Would it be worthwhile trying to track down what had happened to Janet? Or more about my own relatives for that matter? Mum and dad and Kylie?

I needed to speak to Darren again. I put my regulator on. Perhaps I should just let the past be the past.

I was about to leave for the studio when there was a knock on my door. It was a courier with a letter for me: Special Delivery. In an age of worldwide electronic messaging, mail was rarely delivered personally, except on special occasions.

Inside the envelope was a card, tastefully lettered, like a wedding invitation:

Ms Janet Shaw requests the company of
Mr James Lawson
on the occasion of her
Farewell Ceremony
at the
North Canberra Templ of Hevenly Peace,
at Midday on

Wensday the Thirty-First of July,
Two Thousand One Hundred.

So Janet was still alive. What was a Farewell Ceremony? I had seen references to them in the papers, but I hadn't asked about them. I had an uneasy feeling I didn't want to know. It sounded ominous.

At the studio, I showed the invitation to Imogen. She looked sad for a moment, then managed a wry smile. She had received an invitation as well.

'Did you know her?'

'Friend of a friend,' she answered vaguely. But I had the feeling there might be more to it than that.

●

The following Sunday, she took me to see an all-day movie. It was a classic: The Call of the Stars. Billed as 'the most beautiful science-fiction holomovie ever made', it was an epic about the first interstellar space flight.

It was set at the end of the 22nd century, but inspired by a discovery made in the 21st. Astronomers had confirmed that a star several light-years away had planets, one of which might be similar to the Earth.

The movie itself was in three parts, each about two to three hours long. In the morning session, we were with the space travellers as they said goodbye to their friends and relations. The auditorium became the starship as it set out on its great journey. We accelerated for over a year at 1g, the equivalent of earth's gravity.

Traveling at over 99% of the speed of light, we then experienced the effects of relativity. Only a few months passed on the starship while years went by on Earth. In front of us, the galaxy shrank and the stars turned blue. Then we decelerated at 1g, into the solar system of the alien star.

After lunch, in the second part of the movie, we travelled from world to world, moving in towards the sun until we encountered the earth-type planet. It had continents and oceans, clouds and a breathable atmosphere. We found exotic vegetation and strange sea creatures that were like starfish. We had just the hint that in the deepest part of the ocean, there might be even stranger beings.

After tea, Imogen suggested that I wear my regulator for the last part because it was 'poignant'. Having discovered all that they could, the expedition members decided to return home. Arriving in Earth orbit, they had a hair-raising journey through the atmosphere in a couple of slightly damaged space shuttles.

The sad thing was, while they had aged only a few years, everyone back home was about thirty years older. Young children they had known were now adults with children of their own; siblings were now elderly, and parents long gone. Not only that, but the world they had known had changed, in some ways, beyond recognition.

When the movie had finished, Imogen asked me if I wanted to join her and some friends to discuss it over coffee. I said 'No' as I wanted to go home to bed. I didn't dare take my regulator off. I just wanted to sleep.

●

Three days later, Imogen and I went to the airport to catch a flight to Canberra. There were about twenty passengers on board, but no pilot: the Flight Attendant activated the flight program, and served us breakfast while the plane flew us to our destination.

A chill wind blew across the tarmac as we disembarked and entered the terminal. Canberra winters weren't quite as cold as in my youth, but the leafless trees made the place bleak and stark.

While we waited in the car park for our transport to arrive, I saw a strange craft fly overhead, then hover, suspended in mid-air. It was a bug- shaped machine with several small rotors, each whirring at great speed. From time to time, it would emit small jets of air to maintain its stability. Then it flew over to a helipad and landed.

A tall, dark figure emerged. 'Hello, James.' He walked over to shake my hand. 'Welcome back.'

'Hello, Constable, er, Jack.' I pointed to the strange craft. 'What is it?'

'The rotorbug? I'm doing Search and Rescue training. Would you like to see inside her? Ermingtrude won't be here for a few minutes.'

'How do you know that?'

'I picked up her callsign while I was flying over the highway.'

A couple of minutes later, while I was looking inside the deceptively large cabin of the 'rotorbug', Ermingtrude did arrive. I saw Ron get out and greeted Imogen. I heard him ask if I had been briefed. Imogen said, 'Not yet.'

It was good to see Ron again, and Ermingtrude. I patted her bonnet affectionately. 'How are you, my darling?'

'Good, thank you, James,' she purred. 'Welcome home.'

'Thank you.' Out of force of habit, I climbed into the driver's seat. 'And how is everybody?'

'I don't know everybody, James.'

I laughed. 'Same old Ermingtrude.' It was one of the few laughs that I would have for quite some time.

●

The North Canberra Templ of Hevenly Peace was a Japanese-style pagoda that I had driven past several times during my stay at Willow. When Imogen, Ron and I arrived, a young priest in saffron robes ushered us into a waiting room.

A few minutes later, he led us into a reception room. Imogen briefly squeezed my arm.

An elderly woman was sitting in a chair. Her face was pale and wrinkled, her hair nearly gone. Yet she had keen blue eyes, and fixed me with a half-sad, half-ironic smile. 'Welcome, James.'

We hugged each other. 'The last time I held you, you were barely thirty years old.'

There were now tears in her eyes. 'You haven't aged a day. My James, forever young. As you can see, I've aged a bit. But I did save the planet for you. Well, some of it.' She wiped the tears from her eyes. 'So long ago.'

'What happened?' I asked.

'Do you remember a young accountant named Julius?'

'Er … Oh, yes. We hired him just before I started my long sleep.'

'We both continued working for Climate Changers for some time. It wasn't quite the same without you. We started living together, and eventually we moved to a permaculture cooperative down the coast.

'He's gone now. I recently moved back to Canberra for … health reasons.'

'Health reasons?'

'Call it entropy. Basically, I have lived beyond my use-by date. I'm over ninety years old, and despite the difficult times I've lived in, on the whole, I've lived a good life.'

'Oh, yes.'

'But like many people these days, I don't believe in lingering once my time has come.'

I thought for a moment, then nodded. 'I remember my grandad. He went senile. He lived about two years too long.'

'I don't want to make the same mistake,' Janet replied.

We chatted for a while. We tried to reminisce about this and that, but in the strange circumstances, it was one of those forced, stop-start conversations, like being on an awkward date.

I tried to reminisce with her about the times we had together, but she seemed a bit vague: not quite non compus mentus, but her memory was not what it had been. She didn't seem to remember much about the time we had together, but she mentioned Julius and the permaculture collective a couple of times.

The truth finally dawned on me. Her feelings for me were probably much the same as mine for her. She was fond of me, but had she ever really loved me? Julius had become the love of her life, and the permaculture cooperative had been her life's mission.

Eventually, seeing an attendant in the doorway, she rose and gave me a hug. 'Now, it's time for me to go.'

'Go? Where?'

There was that half-sad, half-ironic look in her eyes again. 'I have to drink some tea.'

She motioned to the attendant, who went out to fetch the priest. Together, they escorted her to the door. She paused. 'Farewell, my friends. Julius.' And she was gone.

I caught a brief glimpse of a Japanese garden before the door closed. I was so preoccupied, that I scarcely noticed her Freudian slip. 'What's this about tea?'

Ron and Imogen sat beside me while they gently explained what would happen. Janet would take part in a tea-drinking ritual. The tea contained a special ingredient, which after two or three cups, would make her drowsy. The last thing she would see would be the formal, tranquil beauty of a Japanese garden.

'The Japanese are very good,' Ron explained, 'at developing social institutions for dealing with problems that Western society prefers not to think about.

'Some decades ago, faced with the problem of increasing numbers of elderly people putting strain on the health services at a time of economic difficulty, they established the Temples of Heavenly Peace and the Farewell Ceremony. It gave people a dignified and honourable way of "declaring their innings", as you might say.

'In time, Temples were allowed to be set up in other countries. They are always run on a non-profit basis, by priests specially trained in Japan.'

'Are they compulsory?' I wondered.

'No. But about half the population elects to undergo the ceremony. It is tranquil and painless. And beforehand, it gives them the chance to make peace with their friends and relations.'

'Do any people chicken out?'

'Some. Which is why the first cup contains a mild dose of the ingredient. If the shock of what they are doing hits them after the first cup, they will merely go to sleep for a while.

'In fact, the priests talked many people out of undergoing the ceremony. Young people, for example, who had been jilted in love, or older ones who felt that they were not wanted anymore, but who actually still had much to contribute. Of course, regulators have changed all that in the last few decades. Suicides are now rare.'

After that, we fell silent, each to our own thoughts. I tried to equate the elderly lady with the girl I used to cuddle. Had she deliberately said 'Julius' at the end to make me think she had gone senile, or was it accidental?

Sometime later, the priest returned and asked us to come with him. Janet had passed away peacefully, after the third cup, and now lay at rest in an antechamber. In death, she looked so composed. It had been a dignified end to what had been a dignified life.

As a believer, Janet had agreed to burial according to Gaian custom. She would lie in state for three days before being buried. There would be no tombstone; just a simple plaque. A young tree would be planted over her grave so that she would live on, in a sense, through the nourishment her mortal remains would give to the tree.

For those three days, Imogen and I stayed with the Bushells at Willow Community. It was strange being back in my old room. It was even stranger walking around the park on bleak winter days. All the colour had left the world: gone were the frosty nights and bright sunny days of the Canberra winters of old.

The strangest thing of all was again meeting the likes of Harry, Ramona, Patricia and all my other friends. They seemed like ghosts in a wraithlike world. Perhaps my regulator was protecting me from my feelings within. I didn't dare take it off.

One afternoon, I sat with Ron by the edge of the pond. The willow trees were drooping morbidly over the ruffled waters that lapped against the lank vegetation on the shore. Neither of us said anything: each was meditating, in his own way. Finally, Ron recited: 'The sedge is withered on the lake, and no birds sing.'

●

On the day of the funeral, the weather was more dismal than ever. There were intermittent showers, punctuated by a few pale attempts by the sun to shine through, and the cold, biting wind. Never had the trees looked so stark and black.

At the cemetery, I sat impassively through the funeral service, which was attended by Imogen, Ron, myself, and a few of Janet's friends from the coast. Darren also turned up. I felt no emotion as I watched her being interred, nor as I helped to plant the tree on her grave. Imogen stood beside me the whole time, like a ghost.

Then we wandered over to an older part of the cemetery, where Darren, Imogen and I stood in front of three plaques indicating the burial places of the urns of my mother, my father, and sister Kylie. Maybe it was the cold wind that made me shiver, but it was more like a coldness within. 'I feel as though someone walked over my grave,' I muttered.

'Actually,' Imogen said, 'you just did. You're standing on the plot reserved for you.'

Then she added quietly, 'Remove your regulator.'

I obeyed automatically. At first, I felt nothing. I thought I ought to shed a tear or two, but I was still cold, impassive. As I looked down at the plaques, I tried to conjure up images of the family of which I had once been a part. But I couldn't. There was nothing. They were gone … long gone. For once in my life I was utterly alone. In that dark, bleak place, it was as though a massive weight was pressing down on my shoulders.

Then I blacked out.

CHAPTER TWENTY-ONE

THE WHITE DEATH

Vague shapes drifted before my eyes … movement … redness … a shiny white coat … red face peering into mine … dark hair with silver streaks glowing red. More movement … other white coats in the background … words and other sounds that didn't make much sense.

Someone was groaning. It was me. An Asian man in a white coat was leaning over my face. He was familiar.

'How are you feeling?' The clipped voice was unmistakable.

'Doctor Ohira?'

He bowed slightly. 'You have had a relapse. But you will be better soon.'

Another white-coated figure loomed towards me: brown face, bulging tunic.

'Welcome back, James.'

'Oh. Hello, Mara.' Realising where I was, I tried to sit up; everything was spinning.

Mara and Dr Ohira gently pushed me back down again. 'Rest now,' he said. 'Plenty of rest.'

'Has it returned?'

'The tumour? No. That has long gone. This was shock, pure and simple.'

I tried to reach behind my ears.

'Your regulator is there,' Dr Ohira assured me.

●

When next I awoke, I was back in my old hospital room. The setting sun was casting its sombre light around its walls. Was it the same day as the funeral, or had I been asleep for days? The clock display in the wall told me it was the following evening.

I sat up in bed feeling wretched, depressed. It cheered me up to no end when Helen came in with some soup. 'Like old times, really,' I remarked.

She smiled and patted me on the arm. While I ate my soup, she told me about Gaia's healing powers in times of stress and grief. I was half-inclined to listen. Her voice was comforting, soothing, as she explained the great cycle of birth, growth, decay, rest, and rebirth.

●

Next morning, feeling much better, I was soon up and about. Wandering around the hospital, I caught up with Simon and some of my other old acquaintances. I enjoyed eating with the staff in the canteen. It was a sort of homecoming.

I spent the next couple of days pottering around the hospital. Dr Ohira and his staff performed a few tests on me, said that I was fit, and could leave when I felt ready. Yet I didn't leave immediately. I worked in the greenhouse for a while. I found this relaxing and … renewing. It was as though I had been given a second start in the world of 2100.

The euphoria did not last long. When Ron and Ermingtrude picked me up one sullen morning, my sense of joy blew away with the wind and the intermittent drizzle. The landscape had a sad, stark beauty; the sun was pale, the wind was chill. Where were the sharp, frozen starlit nights and the clear blue, sunny skies of the Canberra winters of my youth?

I asked myself this question more than once during the next two or three weeks. In this time of fog and mists, gusting winds and showers, I settled in as best I could at the Bushells' house in Willow Community.

At times like these, I suppose one might have profound insights into the meaning of life. My only discovery was that I don't have profound insights. I made a token effort to help around the community. I repaired and reprogrammed the cars, probably more to amuse myself than because it was needed.

I stood in the garage one afternoon, looking around at the cars and tires and pieces of junk. It reminded me of another garage in another time. Where I had my first job. I remembered my father saying to me, when he took me there to meet the boss, 'Work hard, son, and one day you'll have a place like this.'

That sent a shudder through my spine: as though the ghost of my long-dead father was watching me. It was one of the few times I had thought about my family since the funeral. Otherwise, I tried not to think about them, or anything else, really.

One day, I helped Roderick, our globe-trotting trade commissioner, to pull down and chop up an old, bare tree that had stood too many winters. I felt sympathy for the tree. Like me, it had lived beyond its time and was now uprooted. It was dry and dead: it would burn well.

In the world of 2100, fossil fuels were still used, but to a limited extent. They accounted for a small fraction of energy production, and added only a negligible amount to global warming. Roderick and Patricia, for example, were amongst the few people who had a fireplace, which they used occasionally in the depths of winter.

Roderick wasn't there to enjoy the burning. He went off to a trade conference in Samarkand or Ouagadougou or somewhere. So I took the opportunity to rekindle my affair with Patricia.

It wasn't lust I wanted so much. During the days I had spent back at the hospital, I had scarcely glanced at Mara. No, I wanted Patricia because she was warm and cuddly.

Not that I was much of a companion. I used to spend hours sitting on the hearth rug, staring into the fire.

'What are you thinking about?' Patricia asked me.

'When I was a kid,' I recalled, 'sometimes in winter, Dad and I would go to the Stromlo forest to collect pine cones and fallen branches. Then we'd go home and make a fire, and we'd all toast crumpets on it.'

Patricia nodded. 'Sounds like fun. We could bake some potatoes.'

We put some potatoes in foil and cooked them in the ashes. They tasted good, but even with butter melting into the potato, it wasn't the same as crumpets. I found myself half-singing, half-humming an old tune.

'I don't know that one,' said Patricia. 'What are the words?'

'Where have all the flowers gone? Long time passing. Or something like that. But I might have the words muddled up.'

I stared into the embers of the dying fire. Long time passing.

●

By the end of August, the bleakness passed. The mists cleared early, and we enjoyed some bright, sunny days.

Ron and I were out walking one day, and I described to him how much the weather had changed since my youth. 'We used to get more days like this,' I told him, 'and clear, starry nights and frost in the morning. We did have a lot of fog, though.'

'But for different reasons,' Ron explained. 'Then, it was the cold weather that caused the water vapour to condense. Now, with global warming, there is more evaporation and more water vapour in the air. So it doesn't take a big drop in temperature to cause mist.'

I nodded. 'We used to have snow then. On the Brindabellas. Sometimes, I went skiing in the mountains.'

'It still snows in the mountains,' Ron replied. 'Not very frequently, but when it does, it is very heavy. When a cold front does come through, there is plenty of water vapour for it to condense.'

'Do many people go skiing?'

'No. It's too unpredictable. But the mountains would be well worth a visit.' He looked at me as though it was a hint. 'Speaking of visits, we shall have several guests tomorrow.'

'Guests?'

'From Sydney. ABC colleagues of mine. For a post-production review of Hamlet.'

Next morning, we drove out to the airport in the community's minibus to pick them up. I knew one or two of them slightly, but at first I didn't recognise the thin, white, figure in the dark coat.

'Hello, James,' she said.

'Imogen? How's Hamlet?'

'All finished.' She said it wearily, as if she was glad it was over. 'How have you been?'

'A bit washed out.' I shrugged my shoulders. 'Life goes on.'

Back at the Bushells' house, while Ron and Imogen and their colleagues were having their discussions, I went out with Lena while she did her rounds. There were no bees to transmit coordinates to, and not many birds to count either.

Later, Ron took the other colleagues back to the airport, but Imogen didn't go with them.

'I'm staying for a few days,' she said.

I soon found that it was up to me to show her around the community and the sights of Canberra. I began to feel there was some match-making going on.

●

Three days later, against my better judgment, I was in a hire car, with Imogen, on the road to Jindabyne and the Snowy Mountains.

It was Ron's idea. He felt that Imogen and I could do with a break. He reminded me of the conversation we'd had about skiing. Imogen, who had been quiet during her stay with us, was keen to go. I had my doubts: I still hadn't warmed to her despite her less aggressive attitude of late.

We had decided not to take Ermingtrude, nor any of the other community cars, because none of them were suited to the rigours of mountain climbing or the problems of slippery roads.

When we arrived at the snowfields, I was disappointed to discover that the days of skiing as a popular winter sport were indeed long gone. It was easy to see the reason why. There were patches of snow here and there, sometimes banks of it, but the vast fields of white of my youth were now a speckled mixture of black, white and grey. For the downhill skiers, there were one or two slopes on which they could test their skills, but it must have been frustrating for cross-country racing.

Nor, it seems, were there enough people interested in the sport for it to be worthwhile to use snow-making machines. Gone also, were the big resort chalets that I had known. In their place were some small cabins, centred around a general store which saw more customers in summer than in winter.

Imogen and I rented a cabin, equipped with bunks, a fireplace, a stove (non-programmable), and little else. Yet it was cosy and would keep us warm. I was able to rent some old skis from the general store, and taught Imogen the fundamentals of skiing, at least as much as I could remember them.

It was then that I discovered a different side to 'the ice maiden', as I was inclined to call her. On her first skiing lessons, she was nervous and giggly, and got embarrassed if she did anything wrong. After a couple of days, however, her determination got the better of her. She became good enough to ski fast enough to sprain her knee when she tripped over.

While she spent the next two days resting, she read a copy of Dickens's A Christmas Carol. It was, in any case, not great skiing weather –mist in the morning, followed by intermittent showers with sunny periods in the afternoons.

I took advantage of these sunny periods to go fishing. I had forgotten how relaxing it was to sit on a riverbank and sometimes jiggle a rod to and fro on the off-chance that a fish would be stupid enough to take the bait.

To my delight, I caught two rainbow trout. We cooked one of them my way. I bought potatoes and cooking oil from the general store, made some chips and grilled the trout. Just like the good old days when Dad and I went fishing. Garnished with tomato sauce, and washed down with a bottle of beer, it was heaven to me. Imogen found it a bit rough, like the actors in our simulated MacDonald's.

We made the other trout into a casserole, with plenty of rice, some stir- fried veggies, and a bottle of vino blanco. That also went down well.

I thought at first that the wine was making Imogen bubbly, until she explained that reading A Christmas Carol had inspired her. She had it in mind to produce another turn-of-the-millennium epic, with Scrooge as a hard-hearted industrialist who was polluting the environment.

'Let me guess,' I chipped in before she could continue, 'the ghost of Christmas Future turns out to be Gaia in disguise.'

'Yes. How did you know?'

'Just a shrewd guess.'

It suddenly dawned on me that beneath her often grim exterior, she was really quite naive. I began to see her in a different light. Up until then, our relationship had been platonic: I hadn't found her arousing and she hadn't made any advances to me.

She was lying on a rug by the fire, wearing a sweater and slacks that fitted her snugly. I wondered what would have happened if I had given her a playful pat on the posterior. But no; I was in the mood for just letting things happen, rather than taking the initiative.

When Imogen's knee improved, we packed some sandwiches and went bushwalking. It was a glorious sunny day, with not a wisp of cloud in the sky. We followed an old, winding, soggy track past a bright orange dome (a ranger's hut), through the scrub to the summit of a nearby hill. There, we gazed out across a valley towards the rows of mountains in the distance. Some peaks were snow-clad; white points piercing into a crystal blue sky.

Imogen squeezed my arm, pointed to a clearing ringed by tree stumps, and suggested it was a good place to have our sandwiches.

It could have been a scene from my time: a young couple, sitting on tree stumps, munching sandwiches, and pouring coffee from a thermos into plastic cups.

I leant back and stretched. 'Ah, this is the life.' I realised that Imogen was looking at me with a curiously intense expression. 'Something the matter?'

'How do you feel?'

'Fine.'

'I mean, internally. Since the funeral.'

'OK. I was flat for a while, but now I'm recharging my batteries.'

'And Janet?'

'Janet? Mixed feelings. It was good to see her again, even though she wasn't the Janet of old. I suppose I can speculate about how our relationship might have been if I hadn't had to go into hibernation. But what would be the point?'

Imogen said nothing.

I shrugged. 'Life goes on. I may regret the past but I can't change what happened.'

'That seems to sum up the people of your time.'

'Thanks very much,' I said wryly.

'It was meant as an observation, not a criticism.' Imogen shivered. 'It's getting cold.'

'They said there was a cold front moving up from Bass Strait. Should be here by this evening. We might get some good skiing weather yet.'

Imogen was gazing out at the mountains. 'It might be here sooner than you think.'

I followed her gaze. The mountains were disappearing behind a mass of rolling, white clouds. 'Bloody Weather Bureau. They still can't get it right.'

'Never mind that. It's coming our way.'

I remembered what Ron had told me. Because of global warming, they didn't get as much snow as they used to. But also because of global warming, the air was more humid. So when a cold front did move through…

'We'd better get out of here.' I quickly gathered up all of our gear.

As we started back down the track, we could feel the first hint of a chill wind. A shiver went down my spine. The hairs on the back of my neck stood up as the sunlight turned to grey. I looked back across the valley. On the opposite slope, the trees were bending double in the wind: a great surge of white was rolling down upon them.

'We'll never make it back to our cabin,' I warned.

Imogen and I stopped for a moment, looking around for some shelter.

'The ranger's hut,' she shouted.

By then, she had to shout. The wind was howling around our ears. We half-ran, half-staggered until we saw the bright orange dome. As we dashed towards it we could barely see. We were being engulfed in a wall of whiteness.

CHAPTER TWENTY-TWO

REVELATIONS

We escaped from one world of whiteness into another. Gasping for breath, we pushed open the door to the orange dome and staggered inside, only to find that its interior decor was white. I pushed the door shut.

While we were regaining our breaths, we looked around us. There was a neatly made bed, a table with two chairs, a tiny kitchenette area, and a videophone. Imogen tried it, but all she could get was static and wavy lines.

'We're cut off.' I looked through the dome's only window. It was blowing a blizzard out there. Snow was already piling up around us.

'Not quite.' She reached behind the phone and pressed a button.

'What's that?'

'An emergency beacon, I hope. It might be a while before anyone can get to us, but we should be rescued eventually.' The roof creaked ominously under the force of the wind and the weight of the snow. 'It's all right. The dome should be able to stand this sort of pressure. It probably gives a bit.'

Outside, the snow was piling up rapidly. Soon, it was up to the level of the window. As it became darker outside, Imogen put her palm on a panel by the door to activate the lights. Then she went to the small kitchenette. 'Let's see what we've got here.'

We found tea bags, soup packets, and a jar of coffee. Imogen switched on the hot water unit on the wall. 'Anyone for chicken soup?'

'How can you think of soup at a time like this?'

'Something to do. It will keep our mind off—'

Above the noise of the wind, we heard the sound of cracking timber. Instinctively, we ducked, until we heard a thud in the snow. It was a few seconds before we realised that we were holding each other.

'Must have been a tree,' I said. I went to the window to check, but it was too dark to see anything. 'Just as well there are no large trees within thirty metres of this hut. But it shows how strong the wind is.'

This place was giving me the willies. I searched my pockets, then rummaged in my backpack.

'What are you looking for?'

'My regulator. I must have left it back at the cabin. I haven't needed it these past few days.'

Imogen pursed her lips. 'I haven't got mine, either. Despite …'

'Despite what?'

'It doesn't matter.'

I paced up and down. How I wished I had my regulator!

Imogen sat down on the bed. 'There's nothing we can do,' she said softly, 'but meditate. And trust in Gaia.'

'You don't believe in all that stuff, do you?'

She thought for a moment. 'As Hamlet said: "There's a divinity that shapes our ends, rough-hew them how we will."'

The dome creaked. 'Yes, well, our ends are rough-hewn at the moment.'

She looked up. 'We must be completely covered by snow. It will take them hours to dig us out. Once they can get to us.'

I was on the edge of panic. 'Have we got enough air to last that long?'

'There's probably a carbon dioxide converter in here somewhere. These domes were built for situations like this.'

Low down, on the wall, I found a device called a CO2 Konverter. This cheered me up. But when I went back to the middle of the dome, I saw that the roof was sagging.

'It's all right,' Imogen assured me. 'These things are tougher than they look.'

I was breaking into a cold sweat. Imogen told me to sit down. How things had changed. Half an hour earlier, I didn't have a care in the world, but Imogen was edgy. Now, it was the other way around. I buried my head in my hands. 'What Hamlet said about divinity. It works both ways.'

'What do you mean?'

'Well, were you looking to Gaia for some sort of comfort?'

She furrowed her brow. 'In a manner of speaking, as a metaphor, but—'

'Because Gaia, nature, is a very dangerous goddess. Peaceful one minute, violent the next. We've just seen that.'

Imogen's eyes lit up, the way I had seen Helen's do sometimes. 'Yes, but it's magnificent, isn't it?'

'If this roof caves in, we'll be a couple of magnificent corpses.'

'Have a little faith—'

'I don't believe in that sort of thing.'

'—in structural engineering. These domes were designed for precisely this purpose.'

The roof creaked. 'I just wonder if this is some kind of divinity. The other kind. Am I being punished?'

'Punished?'

'For what I did. Look, my life before I came to this time was all about making money. Many people would say that's wrong, but I never wanted to be poor again. And I wasn't to know I'd get a brain tumour, which could have happened to me whether I made zillions or zilch. How was I to know that it would turn out like this? I just wish I could turn back the clock and stop the whole damned thing from happening.'

'You can't,' insisted Imogen. 'The moving finger writes, and having writ moves on.'

'Oh, great,' I snapped. 'I get thrown into an alien world full of do-gooding social workers, lousy cars, and booze that costs a fortune. And you can't even get a decent Big Mac. So here I am about to be crushed to death in a snowdrift while some hard-nosed bitch quotes poetry at me.'

To my astonishment, Imogen burst into tears. 'Hard-nosed bitch? Is that what you think of me? Well, perhaps I'm being punished too.'

'I'm sorry.' I could stand up for myself against blokes who were a bit aggro, but I was defenceless against blubbering women. I dabbed her cheeks with my handkerchief while I put my hand gently on her shoulder. 'I guess I'm being silly. I can understand why the powers that be might have it in for me, but I can't imagine that you would do anything bad.'

'Maybe I have,' she blurted. 'There's something I've been meaning to tell you.' She dried her eyes and looked up at me. 'I've been wanting to tell you for some time.'

I looked around me. The room was misshapen. 'Now is as good a time as any.'

'Let's have some soup, first. I need to gather my thoughts.' She sniffed.

As I stood there, making the soup, the roof creaked again. I wondered if there was a God of Structural Engineering I could pray to. Imogen, meanwhile, regained her composure.

'Let's start with your regulator,' she suggested, after having a few sips.

'What about it?'

'Did you know that regulators were in public use over forty years ago?'

'So?'

'You could have been revived much sooner. Maybe not straight away. But regulators were being used to revive people from hibernation by the 2070s.'

'They said mine was a difficult case. Dr Ohira waited until he was sure it would work.'

Imogen shook her head. 'No more difficult than any other case. Tumour or not, the regulator would have restored the neural pathways that you had before you went into hibernation.'

'Then why wasn't I revived sooner?'

'Janet was your guardian for most of the time you were in cryosleep. When she was contacted about reviving you, she declined.'

Stunned, I sat down on the edge of the bed. 'Why?'

'Because, by then, she was in her sixties. Maybe she was worried about how you would feel if you were revived to find she was then nearly thirty years older than you. Or maybe she feared, since she was happily partnered with Julius, that seeing you again would revive her feelings for you.'

My whole world seemed to stop at that moment. 'Oh.'

'About two years ago, shortly after Julius died, she realised that senility was starting to set in. So she said farewell to her community and came to a hospice in Canberra. She signed a farewell agreement while she was still of sound mind. She handed over her guardianship of you to Darren, on the understanding that you not be revived until after her death.

'Darren is a fine and upright man. A man of principle. You were a great dilemma for his conscience. On the one hand, he felt that you had the same right to life and liberty as any other human being. He saw your hibernation as a form of imprisonment. On the other hand, there were Janet's sentiments.

'Then one day, at the ABC, he met Ron Bushell. They discussed the difficulties of doing accurate historical re-enactments. Ron mentioned that part of the problem was that although there might be plenty of artefacts and records from any time period, say, the early twenty-first century, they didn't tell you what people actually felt and thought. What it was really like to live then.'

'What about the cloud?'

She looked towards the window. 'I guess it will pass over soon.'

'I mean the cloud. Where all the social media stuff was stored. You know, like Google, Facebook, TikTok, Youtube.'

'I've no idea what you're talking about.'

It occurred to me that I hadn't found them online. Apart from two big service providers, who had merged to become Macrosoft, they must all have become extinct during the collapse of the global economy. And there would have been no one who could afford to maintain the cloud.

I took a sip of my soup. 'There must have been old people around he could have interviewed. Darren himself, for instance.'

'Yes, but they have lived through the period since you went into hibernation, and their views and memories of the past have been conditioned by that experience. What Ron needed was an original, fresh mind unaffected by all of the changes that have happened since then.'

'Me?'

'Ron wanted someone for the 2100 History Project. Darren may have steered him around to that way of thinking, of course. It gave

him an excuse to have you revived, for the sake of historical research.'
Imogen sipped some more soup. 'There's more, of course.'

'More?'

'As part of the project, it was important to study your reactions.
The way you behaved, the things you said. If it could be determined,
what you thought and felt. But you had to be unaware that this was
happening.'

'So?'

'Some of the things that have happened to you since you were
revived have been arranged.'

I felt I was losing my grip on reality. 'Explain.'

'The incident in the holoroom with the cricket match, for example.
When Helen conveniently took your regulator away from you.'

'Helen was involved?' I said incredulously.

'In a small way. Ron and Darren had discussed the project with
Dr Ohira some time ago. He was most enthusiastic. Helen and Mara
were acting on his instructions. They saw you as a valuable source of
physiological and psychological data.'

'Mara? You know about her?'

I thought back to our night of passion in the holoroom. Had
she arranged that to gather psychological data, or for more obvious
reasons? Perhaps it was better not to know.

'Anything else?' I asked tersely.

'At Willow Community, of course, we were able to examine how
you interacted in a co-operative setting.'

'So Patricia and Lena and the kids were in on it too?'

Imogen nodded. 'To a limited extent. Ron, Dr Ohira and I were
the ringleaders, so to speak.

'You did present us with two unexpected bonuses. We knew that
cars were important to people of your time, but we didn't realise that

you had been a mechanic. The cars gave you a chance to contribute in your own way.'

'Yeah, I enjoyed that.'

'The other thing that intrigued us was your reaction to the globe burning ceremony. The one occasion when you were allowed to be violent, you walked away.'

'That was crazy. There was no need for that sort of thing.'

'But there is.' Imogen finished her soup. 'As you have probably noticed, compared with your time, we are more open about sex, but more inhibited about violence. Yet we recognise that people have aggressive instincts. So once in a while we "let off steam" as you would say, in a ritualised manner. As the globe burns, we are able to share the experience of casting our hatred into the flames.

'That is the main thing that stands out as the difference between us and people of your times. Apart from the odd war or football final, you seemed to have a limited appreciation of the concept of shared experience. You each lived in your own little worlds which you generally managed quite well, as we observed when you were able to live on your own in Sydney. Yet all the time, the bigger world around you was falling to pieces.

'That is why we don't blame you or anyone else personally for what happened to the world.'

'Thank you, er … I think.' I still had the feeling I was being matronised: poor dear, I really couldn't help being a greedy, environmentally unfriendly brute.

Imogen sighed. 'Finally, there was the meeting with Janet. She originally didn't want to meet you, even though Darren, Ron and I thought it was important. But she agreed, at the last moment, so to speak.'

'It was difficult to know what to make of her,' I explained. 'Last time I saw her, she was so much younger.'

Imogen dabbed her eyes. 'As for the funeral, I … I didn't realise you cared so much for other people. You always seemed to be so self-contained until that moment. I knew then that we had to stop. Ron and Dr Ohira agreed, which is why I'm telling you now.

'If you think you are being punished for your sins, James, then perhaps I am as well.' The roof above her creaked. She looked up. 'The snow must be moving. It was creaking on your side a few minutes ago. The blizzard may have stopped.'

I tried to look through the window. There was nothing but darkness. We were cocooned in a bank of ice.

●

I paced up and down for a while, trying to take in what Imogen had told me. Looking back on the last eight months, I could see that many things that happened to me did fit a pattern. I'd always had this feeling that somehow others were controlling me. They always seemed to know what I was up to.

The roof creaked above my head. Yet it bulged outward rather than inward. The blizzard was definitely over. It was surely just a question of time before we were rescued.

Realising that it was getting warm, I took off my jacket. Imogen had also removed hers. She was wearing a tight-fitting blouse. I realised that she wasn't as flat-chested as I had thought. She unclasped her hair: such lovely, dark, wavy hair.

She came over to stand beside me. 'How do you feel?'

'Strange. I don't know if any human being has ever experienced what I've been through.' I looked at her and smiled. 'I suppose I should feel angry, but I don't. As for being kept in hibernation for all those extra years, perhaps it was for the best.

'Remember that movie we saw, where the astronauts went off to another star, and when they came back, everyone they knew at home was old. I think it would have been like that for me with my relatives. Maybe it's best that I didn't see them again.

'As for all the experiments you've been conducting on me, well …' – I blew out a stream of air – 'I had no idea I was so … special.'

Imogen beamed. 'Really?'

'Yes. I mean, no one's ever made a fuss of me like that before.'

Imogen bowed her head. 'Am I forgiven?'

'Mm? Yeah, you're forgiven, all of you. I don't feel aggro towards anyone.' I patted her on the shoulder. My hand lingered. 'I'm sorry I called you a hard-nosed bitch.'

'That's all right. I was nervous with you. I wasn't sure how to react.'

'And the burden of command, I suppose. With directing Hamlet. It must be a big break for a young kid like you.'

She looked at me in surprise and indignation. 'I'm twenty-seven years old, James.'

For the first time, I really examined her face. Yes, she was a bit older than I thought. Somehow her eyes were gentler, softer. I barely noticed that I was fondling her hair.

●

During the night, I had a strange dream. The whole of the last eight months seemed to flash before my eyes – backwards. It was as though I was watching a videotape of my life in reverse. It went all the way back to my flat and Janet. When I awoke, I could feel Imogen, soft and warm, pressing against my side. I stroked her, and realised that she was the most precious thing in the world to me.

I pressed my thighs into hers. Imogen opened her eyes and looked surprised: 'Again?'

'Why not?'

Just as we were getting into our stride, so to speak, I stopped dead.

'What's the matter?'

'An idea just struck me.'

'I hope it's not too painful.'

'It isn't.' I let the idea pass while I got back to more pressing matters. It was a great idea. It should work, and the financial returns could be good. Shared experience? Yes … yes … oh, yes …

As we lay back in each other's arms, I started to tell her my idea. I was interrupted by a knock on the door.

CHAPTER TWENTY-THREE

RECONSTRUCTION

J ust a minute,' I called out. Dressing hastily, I went to the door. As I pulled it open, I was struck by a blast of cold air and blinding light. Standing outside the doorway, silhouetted against the rising sun, was a tall, dark figure in a bright orange jacket.

'Good morning, James,' said Constable Wilberforce.

'Are we glad to see you.' I shook his hand as he walked in. Imogen was still dressing. Neither she nor Jack seemed concerned. He walked over to the emergency beacon and switched it off.

Minutes later, having packed our gear, we followed him through the snow and slush to the strange rotorbug that I had seen him testing at the airport. As we took to the air and headed back towards the ski lodges, we could see the devastation wreaked by the blizzard: trees were uprooted, buildings were half-buried in drifts and the slopes were covered in snow and debris. No wonder people didn't ski much anymore.

We decided to accept Jack's offer of a ride back to Canberra. Gathering the rest of our things from the chalet, we settled our account. I arranged for our hire car to be dug out of the snow so that it could drive itself back home. Then, we were airborne again.

'You missed all the fun,' Jack told us, 'when the storm hit Canberra.'

'Did it snow?' I asked.

'Yes. First time in years. Quite heavy it was, too. Snowball fights broke out all over Canberra. Even the politicians on the hill went outside to throw snowballs at each other.'

'Serves 'em right,' I quipped. We both laughed.

When we arrived back at Canberra Airport, the snow had already melted. Imogen and I didn't feel like throwing snowballs anyway. We went back to the Bushells' place.

After a couple of warming ports, I decided to tell everyone about my idea. 'I was thinking about not being able to turn back the clock.' I looked at Ron and Imogen. 'Yet isn't that what you try to do? With all these historical re-enactments, I mean.'

Ron was uneasy. 'There is a difference. We don't turn back the clock in the sense of trying to change history. We try to explain to people what things were actually like, so that they can better understand their heritage.'

I turned to Imogen. 'Is this all part of what you mean by "shared experience"?'

'In a way. The re-enactment of the first fleet landing, for example, was an early shared experience between black and white. Although it meant different things to different people.'

'Well,' I went on, 'there's an experience that I would like to share with everyone. It might help people to understand what life was like in my times.'

They were all ears.

'I would like to tell the story of my life, up until I went into hibernation. You can do your historical re-enactments, but I can do it from memory. A first-hand account of what life was really like in the early years of this century. To use an expression from my time, call it my "personal statement".'

'Personal statement? That's very good.' Ron nodded in approval. 'A Christmas or New Year special, perhaps.'

Imogen shrugged her shoulders. 'I did have an idea for adapting A Christmas Carol. But Dickens can wait.'

Ron leant back in his chair, and steepled his hands under his chin. 'It will mean a lot of hard work, James. Plenty of research. You can't just rely on memory.'

'I know. But we've got four months.'

Ron turned to Imogen. 'Can he act?'

'A re-enactment? Maybe. If it's the story of his life, we'll need to use younger actors for his earlier years.'

'Then I shall speak to the ABC programmers. Scheduling would be tight and it may not have popular appeal. One of the special channels, perhaps.'

By now, I had gotten used to the disconcerting tendency of late-21st century people talking frankly about other people as if they weren't there. It was a way of paying them a compliment.

Ron looked at me for a thoughtful moment. 'All right. We'll prepare a proposal and put it to ABC management.'

●

Imogen and I returned to Sydney to set up a house together in the Hamlet Hamlet. Spring was in the air; the world was abundant with life and colour. Having cast aside our inhibitions, we were a high-spirited couple. Imogen was the life and soul of the many house parties in which we indulged.

It wasn't our only form of indulgence, of course. I had to repair our bed three times.

Eventually, we settled down to some serious research. In my mind's eye, I could see the house where I grew up. We visited the site where it had been located in Canberra. Long gone, it had been replaced by a community; the suburb was barely recognisable.

I could also remember the Climate Changers office (also long gone), the flat where Janet and I lived, and the clinic where I had learnt the dreadful news about my tumour.

To help me describe them in detail, Imogen first got me to relax, then to go almost into a trance. She made me recall every fine detail, even down to the colour of the files at work, and the design of the settee in the flat.

Next, we set to work on a large computer screen, which, to my delight, worked in 3D. It consisted of a series of screens, one behind the other, which were transparent until computer-generated images were imprinted on them. They could be enlarged, contracted, moved around, recoloured, until everything came flooding back into my memory.

Then we did the same with the people I had known: Janet, my parents, Kylie, little Darren, my staff. Gradually, they took shape before my eyes. It was unnerving.

We had to go further. How did they walk? What little mannerisms did they have? What did their voices sound like? Over a fortnight, we created electronic ghosts from my past.

It would have helped if some photographs or other family relics had survived. But any photographs would have long since faded, while USB sticks, clothes and other mementos had been scattered and lost. My mind was the only link with my past.

This saddened me in a way, yet the 3D computer system had its compensations. One night, I had a conversation with my father, face-to- screen, as it were. I explained to him what had happened to me. I had offered him a job with Climate Changers as a handyman, but he'd been too proud to accept working for his son.

I also re-created my mother, who said she was glad that I had found a nice girl to settle down with, and when was little Darren going to have a playmate? I told her that Imogen and I weren't quite ready for that yet, but that Darren had gone on to be a success.

The one person I found it hard to conjure up was Kylie. I remembered her as a sweet kid, with freckles, and an impish expression in her eyes. I used to call her 'baby face'. Even at 22, married and with a baby, she could still pass for sixteen.

I contacted Darren, who gave me a photograph he had taken some twenty years earlier of his mother, shortly before her death. I didn't recognise her: years of care and ultraviolet radiation had worn away her baby face, making her haggard and grim.

Reluctantly, I let Kylie go. We would have to make do with the best resemblance of her that I could muster. Then, one night, I saw her in my dreams – an eight-year-old sitting on a swing, teasing me by calling me Jamie. I also saw her, aged 18, at a disco, trying to chat up this guy while being hopelessly distracted by her friends.

I woke up, went to the computer, and produced a likeness of her.

Another person with whom I had problems was Janet. I could get the basic shape of her right, yet there seemed to be something missing when I tried to capture her mannerisms. I realised how little I had understood about her.

One evening, I was playing with her face, elongating it a trifle, thinning it a bit, changing her hair colour. A face I thought I recognised stared at me from the screen. I made a few more adjustments and … I had re-created Imogen.

Was Imogen a latter-day Janet? There were some similarities. Both could be very practical and business-like, and both were crusaders for 'saving the planet'. Both insisted that I do my share of the housework.

There were two important differences. Unlike Janet, Imogen did not try to 'reform' me. She accepted me as I was. I wasn't sure whether this was because of the human relations training that people of her generation received, or whether it was because she still saw me as an interesting specimen to be observed. The second important difference was that Imogen soon realised that the way to twist me around her little finger was to stand provocatively in front of me and play with the buttons of her blouse: I loved it.

While Imogen and I were trying to re-create my past in one way, I managed to re-create it in another. One bright, sunny Saturday morning, I saw Damon, one of our housemates, dusting off a set of cricket pads and flannels. I picked up his bat and practiced a few strokes.

'You've played the game?' he asked, pleasantly surprised.

'Used to play Second Grade in Canberra. Got the occasional First Grade game, but—'

'You must come along and meet the team. They'll be thrilled to meet someone who played in the age of real cricket.'

Damon's team was part of the South Sydney Cricket Club. They played in a social league, but Souths also had teams in the district competition.

Neither the level of competition nor the game itself were the same as in my day. At the junior level, the game was played in only a few dozen schools in the conurbation, as a 'traditional sport'. Above that, there were about as many teams again, playing in a social league or at the district level. Like so many of the sports I had known, cricket went into a marked decline in the wake of the Second Great Depression and the social changes of the forties and fifties.

In an effort to keep the game alive, the organisers changed the rules to make it more of a 'family game'. They had mixed teams, and played with a softer ball than the leather cherries I had known. They didn't bounce as hard off the pitch, and tended to 'prop' a little. This meant fewer bouncers but more skied catches.

My gut reaction was to think the softer ball was a bit 'sissy', until I remembered the odd painful blow to the groin I had received in my day. I decided that maybe the softer ball wasn't a bad idea after all.

I played three social games with Damon's team. By that time, I had gotten the hang of the new version of the game. Because of the softer ball, there wasn't much point in even the heftiest of blokes trying to bowl faster than a gentle medium pace. I was secretly glad of this. Truth to tell, I'd been getting to the stage where I couldn't handle the quicker deliveries as well as I used to. The other thing that helped me was wearing my regulator, which meant that I didn't get too excited or frustrated. I was able to concentrate a lot better.

Towards the end of September, I was asked if I would like to try out for the Second Grade side in the district competition. The captain told me, almost apologetically, that it meant we would have to train one night a week, something that was unheard of in the social grades. I didn't mind in the least, and soon made my debut in the Seconds.

It was at this time that Ron came up to Sydney to join us in discussions with the ABC about the budget for my proposed 'shared experience' with the people of 2100. The ABC managers were sceptical at first. They thought that the idea for the storyline was interesting, but wondered about my abilities as an actor. I was annoyed about them calling it a storyline, as if it was something I had made up. I wanted to re-enact things that had actually happened to me.

Management finally agreed to a low-budget production, running for half an hour, to be broadcast on one of the special channels. In other words, they didn't think it was 'commercial'.

With my help, Imogen and Ron worked out a script. There would be a series of short scenes describing what had happened to me in my life, interspersed with some actual footage from the time. The last and longest scene would show me saying farewell to my friends and relations, and going into hibernation – a subject that might fascinate the people of 2100.

They used the footage Ron had presented me with on my 100th birthday, of the circumstances of my birth, and of my then youthful parents. There was also some footage of Sydney Harbour, as it had been in 2000.

As far as my scenes were concerned, Imogen planned to use a technique called 'modified cinema verité', in which we would shoot the shorter scenes three or four times, and then edit them on computer to get the best result.

'It has to look a bit rough,' she explained, 'without being boring. I'm in two minds about whether to ask Nigel Campbell to give you acting lessons. We want you to come over as natural.'

Nigel did agree to give me some acting lessons, and to play the 'walk on' part of the doctor who gave me the bad news about the tumour.

I went to my first lesson with some trepidation. During the production of Hamlet, Nigel didn't mince words and could be devastatingly sarcastic. When he insisted that I not wear my regulator, I was even more nervous.

'I'm not going to teach you how to act,' he explained. 'Instead, you're going to help me rehearse my part.' Even allowing for his natural arrogance, this annoyed me. He reached for the script that

Imogen handed to him. 'Now, we'll improvise a bit, just to get a point across.

'Imagine it's the clinic, the tests have been done, and I'm about to give you the diagnosis.'

I looked at my copy of the script. 'Well, doctor?'

He shook his head. 'Not good news, I'm afraid. It is inoperable.'

'So. How long have I got?'

'No, no no. That won't do at all. I've just given you the most devastating news you've ever heard. How did you react at the time?'

'It felt almost like a physical shock. I think I was dizzy for a few seconds.'

Nigel reached for his pen and my script. He inserted a note:

JAMES (Sits down. Puts head in hands for a few seconds): How long have I got?

I did as he instructed. 'How long have I got?'

'No, no. That's not anxious enough.' He paused. 'You still have regular brain scans, don't you?'

'Yes. But the scans are clear.'

'Supposing, next time you have a scan, they were to tell you that your tumour had returned.'

'Well, I guess they'd have to give me some more nanites.'

'What if they told you that this time, nanites wouldn't help?'

'Is that possible?'

'Perhaps.'

I could feel the terror of the tumour returning, and I did feel a bit dizzy. I put my head in my hands for a few seconds. 'I, er … I, er … How long have I got?'

'That's better. Now we're starting to get somewhere.'

CHAPTER TWENTY-FOUR

RESOLUTIONS

The longer my relationship with Imogen lasted, the better it got. She was always full of surprises, both in the things she did and in her understanding of me.

One day, around the middle of October, I was working on the graphics screens, when a message flashed on the screen telling me to turn on the voice link.

Janet's face appeared on the screen, and I heard her faded voice as well. There was something about a permaculture commune down the coast, but the rest was difficult to hear.

I sat there for ages, not knowing how to react. I was still sitting there when Imogen walked in. She could tell immediately that I had seen the computer sequence.

'Darren was executor of Janet's estate. He found that in her personal effects,' she told me. 'It must be very old. I'm afraid it's deteriorated over time.'

Imogen handed me a package. As I unwrapped it, she said, 'Ron and I believe that we have found out all that we reasonably can about the physical circumstances of your life. As for your feelings, what you need is something that will jog your memory.'

Inside the package was a leather-bound exercise book. 'And this is from Ron.' She handed me a smaller package which contained a pen.

'Thank you. They're lovely gifts. Is there a special reason for them?'

She smiled. 'You can lead a horse to water …'

I got the hint. That evening I sat down and started to write. It was difficult at first, but after a while all my memories came flooding back to me. It also occurred to me that if the teleplay went down well, there might be a market for a book on the story of my life.

Speaking of markets, I found time to research my other idea. I learnt about plastics, and about how coatings of micros could be used in lieu of paint – micros that would change colour as the temperature changed.

I found that there was a plastics manufacturer in Sydney that produced fitballs. There wasn't a big market for them, apart from the globes for the annual burning ceremonies on Black Friday, but there was enough demand for them to be profitable.

I explained my idea to the factory manager, who thought it was 'novel', though he wasn't sure how well it would sell.

'I'm willing to put some capital into it,' I explained, remembering that I still had 20,000 Australs in my account, 'and into marketing.'

He agreed to get his designers to work on it, and I paid him to produce a prototype by the end of the year. I also prepared and lodged documents with the Patent Office.

●

Towards the end of the month, we began shooting the telemovie based on the story of my life, starring me. The production had a weird beginning. I was introduced to Jennifer Laswell, an actress who bore a striking resemblance to Janet. She even captured Janet's slow, thoughtful, pedantic way of talking. More than once in the weeks to come did I inadvertently think she was Janet.

The production team did a mock-up of a replica of my Climate Changers car. It was built purely for show. The front doors could open and 'Janet' and I could sit in the front seats. The shaft of the steering wheel fitted into a hole in the dashboard but was only connected to a clamp. It was like a big kiddie car, except there weren't any pedals.

They filmed Janet and I getting out of the car. Then we were taken to a simulator, where I pretended to drive to work while listening to the radio.

Imogen had unearthed some radio news files from the ABC Archives. From these, she put together a composite news bulletin from my times. There was a war somewhere in Africa, a murder in Sydney, there were arguments about carbon quotas, and governments were cranking up quantitative easing to forestall a credit crisis.

Production of my epic melodrama was slotted in between more important projects. It wasn't until the later part of November that the next scene was shot.

The eeriest thing was meeting my 'family'. They hired two adult and two juvenile actors to play Mum and Dad, my sister Kylie, and eerily, me, played by a 12-year-old named Jason. I could see a resemblance to my family, but not a really close one.

'I realise you'd like them to look more like your family,' explained Imogen, 'but the most important thing is their acting ability. Portraying what your family said and felt is the crucial thing.'

The actors were needed for a couple of scenes before and after Dad's accident, which they simulated with a mock-up of an ACTION bus of that era, and a stunt cyclist. The scenes showed how Dad's personality changed from cheerful to moody. There was also a scene, shot with an actual class at a local school, who got a buzz out of dressing up in quaint 2000s costumes, in which Kylie and I were too poor to go on an excursion.

They did some of the scenes using still photos from archives, with my voiceover explaining my growing up in Sydney and Canberra. They had even found and showed a photo of me, aged 15, while I explained that I had decided that the most important thing in life was to make lots of money. We had to mention cricket, of course, and players from the South Sydney Cricket Club had fun dressing up in the old 'whites' for a sequence where I batted and bowled a bit.

I had the eerie experience of re-creating one of my first jobs, when I had to climb up onto a roof to help install solar panels. After that, it was back to some more photographs, while I explained about getting my degree, designing an app, working for an energy monitoring firm, and eventually setting up Climate Changers.

We shot one or two scenes in a replica of my office, explaining what we did and why it was so important. I was keen to show that I was someone whom the people of 2100 would regard as a hero – one of the people who led the fight to combat climate change.

We had one short scene where Janet came to join us as a secretary. We added some romance as it became clear Janet and I were falling for each other.

It filled my heart with joy that they actually managed to find one of our Climate Changers ads, which they ran as the sort of 'intermission' in the middle of the program.

All of this took up the first quarter-hour of my story. The rest, starring me, was about my relationship with Janet, the tumour, and going into hibernation.

●

Re-creating my old flat was an eerie experience, like summoning up a ghost. At first, I could only remember the barest details. With Imogen's persistent questioning and the aid of the 3D graphics computer, I was able to extract the finest of details from my memory banks.

We re-created the living room, kitchenette, bathroom and bedroom, down to the exact colour pattern of the sofa, the brand of environmentally friendly dishwashing liquid that Janet and I had used, the touches of mould on the plastic shower curtain, and the slight hiss in one of the speakers in the stereo in the bedroom. The carpet in the living room was specially stained to make it look as though there was a well-worn path from the front door.

By one Saturday evening in late November, I was so used to it that I said absent-mindedly to 'Janet' that I was going down the street to get a pizza. (That was our Saturday evening indulgence back in my day.) Everyone on the set laughed.

Jennifer Laswell, Imogen and I decided to spend the night in the flat, prior to shooting in the morning. Imogen and I took the bed, Jennifer the sofa.

When I awoke, I half-heard on the clock radio that there was a war in Africa somewhere, the road toll for the year was a thousand and something, and the weather outlook was fine.

Automatically, I reached over and groped Janet's warm, chunky body. 'Not now, darling,' came the muffled reply. 'You're first in the bathroom.'

I staggered off to the bathroom, relieved myself, then did battle with the electric shaver, all of which seemed a bit odd for some reason. 'Funny, I thought it was Sunday.'

This thought stuck with me while I showered. I dried myself, wrapped the towel round my middle, and went back to the bedroom. Instead of going to the wardrobe, I groped around on the dresser.

'What are you looking for,' Janet asked.

'My regulator, I—'. I stared at her. She wasn't Janet. Neither was she Imogen. I turned bright red. 'You mean we—?'

'Keep going,' she hissed. Then more loudly, 'Don't forget to put out the recycling bins for the permaculture cooperative.'

'Yeah, OK.' I rummaged through the wardrobe for a shirt. 'I should be getting the results from the scan today.'

'Good luck,' she said drowsily, then got out of bed and headed for the bathroom. She was stark naked. It wasn't just her face that resembled Janet. 'Erm, actually,' I said quietly, 'Janet used to wear a nightdress. She was a bit of a prude.'

'You can talk,' said Janet who was Jennifer, and closed the bathroom door.

I fried the free-range eggs that morning. The people of 2100 were used to programmable ovens and hotplates. I was one of the few people who still knew how to use an old-fashioned skillet on the electric rings.

Over breakfast, we discussed our plans for the day. Both of us were concerned about what the scans might reveal. We decided to adopt a 'wait and see' attitude. As we were getting up from the table, she said, 'Bins.'

'Oh, yeah.' I took five brightly coloured recycling bins outside, much to the surprise of the ABC staff. They were even more surprised when I took them back in again, for the re-run. We replayed the scene that afternoon, and again the following morning and afternoon. By then, Imogen was satisfied.

Not until that evening did I confront her about the previous morning's experience.

'That was very sneaky of you,' I protested.

'Yes it was.' Imogen grinned. 'Putting a naked woman in your bed.'

'Well, I mean, Janet and I usually didn't, on a weekday morning, but sometimes we did … I suppose Jennifer wouldn't …'

'Wouldn't what?'

'Erm, make love.'

Imogen looked at me mysteriously. 'You'll probably never know, James.'

●

The scene at the clinic, when 'Doctor' Nigel Campbell gave me the bad news, went off quite well. So, later, did the scene back at the flat when I told 'Janet' the bad news. To my astonishment, she produced some real tears. In fact, the whole thing was starting to become ominously real.

The scene where I told other members of the Lawson clan about my terminal condition was also eerie. It involved the same two adult actors, made up to look older and greyer, and an older actress to play the adult Kylie. We also got a young lad in to play the ten-year-old Darren, and with the real Darren's permission, replayed the scene where he and I had discussed what would happen to my soul, if I had one.

●

Around the middle of December, we had an eerie experience. The best place to shoot the hibernation scenes was, of course, at the Cryosleep Centre. For twenty years, it hosted only one sleeper – me, which would have been a frightful waste of resources. It was still being used for experiments, amongst other things, in food preservation and the study of materials at very low temperatures.

On the drive out to the Centre, I was feeling buoyant. Dr Ohira had performed another brain scan on me. In stark contrast to the scene I had played out with Nigel Campbell, this scan showed no sign of the tumour returning.

We had to shoot two scenes at the Cryosleep Centre, as well as one on the road, on the way there before I began my long sleep, including footage of what the view would have been like sixty-five years earlier.

It was strange going back into the place that had been my home/prison/bed for all those years. Most of the 'coffins' in which we had slept had since been removed, so they had to use clever camera angles to make it look like a room full of sleepers. On these out-of-studio shots, we had to use cameras.

One short scene, where I was shown over the facility by the Centre manager and we discussed energy conservation measures when I was running Climate Changers had to be inserted into an earlier part of the story.

In the final scene, all of my 'relatives', indeed, all of the cast were there to say their farewells. There was a certain poignancy to this because it really was the last time the cast would be together. I said my farewells to them all, the staff gave me an 'injection' and I nodded off to sleep.

The last scene showed my relatives and Imogen watching while a dummy of me was lowered into my 'coffin' and the cooling controls activated. I watched this scene from behind the camera. It was something I had never actually seen in real life.

And then it was done.

●

On Christmas Eve, a large box turned up on our doorstep.

'What is it?' asked Imogen.

I winked. 'We'll find out tomorrow.'

I put it on the tiled floor in the bathroom, so that it would cool down during the night, hopefully to around 15 degrees.

Next morning, I eagerly opened the box, and out rolled a large, plastic globe of the world. It was cool, and depicted the Earth as it was during the ice ages – great amounts of white spread across the continents, and the continents were larger because of lower sea levels. Imogen was impressed.

'Wait till it warms up,' I insisted.

By the time it had warmed up to 20 degrees, the ice caps began to melt and chunks of land disappeared into the sea. The ball soon resembled the world I had grown up in.

'Oh, that's clever,' said Imogen. 'How is it done?'

'Heat-sensitive micros in the paint that change colour as they warm up. At fifteen degrees, which was the mean Earth temperature during the ice ages, it looks like the Earth did at that temperature. At twenty degrees, it looks like the temperate world the earth is at that temperature.'

We took turns sitting on it, rolling it around, and throwing it to each other.

As it warmed up more, to 25 degrees, the ice caps disappeared altogether, and land masses contracted even further. 'I got the idea from our old Climate Changers logo. The fitball now resembles what the Earth will look like at that temperature – a hot house world – a sort of reminder of what will happen if we fail to prevent global warming.

'Now, supposing we were to use these for the globe burning ceremony. Put them out in the sun, and people could see it warm up from ice age to temperate to hot house before we set fire to them.'

Imogen was thoughtful for a moment. Then her eyes lit up. 'Yes. I can see it might work.'

'Think of how many we could sell each year. This could be a gold mine.'

Imogen frowned. 'Is that what you want?'

'To be rich? Doesn't everybody?'

She shook her head. 'Being financially comfortable is fine. But beyond that, surely being at one with nature and enjoying the fellowship of a community is more important.'

As I looked at her, I realised there was the great divide between my era and hers. I grew up with the notion that to be rich was glorious. I assumed it was what everybody strived for. I also assumed, based on what Ron had told me about economic necessity, that the reason the people of 2100 put more emphasis on community life than wealth creation was because they had little choice. It was beginning to dawn on me that the reason people were now more community-oriented than materialistic was because they wanted to live that way.

I wondered how our different attitudes to wealth would affect our longer term relationship. 'Well,' I hedged, 'we don't want to get ahead of ourselves. We can't assume these balls will be a big success.'

Truth to tell, I had already done some calculations. If things worked out, we could sell at least 100,000 balls a year. I had struck a deal with the manufacturer that if we went commercial, I would get royalties of one Austral per ball. Once I had recouped my investment costs that would mean an income of A100k per year – a nice little earner.

I decided it was best not to tell Imogen that now. The money would initially come in slowly, but build up later on. That would get her used to the idea of being rich.

●

On the evening of Leap Year Day, we had a party to see in the New Year. We invited all our friends, and they took turns on our 'world ball' which they found great fun. I could have taken several orders that night.

That set me thinking. Maybe there would also be a market for our balls in gyms, and in people's homes. A world ball in every home in Australia? Hmm. Make that a million Australs per year.

When we finally saw off our guests and went to bed, I was feeling full of myself. Our lovemaking was particularly enjoyable that night.

Later, I dreamed a strange dream. I was back in my old apartment of sixty-five years earlier, with Janet. It seemed so real that when I woke up, I was disoriented. I staggered to the window. Something didn't seem right. I couldn't remember when I was. Feeling dizzy, I sank to the floor. All I wanted to do was to sleep forever, back in my cryonic capsule.

A blurred figure loomed over me.

'Janet?'

'Not quite.' Imogen helped me to my feet, and led me out into the brave new world of 2101. The twenty-first century was over.

END

ABOUT THE AUTHOR

Robert Phillips grew up in Adelaide, where he started writing for theatre. He has had plays and sketches performed in Adelaide and Canberra.

Moving to Canberra, he became an aviation risk analyst. His published books include a full-length science fiction play (Technocraton, Heinemann,1976) a book about risks in everyday life (A Risky Life, Halstead Press, 2014) and a post-post-apocalyptic comedy novella (Canberraesque, Busybird Publishing 2017).

Apart from technical papers on aviation safety, he has published historical articles and short stories.

He lives in North Canberra. His website is:

www.robertphillips.com.au.

Canberraesque
Robert
Phillips

CANBERRAESQUE

Post-post-apocalyptic society can be fun.

n the 23rd century, as Gaia's Curse starts to lift, Canberra is divided. Leaders of local communities revel in grandiosity in a political landscape pervaded by lust, betrayal and power struggles.

The nefarious Baron von Belco and his Coalition of the Largely Unwilling attempt to conquer North Canberra, resulting in the most embarrassing battle in military history. The Governor of Gungahlin just wants a quiet life, despite the machinations of his power-hungry Secretary. The demented Mud People of EPIC go on an epic journey to find the earthly paradise of Wagga Bay.

The Weston Union attempts to secede from the domains of the Warlord of Woden. Meanwhile the temptress Jezebel, Begum of Jerra, conspires to overthrow dear old Queen Doris of Queanbeyan. The Peoples Soviet Republic of Tuggeranong tries to liberate the peasants held in feudal servitude to the aristocratic Count of Condor, who is under siege by chicken rustlers. South Canberra remains as confusing as its street layout.

Yet Canberra is pervaded by the far-sighted legacy of a man long gone – a legacy and a prophecy.